# THE V V AGENCY

# THE V V AGENCY

By

Mike Befeler

Oak Tree Press  Taylorville, IL

Oak Tree Press books may be purchased for educational, business or sales promotional purposes. Contact Publisher for quantity discounts

First Edition, April 2013

ISBN 978-1-61009-073-5
LCCN 2013933631

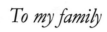

*To my family*

# Acknowledgements

I want to thank my critique group, in particular Donnell Ann Bell. In addition, kudos to Sunny Frazier and Billie Johnson of Oak Tree Press.

# Chapter 1

Glad to have Vanna out of the way for a while, Van heard the door creak. He jerked his head up from his paperwork, and a blonde bombshell sashayed into his office. Va-va-voom. She had sumptuous legs visible practically to her hips, sparkling hair flowing down to her shoulders, a well-filled sweater out to . . . well out to there, and azure eyes like deep wells he could fall into and never find his way out. It was all he could do to keep saliva from dripping out of his mouth.

He sniffed the aroma of jasmine and plumeria as images of tropical beaches popped into his mind. This day had definitely started well with the promise of things to come.

She stopped and gave him the onceover as well. Hopefully, she wasn't disappointed. Van had what his lovers had complimented him on—six feet of muscle; a handsome tanned face; tight butt; and wavy black locks. Not that he had ever hung around after one of his trysts, but that wasn't a circumstance he could help.

He met her unflinching gaze. "What can I do for you?"

She bit her full, pouty lip and then let out a heartfelt sigh. "I came to your agency because I understand a woman private investigator works here."

"That's right. My partner, Vanna."

The bombshell's eyes clouded over, ever so slightly. "I'd like to meet with her, please."

Van figured Vanna and this woman would get along. Vanna had a way with wild animals, and the blonde gave no vibes of being tame. "I'm sorry, but you're stuck with me right now. Vanna won't be back in the foreseeable future. May I offer you a donut, coffee, tea . . ." He resisted the urge to add, "or me?"

"No." She sagged, not that it detracted from the luscious picture. "I really hoped to work with a woman."

"Please, sit down." Van waved toward one of the two upholstered brown chairs facing his desk. The only other furniture in the office was a four-drawer file cabinet. The walls displayed an eclectic array of animal photographs. Van wouldn't have put anything on the walls, but Vanna had insisted on pictures of deer, bear, elk and moose. She thought it gave a rugged look to the place to enhance the image of a top PI outfit.

Van pushed aside the vision of himself as a fox ready to pounce on an unsuspecting rabbit. "Tell me what brings you here. I can assure you I'll help you until Vanna returns. We work very closely together as a team and nothing will be lost between us."

She sidled into the seat, her short, slinky skirt hiking up to reveal enough thigh to make Van's heart beat a ragged tattoo. She gave him a come-hither look. "I'm Gloria Blendheim. Do you mind if I smoke?" She reached for her purse, a small black job with a gold handle.

Van held up his hand. "I'm sorry, but I'm allergic to cigarette smoke." Not exactly the truth but necessary. A whiff of a Marlboro made him as horny as hell, and he had a policy of never getting involved with a client. He could already feel the sparks passing between them. He couldn't risk this getting out of hand, so to speak. Besides, he and his partner had a strict policy of no smoking in their office. The effect on him was one thing, but cigarette smoke made Vanna puke. He appreciated all the non-smoking ordinances being passed in and around Denver. He could now go into a bar without turning into a letch, not that he frequented bars that often. When he did, only seltzer water. Booze had a debilitating effect on him.

"Oh." Her wide eyes met his as she pushed the pack of smokes back in her purse and returned the bag to her lap. She sat there demurely, waiting for him to say something.

"Tell me, Ms. Blendheim, what brings you to our humble agency?"

"You can call me Gloria." She graced him with such a charming smile that his knees trembled under the desk.

"And I . . . I'm . . ." He couldn't remember who the hell he was. Then the right brain cells connected. "Van."

She looked around the room, and then her gaze bore in on him. "Van and Vanna. The V V Agency. The two partners. I get it now."

No, she didn't, but that was another story.

She tossed her head to the side, and her mane flowed like liquid gold. Van told himself to maintain focus. This woman reeked of danger, sexuality, sexuality and sexuality. A puff of smoke and he would have been all over her like snow on pines during a Colorado snowstorm. His fingers itched to touch her cheek. He firmly planted his palms on the desk to control the twitching digits.

She let out another deep sigh. "I have a little problem."

Van tried to imagine what this might be. Man problems? Money? Fraud? Definitely not loneliness. "Define little."

"Someone murdered my husband Cornelius last night." She reached in her purse and extracted a monogrammed hanky and dabbed at a tearless eye.

"Have the police been notified?"

"Oh, yes. They've been investigating. And that's why I'm here. They consider me a suspect in his death." Her bountiful chest heaved, and a sob emerged from her ruby red lips.

Van resisted the urge to step to the other side of the desk to console her. That foolish idea had too much danger associated with it. He took another deep breath. A murder case. He hadn't worked one for a few months. He could use something else besides checking on cheating spouses. This had possibilities. Homicide. Beautiful broad. Intrigue. He pushed a box of tissues toward her, but she waved it off, staying with the hankie.

"Cornelius took such good care of me, and now he's dead. I never would do anything to hurt him, much less kill him." Her pleading eyes met Van's gaze. "But the police are suspicious. They won't leave me alone. That's why I'm here to solicit your assistance. I need to hire your agency to help prove my innocence."

"It's up to the cops and the DA to prove your guilt and your lawyer to demonstrate you can't be proven guilty beyond a reasonable doubt. To support this we only have to show that you didn't have means, opportunity or motive to kill your husband."

Her chin shook.

Van hated to see that expression on her face. He wanted to bring squeals of delight out of those succulent lips. He reminded himself he was a professional.

She turned her doe eyes on him again. "That's the little problem. The detective says I had all three. He grilled me unmercifully last night. When I got up this morning after a sleepless night, I decided I needed some assistance. That's when I inquired and learned of your investigation service. You will help me, won't you?"

Van thumped his fist on his desk. "You've come to the right place. I'll put the full resources of The V V Agency behind resolving your problem. Let's start with the circumstances surrounding the murder. Tell me what happened."

Gloria dabbed one last time and then stowed the hanky in her purse. "Last night I attended a reception for board members and patrons of the Denver Cooperative Art Alliance—our annual recognition event to thank contributors who support the arts. It's one of the charities I'm involved with. We had a wonderful evening of excellent food, champagne and sparkling conversation. That all changed when I came home at approximately ten-thirty. I found . . . I found Cornelius dead in his den." Her lip quivered.

Van pushed the tissue box her way again, but she resolutely waved it off.

"How did he die?"

"Shot. Shot in the back of the head." Her lip trembled. "And . . . and I couldn't find my Smith & Wesson Centennial 442 Airweight . . ."

"So you pack?"

She nodded. "I took the training course and have a permit to carry a concealed weapon. You have to be so careful in this city."

Van whistled. "Where was the gun when you left the house last night?"

"That's the strange part. In my rush to get ready for the reception, I never transferred it from my day bag to my evening purse, so it was left in my dressing area. Someone discovered it and might have killed my husband with it because it's disappeared."

"So you find your husband dead and your handgun's missing."

"That's not all. When the police had me check the den, Cornelius's own gun wasn't there. He keeps a SIG P210 in a desk drawer."

"And who uses that weapon?"

"Only Cornelius. But I cleaned it for him two days ago."

Van saw the challenge he would be up against here. Two guns missing, hers and one she had handled. A shitload of means and opportunity. "Okay, regarding the motive for the crime?"

She gulped. "That's another little problem. Cornelius is forty years older than I am. I stand to inherit the majority of his fortune worth over a hundred million dollars."

# Chapter 2

"I see your little problem," Van said to Gloria Blendheim. "Everything points to you as the murderer. So, did you whack your old man?"

She sat up stiffly in the chair and didn't blink. "No, I did not."

Van nodded. "Okay. I had to ask. And you still want me to take your case?"

She scrutinized him for a moment. "I need someone to find the real murderer. I'm concerned that the police are only after me." She paused and sucked on her lip for a moment. "I'd prefer to work with Vanna, but I guess you'll do. Yes."

"With that resounding endorsement, let's get started." He explained his fee structure, including a retainer of a thousand dollars. This didn't faze her in the least. With a hundred mill, she wouldn't sneeze over a few thousand for a PI at seventy-five bucks an hour plus expenses. "I'd like to check the crime scene and have a little chat with the police."

"They still have my house sealed off. I had to sleep at a hotel last night. Fortunately, the Adams Mark could accommodate me on short notice."

With the size of her inheritance they would have kicked the Queen of Sheba out of a room to make a place for her, whereas if he tried to get a room late at night, he would have ended up in the janitor's closet or bedding down with the homeless people outside the Denver Rescue Mission on Lawrence. "Okay, I'll take a look at the house later. Who's the detective on the case?"

Gloria scrunched up her nose as if she had smelled a sweaty athletic sock. "Mulhaney."

"He's a good cop. Tough but fair. I'll have a little chat with him and see what I can learn."

"I can't imagine him divulging anything," Gloria said. "He asked lots of questions but didn't answer any I put to him."

"Don't worry your pretty head over it. I have my ways of getting the information we need. I assume you've lawyered up?"

"Yes, Donald Hallett of Hallett, Jones and Clancy represents me. He's kept me out of jail so far."

"Good. Reputable ambulance chaser. He'll do a fine job for you. I'll let him work the foreground while I cover your . . . uh . . . the background," Van stammered. "With your permission I'd like to speak with Donald."

She shrugged. "No problem."

"What living relatives does Cornelius have?"

"Only his son, Huntington. He lives in Golden."

"How did father and son get along?"

She grimaced. "Not well. Huntington and Cornelius became estranged a year ago. They didn't see each other very often, and when they did, it usually led to a heated argument."

"What did they argue about?"

"The usual stuff. Money, women, that sort of thing."

Van jotted a note. "Now, what else should you tell me about the case?"

She held her thumb and index finger a quarter of an inch apart. "There's one other itty bitty problem."

Van gave an eye roll. Okay, here it comes. "Which is?"

She cast her gaze down to the floor as if inspecting to make sure it didn't harbor any unwanted creepy crawlers. "I was having an affair but ended it yesterday. You see, my husband and I had a very happy and modern marriage. We had reached an understanding. As long as I paid attention to him when he wanted me, he didn't care what else I did. Besides, he was used to having other women and had been so busy with his business deals lately that I pursued an outside distraction. I'm a hot-blooded woman and needed an outlet."

"I understand." Van only wished he had been the avenue for her outlet. But that would have caused other problems. "And who was this affair with?"

"Do I have to tell you his name?"

"Only if you want me to effectively pursue this case."

She raised her gaze from the floor and met his. "I find it difficult to discuss. His . . . uh . . . name is Bentley Graves."

Van whistled again. "The big honcho real estate developer?"

"Yes. We met on the board of the Denver Cooperative Art Alliance. We'd been seeing each other regularly, but I broke off our relationship right at the beginning of the reception last night. I'd had enough of him."

"Did you speak to him after that?"

"No. I saw him at a distance. We completely avoided each other, but I did notice he left early."

"Have you told anyone about this affair?"

"No. You're the first."

Van tapped a finger on his desk. "And you stayed at the reception until what time?"

"Ten. Then I drove home."

"Are there other witnesses to you being at the reception?"

She smiled. "Oh, yes. I spoke with all the other board members, and Gladys Roons saw me leave."

Van scribbled another note. "Good. I'll check that out as well. Any other little surprises?"

She wrinkled her brow. "No. That's everything."

"Give me your contact information." He slid a pen and pad of paper toward her.

She grabbed the pen, wrote the information and then looked up to meet his eyes. "Thank you for agreeing to help me." She stood, reached across the desk and gave him a warm handshake.

He thanked the gods of lustful detectives that a desk remained between them with no cigarette smoke in the air. This was taking all his resolve and then some. "Don't go out of town while the police investigation continues. Let me know when the cops release your home. If you have any questions in the meantime, you can call me here or on my cell." He pushed his card across the desk to her.

She picked it up, regarded it closely as if memorizing the content, dropped it in her purse, turned and glided out of the office.

Her tropical fragrance continued to tickle his nose. He took in a deep breath and slowly exhaled. Some broad. Interesting case. He'd use his special abilities after dark to scout things out.

# Chapter 3

After reviewing his notes, Van picked up the phone and placed a call to the Denver Police Department.

"Detective Mulhaney here."

"Hey, you old flatfoot, Van Averi here as well. You have a minute?"

"I'd prefer to speak with your partner."

Van looked upward and stifled a groan. Mulhaney was always hitting on Vanna. She didn't like the guy, but Van actually got a kick out of the crusty detective. "Sorry, she's not around at the moment. You'll have to put up with me instead. I understand you're working the Blendheim case."

"What of it?"

"Gloria Blendheim hired our agency. She says you're too busy chasing her butt to catch the real murderer."

Mulhaney let out a rush of air that sounded like a Chinook wind. "Give me a break. Although she does have an attractive tush, she's in deep crap. Good as convicted. I'd suggest you find a better client. Otherwise, word will get around that you represent people who end up serving life sentences."

"I'll take my chances. So, what's the poop? What evidence do you have on her?"

"Yeah. Good luck me giving you anything you'd turn around to help that broad weasel out of this mess. Tell you what. You can track the case when it goes to court."

Van drummed his fingers on the corner of his desk. "Come on, Mulhaney. You don't really think that sweet young thing shot the old man, do you?"

"Yes, and all the evidence substantiates it."

"Which is?"

"Forget it, Van. I'm not telling you squat."

Van groaned. "Okay, Mulhaney. I thought I'd give you a chance first. We go through this same routine every time. I'll find out what I need to know without you."

There was a pause on the line, and Van could hear a hack, followed by a spitting sound. He wondered if Mulhaney kept a spittoon near his desk. Most likely the wastebasket.

"Averi, you have an uncanny knack for discovering confidential information, but you'll have to do it without anything from me." The line went dead.

Van hung up and rubbed his hands together, thinking how much fun it would be to snoop into Mulhaney's police reports. The guy would never figure out how he did it.

He next tracked down the phone number for Gladys Roons. She answered on the fourth ring. "Ms. Roons, This is Van Averi from The V V Agency. I'm a private investigator and have a few questions for you."

"Oh, my. Does this regard that insurance case?"

"No, ma'am. I want to discuss Gloria Blendheim. I understand you saw her last night at the board reception for the Denver Cooperative Art Alliance."

"Oh, yes. She attended. A very attractive woman. And she makes such good suggestions on our board."

"Did you notice when she was at the reception?"

"Let me think. Well, I saw her when I arrived around eight-thirty. And I remember waving to her when she left."

"Do you recall the time?" He wondered if she would verify Gloria's statement of leaving at ten.

"Oh, yes. I don't wear a watch, but there's a large clock over the doorway. It was exactly ten o'clock."

"Could she have stepped out of the reception for a while between the times you arrived and when you saw her finally leave?"

"Oh, no. I spotted her numerous times during the evening. She usually had quite a collection of men around her. Oh, my, I remember back in my day, I attracted a crowd myself. I had my fair share of men paying attention . . ."

He listened to her ramble on for five minutes. When she finally paused, he had a chance to say, "Thank you, Ms. Roons. You've been most helpful."

Van spent the rest of the afternoon speaking to other board members who confirmed Gloria's presence at the reception. No one else had noticed the time she left at the end of the evening besides Gladys Roons.

Then he tracked down Bentley Graves's home address.

Next on his list, he located the address and phone number for Cornelius Blendheim's son Huntington and gave a call. The phone cut over to voicemail, and Van left his name and number.

Finally, a call to Donald Hallett. After explaining to Hallett's administrative assistant that he had been retained by Gloria Blendheim, he was put through to the big guy.

"Van, how the hell are you?"

"Surviving. I understand we're both working to keep Gloria Blendheim out of the slammer."

Van could hear a burst of air over the phone. "That woman ended up in quite a jam. I spent most of last night keeping the Denver PD from incarcerating her. Glad you're helping out."

"Can you spare a few billable minutes to meet with me?"

"Sure. Sure. Come on over. I can see you in an hour."

\* \* \* \* \*

Later, as Van stepped outside, a gray tabby appeared from the nearby alley. The beast approached, and as its yellow eyes bore into Van, the cat hissed loudly and doubled in size.

Watching its hair puff out in all directions, Van froze. "Uh . . . nice kitty."

The cat lowered itself to sidewalk level and crept toward him as if Van were a giant mouse ready for the plucking.

Van tentatively reached toward the gray feline, which took a swipe and connected.

"Ouch!" He drew back, clutching his hand in pain.

Next the cat lashed out at his leg, and Van danced backward to avoid more claw marks. He was saved when a dog barked and the cat scampered away.

Van spat on his hand and rubbed saliva into the wounds. Given his way with animals, he needed to stay as far away from them as possible.

\* \* \* \* \*

Fifteen minutes later Van strolled into the Equitable Building on Seventeenth Street. He loved the lobby of this place with the high arched ceiling, polished marble floor and brass handrails. Built in 1892 this building had more class than the modern skyscrapers with all their glass and steel. Some day he'd like to locate the agency here, but for now it exceeded his price range. And besides, he and Vanna had a good setup in Lodo with their office and lofts. They had bought when lower downtown Denver prices were reasonable, and their investment had increased in value.

Exiting on the seventh floor, he strolled to the office of Hallett, Jones and Clancy, identified by six-inch-high gold letters. An attractive brunette displaying sparkling eyes and long lashes greeted him. As she led him to a conference room, he decided he could watch her sway in front of him all day long. She left him alone in a conference room with gossamer curtains covering large windows providing natural lighting reflected off a polished twenty-foot-long oak conference table. He'd need to punch out two walls to accommodate a piece of furniture this size in his office.

Moments later Donald Hallett strolled in. In his sixties with his well-trimmed silver hair above an immaculate gray Armani suit that did its best to hide his protruding gut, Donald looked like he could be a top business executive, politician, mob boss or shyster. Van figured the guy would have succeeded at any of the four but had chosen the latter as a preferred approach to pick pockets.

"May I offer you some coffee, tea . . . bourbon?"

Van waved him off. "I'm fine. I know you're a busy man, so let's get right to the point. Gloria Blendheim stands to inherit a lot of money and is in deep shit as a suspect for the murder of her husband. I've spoken with her, and a lot of circumstantial evidence points to her. She professes her innocence, but her alibi's not ironclad."

Donald chuckled. "I always like how you net things out, Van. You obviously don't get paid by the word."

"Never have, never will."

"Yes. The police are breathing down her pretty neck."

Van looked across the table, which didn't have a nick or scratch. He could shave by the reflection from its surface. "She told me she would inherit over a hundred mil. That really the case?"

"I'm afraid so. She gets the majority of the estate with a pittance going to Cornelius's only other heir, his son Huntington."

Van arched an eyebrow. "That's unusual. What happened between father and son?"

"They had a little blowup at the time Cornelius married Gloria. Huntington didn't approve of his dad playing house with such a young woman. So Dad took it out on him by cutting his portion of the inheritance to less than five million dollars."

"Tough life. I hate it when you get stuck with chump change like that. But it could at least provide pocket money for the kid."

"Huntington remains angry to this day at both Gloria and Cornelius. He wanted the big bucks, and it irritates him that he has to settle for a small percentage of his dad's total wealth. Expectations can cause problems between people. He feels he's owed more than he'll be getting."

Van stared at Donald. "Angry enough to whack the old guy?"

Donald shrugged. "Hard to say. He threw a valuable vase at Cornelius one time. That was the final incident before Cornelius changed his will."

"How will you keep the cops away from Gloria?"

"That's where I need your help. So far they have no conclusive physical proof to implicate her in the crime. As you summed up, lots of circumstantial evidence and speculation. Like Gloria, I'm concerned that the police aren't doing enough to chase down other suspects. I figure you may be able to turn up some additional leads and take police attention away from Gloria."

"You the one who steered Gloria to our agency?"

Donald grinned. "Could be."

"I'll see what I can do. You keep her out of jail for the time being. I have some interesting characters and information to check out."

"Good. Keep me apprised." Donald stood, reached across the table and shook Van's hand.

* * * * *

Back at his office Van received a return call from Huntington Blendheim. Van explained he was a private investigator looking into circumstances surrounding the death of Cornelius Blendheim. Huntington agreed to see him at two the next afternoon. Fortunately, Huntington didn't ask who had hired him.

* * * * *

That night after dark, Van prepared for some significant investigation into the Blendheim case. As Mulhaney had noted, Van did have an uncanny ability to track down information. He sat on the bed in his apartment and removed all his clothes. When he was completely naked, he removed his one piece of jewelry, a ring. As it slipped off his finger, his whole arm disappeared from view.

He remembered when he had first discovered this power—right after learning the other significant part of being a transvictus. He had left the orphanage to go out by himself into the woods. He came to a stream to wash off. After removing all his clothes, a ring he had found and worn since he was eleven slipped off his finger and, poof, he disappeared. Making that discovery as a thirteen-year-old kid would have been quite a surprise, but nothing compared to the shock of the significant transvictus side effect he had earlier encountered.

Although Van could use the power of invisibility during the day, he preferred only to employ it at night. Daylight presented risks—less chance of a screw up after dark. He chuckled at one of his early misadventures. After removing his clothes and ring one time at the age of probably fourteen or so, he had turned invisible and taken a walking tour of the girls' wing of the orphanage. He watched several of the girls change into swim suits for a trip to the pool. Then one of them threw a pair of underwear which landed on his head. Suddenly, a naked boy appeared in the girls' dorm, replete with panties on his head. Fortunately, this had hidden his face. They screamed, and he tore the panties off his head, pitched them away to resume his invisibility, before scurrying out of their dorm.

Van also refrained from driving a car when invisible. This had led to too many accidents when other motorists noticed a car with no driver, became distracted and bashed into telephone poles. He had vowed to use his unusual ability judiciously and to make sure he didn't give himself away or cause any harm.

He enjoyed the warm summer evening while strolling from his Lodo loft to police headquarters. Once he had to duck out of the way of a homeless man who almost staggered into him. No sense giving the guy a new trauma to add to his existing troubles.

Arriving at the fortress-like Denver Police Department building, he tailgated in behind a plainclothesman and headed to Mulhaney's office. The guy kept his desk in a mess but seldom worked nights, so Van had the place to himself. He sat in Mulhaney's swivel chair and began sorting through papers on the desk. Anyone looking at the chair would have seen a strange indentation but nothing more. He heard footsteps passing by and halted his search. He liked to circumvent potential problems—people spotting papers floating in the air. That type of optical illusion tended to raise the wrong kinds of questions, particularly in a police department.

Once the footfalls receded in the distance, he resumed his search. He tossed aside a donut wrapper, a paper cup with coffee crud solidified in the bottom and *The Denver Post* sports section, before continuing through the mound of reports.

Finally, an inch into the pile he found the Blendheim case report. Van scanned through it and would have whistled at what he read, except he didn't want to arouse undue attention.

Gloria was in deep doo-doo. The victim's blood was found on her dress, and a neighbor walking by had overheard her cussing at her husband in the front yard near the street earlier in the evening. That angelic woman, who had caused heart palpitations in his office, apparently had quite a temper when pissed off.

Cornelius had died from a bullet to the back of the head. No gunshot residue on the victim's hands, and the location of the bullet entry wound and lack of the gun being found eliminated a suicide. The 38 bullet matched the caliber that could have been fired from Gloria's registered Smith & Wesson Centennial 442 Airweight.

Furthermore, old Blendheim had changed his will a month before, turning over the majority of his pilfered cash from shady financial deals during his lifetime to his bride of one year. Van shook his head. Didn't look good for the broad.

No one reported hearing a gunshot—understandable because of the size of the Blendheim estate and with no staff on duty that night. Van now understood he was up against a thick and high brick wall.

As he continued reading, it looked like an altercation had taken place in Cornelius's den before the murder. Papers were strewn on the floor, items had been knocked off the desk including a small battery-powered clock. The clock had been damaged in the fall, knocking out the AA-battery. According to the police report, the hands on the clock were stopped at approximately seven minutes after ten.

Gloria had placed a 9-1-1 call at 10:28. Mulhaney's notes indicated he suspected she had shot her husband and then waited approximately twenty minutes before calling.

Van gave an invisible smile. One chink had appeared in the armor of Mulhaney's case against Gloria. She had been seen by Gladys Roons leaving the reception at ten o'clock. The damaged clock indicated the murder took place at seven minutes after ten. Gloria couldn't have driven home that quickly. He'd test the commute time later.

The one other interesting piece of information—one of the crime scene techs noted the aroma of Shalimar perfume in the den where the body was found. Van would have to poke at that issue as well. He couldn't claim to be an expert on perfume, but he didn't think he had sniffed Shalimar when Gloria came to his office earlier.

Resisting the urge to leave some mystifying souvenir of his visit to confound Mulhaney, Van's rationality won out, and he departed, making sure to avoid any collisions with unsuspecting denizens roaming the halls.

Next stop, Bentley Graves. His mansion would take him all night to walk to, so Van tailgated onto a bus and took a seat in the back where hopefully no one would try to sit in his lap. With two more transfers, he ended up within six blocks of his destination in Cherry Hills Village and enjoyed the stroll the rest of the way. He had certainly become an expert on the Denver public transportation system with his nighttime escapades.

Entering Graves's house presented no problem. If someone answered the door, Van had a tried-and-true method.

He couldn't go through walls or anything, but by putting some object such as a potted plant three feet from the door and ringing the doorbell, the occupant invariably would step outside to inspect the object, which allowed him to slip inside unnoticed.

At Graves's manse, Van walked through the grounds and stopped to peer in a window of the four-car garage. A Mercedes, BMW, jet ski and an MV Agusta F4 CC motorcycle nestled inside. The guy had expensive tastes with silver as his color of choice for each mode of transportation.

Van traipsed through a garden area large enough to give the Denver Botanical Gardens some competition and found a two-foot-high ceramic cupid statue. He hefted it up, chuckled at the thought of a neighbor seeing a flying cupid, carried it to the front porch and placed it so it would be visible from the doorway. Then he rang the doorbell and stepped aside to watch. A buxom blonde, who would give Gloria Blendheim a run for the money, answered the door and peered out. She wore a half-opened red robe over a short pink nightgown with enough thigh showing to cause Van to cover his mouth so his gasp wouldn't give him away.

She spotted the cupid. "What the . . ." She stepped outside to inspect it. Van wanted to take the time to ogle her, but with work to accomplish, he simply slipped inside the house.

"Bentley, have you been screwing around in the garden again?" she shouted back into the house.

"No, Eva." Bentley padded toward the door, wearing black house slippers and a smoking jacket. The guy had a pot belly, hook nose and less hair than a shaved Chihuahua. Van couldn't figure what these broads saw in the guy. He guessed money could be the reason for Eva, but why had Gloria jumped in the sack with this loser? Maybe something concerning power. Or had he happened upon a coven of nymphomaniacs who hopped in bed with any man who had the proper equipment between his legs? Hell. Who could figure out women?

Inside the house, Van waited for Bentley and Eva to return to the living room. She dropped on a couch in front of a sixty-inch wall-mounted plasma TV to watch a Seinfeld rerun, and Bentley plopped into an easy chair to read a report of some sort. Time for a little reconnoitering.

Van tiptoed through the house to get the lay of the land. A kitchen larger than his own loft, a billiard room, two guest bedrooms and a den were on the first floor. Making sure the residents still remained engrossed in their separate forms of entertainment, Van entered the den and sorted through papers on the surface of a large roll-top desk. The usual bills, several real estate contracts, a Merrill Lynch statement. Van gasped at the size of Bentley's holdings in this one account. The guy had weathered the stock market downturn in style.

Looking through the drawers, he found the usual collection of pens, pencils, sticky notes, calculator and stapler. Boring. Boring.

Van had just started sorting through the file cabinet when he heard footsteps. He quickly closed the drawer.

Bentley stomped into the den and dropped his oversized butt into the chair. He booted up his computer. Van stepped right behind him and watched as Bentley slowly finger pecked in the password r-i-c-h-p-o-w-e-r. He brought up several commercial real estate listings, surfed two porn sites and logged off.

As Van stood behind Bentley, his fingers itched to tweak the guy in the back of the head, but he resisted the urge.

With a grunt Bentley raised himself out of the chair and ambled back toward the living room.

Van waited a moment until he heard Eva whine. "Where's my scotch?"

"Go get it yourself," came the reply.

Van shook his invisible head. The honeymoon was over. He returned to the file cabinet and thumbed through a number of manila folders. He found one labeled "Denver Cooperative Art Alliance." He removed it and inspected the contents. A letter from the president reminding members to continue to solicit donations from their friends and contacts, followed by the minutes of the last two board meetings. He yawned. As exciting as watching toadstools grow in the backyard. Then he found a list of board members. A thick black mark underlined Gloria Blendheim's name accompanied by two exclamation marks. Subtle guy. Nothing else of interest in the folder. The remainder of the file cabinet provided no useful information.

Five minutes later, he heard Eva say, "I'm going up to bed."

"I'll join ya," Bentley replied.

Van headed out to the living room to watch.

Bentley set no alarm system and didn't even bother to turn off the lights before he trudged upstairs right behind Eva, giving her a pat on the rump.

Worked fine for Van. He could wander around to his heart's content and leave when he wanted with no alert being sounded. He made a pass around the living room, picked up the report Bentley had been reading and scanned through it until his eyes glazed over from the columns of housing statistics.

Once the toilet had flushed twice upstairs, he returned to the den and logged onto Bentley's computer. With password accepted, he checked Bentley's calendar. It showed the Denver Cooperative Art Alliance reception the evening before. Nothing else was scheduled that night.

Then on to email. Scanning email traffic for the last few days, Van's eyes riveted on a message from the afternoon of the murder. It stated, "Be at my place at eight-thirty," and bore the email signature of Cornelius Blendheim.

# Chapter 4

Time for a little fun. Van flexed his fingers and forwarded the message setting up a meeting between Cornelius and Bentley. Detective Mulhaney would get a kick out of reading it but would be perplexed over why it had been sent to him.

Then he deleted this communiqué from the sent message folder. Mulhaney could take it from there, and Bentley would be none the wiser. He still couldn't believe the guy hadn't deleted the original message, which made him a suspect the night of Cornelius's murder. Must have been too busy with all of his real estate finagling to take care of it.

With enough entertainment for the evening, Van logged off and wiped the keyboard with a tissue. He might be invisible, but he still left fingerprints. Then he went to the front door and let himself out. Looking up at a clear sky, he tried to make out a few summer constellations, but the ambient light made the effort futile. No wind and still warm enough not to cause him a problem wandering around with no clothes on.

He started whistling *Some Enchanted Evening*, then thought better of it in case some late night dog walker became freaked out at whistling appearing from thin air. He strode along the sidewalk but came to an abrupt halt when something squished beneath his right foot.

Damn. Speaking of dog walkers. The one hazard of walking around barefoot.

After wiping his foot on an immaculately trimmed bed of bluegrass, he continued unhampered to the bus stop. The first bus that came by didn't even slow down. He thought he might have to find a homeless man to roll for his clothes, but when the next bus appeared, a frumpy woman exited, giving him the opportunity to clamber aboard and squeeze through before the door slammed shut. Then he retraced his route, thanks to the Denver Regional Transportation District. He'd have to make an anonymous donation to RTD one of these days for all the free transportation they provided him. On the other hand, he contributed his fair share of sales tax dollars to support Denver transportation. All was fair in love, war and private investigation.

When Van returned to his loft, he thoroughly washed his foot, dressed to regain visibility and drove over to the Danvers Building where the Denver Cooperative Art Alliance reception had taken place. From there he timed the drive to the Blendheim estate. Twenty-three minutes. He drove back to the Danvers Building. Twenty-two minutes. He repeated the trip to the Blendheim house, driving as fast as he could. Twenty-one minutes.

Given the time of night, he had no interfering traffic and didn't think anyone could make it much faster without being stopped for speeding. That told him Gloria could only have reached her home at ten-twenty or later. It also fit the timeframe of Gloria calling 9-1-1 at ten-twenty-eight, approximately twenty minutes after the police estimate of when Cornelius had been shot.

This supported Van's contention of Mulhaney being off base in suspecting Gloria. He liked to believe in his clients. It made the work easier.

\* \* \* \* \*

Van awoke in the morning with a start. The vivid image of a reoccurring dream pulsed through his brain. Where did this strange image come from? He remembered slithering along the ground through tall grass, over rocks and coming to a closely cropped pasture. In the middle of the field stood a single lamb, pure white and motionless. He approached it at ground level until he was inches away from its hind hoof. The lamb did not move. He opened his mouth and bit the lamb's hoof. The lamb gave no resistance, just held its ground in the same place.

He remained in bed and replayed the vision again in his mind. Same sequence every time he had this dream. Always sneaking up on a lamb and grabbing a hoof in his mouth. Weird.

He stretched, jumped out of bed, changed, downed a cup of coffee and headed downstairs to his office to bill a client whose wife had not been cheating on him. After two days of surveillance, Van had determined she merely had a gambling addiction and frequented the casinos of Black Hawk to spend her hubby's hard-earned money on slots.

He spent the morning catching up on paperwork and with no new blonde bombshells gracing his threshold, he grabbed his usual hot dog at Steve's Snappin' Dogs before driving to Golden to meet with Huntington Blendheim.

Huntington lived in a new residential neighborhood with two-story houses crammed like sardines in a can, employing the California rabbit warren-style of architecture. A red Mini Cooper rested in the middle of the open two-car garage. The lawn sported brown patches between splotches of green that stood six inches too tall. Through a front window he could see a torn curtain and the front door looked like someone had tried unsuccessfully to kick it in.

Charming place.

Cornelius's son looked nothing like the pictures Van had seen of the old man. Huntington was in his thirties, bore a scraggly goatee with bagel pieces still embedded, stood all of five-foot-three and wore a dirty gray robe as if he had woken up moments before. He held a glass containing some dark brown gunk.

Van entered a living room strewn with movie magazines and old newspapers. The interior had the ambience of a landfill. A coffee table displayed a torn chip bag leaking its contents, an overturned Big Gulp cup and a half-eaten Twinkie. A dozen empty See's Candies boxes littered one corner of the room. Huntington was even more of a slob than Mulhaney.

"Have a seat." Huntington waved toward an old green couch

covered with junk mail and promotional flyers.

Van cleared a spot and lowered himself, first checking to make sure nothing was alive and moving. When not attacked, he settled onto an uneven cushion. "I'm sorry about your father's death."

Huntington plunked down into a dark blue armchair that leaked stuffing from what could have been a knife slash. He didn't bother to remove the magazines scattered on the cushion. "It was bound to happen. At one time I would have mourned the loss. Not anymore. Good riddance."

Van scanned the living room to make sure no rodents scurried out from underneath any of the trash on the rug. "What happened between you and your dad?"

"Gloria. That bitch." He looked up with red-lined eyelids. "I was dating her and introduced her to my father. She decided to go after the source of the money rather than me. The damn gold digger." He picked up a magazine and flung it across the room, striking a lamp which teetered before making a cushioned landing on a pile of newspaper.

Interesting. Gloria had neglected this little detail of an earlier relationship with Huntington. He needed to have a little heart-to-heart talk with his client. "How long ago did this happen?" Van couldn't see the taller Gloria dating this doofus. Maybe she had planned the handoff to Cornelius the whole time.

He took a gulp from the glass and stuck out his tongue. "A year and some. She dumped me, planted her hooks in dear old dad, and they married two months later. She also conned him into changing his will, so I get next to zilch while she inherits a fortune." His fingers played with his goatee. "She probably knocked him off because she hadn't been able to get him to have a heart attack yet."

Van watched Huntington, who twitched as if on the verge of having a seizure. "I understand you're Cornelius's only offspring."

He took another sip and slammed the glass down on the coffee table. "Yeah. He divorced my mom right after I was born. Took up with a younger woman. Went through a number of them but must have shot blanks after me." Huntington scratched his hairy leg. "I was sitting pretty until Gloria came along."

"And your mom?"

He gave a dismissive wave. "She died right after I turned ten.

Suicide. Apparently she never recovered from the divorce. My father had a way of tossing women aside. One minute he's in bed with them, the next authorizing his lawyer to serve them divorce papers. Quite a guy."

"Did you live with your father at all?"

Huntington picked up his glass again and took another swallow. "After my mom died, he took me in. Treated me like a servant rather than family. I stayed with him until I went to college. No way I'd go back after that."

Van leaned forward. "Did you kill your father?"

Huntington dropped the glass and it shattered on the coffee table. "What the hell are you asking? Of course not." He waved a shaky index finger at Van. "But Gloria, the bitch, probably did."

Van sniffed the air and smelled the distinct odor of rotting vegetables. He wondered if Huntington's neighbors had placed a call to the state health department yet. "What were you doing the night before last?"

"Sitting here."

"Anyone see you?"

"Not unless there's a peeping tom in the neighborhood." He kicked at a book lying near his foot. "You working with that lawyer, Hallett?"

"I met with him yesterday."

He nodded. "I hope he's honest. I don't want to be screwed out of any more inheritance."

"He's reputable." Both of Van's arms started to itch. "The police spoken with you?"

"A detective named Mulhaney came by yesterday morning. Asked some of the same dumb ass questions you did." Huntington jumped up and looked at his watch. "I have to meet someone. You can let yourself out."

Van stood up and dropped a card on the coffee table, careful to avoid the glass shards and globules of dark liquid. "Give me a call if you think of anything else related to your father's death."

\* \* \* \* \*

Returning from his little expedition, Van resisted the urge to take a long, hot, steaming shower and settled in for a late afternoon of matching expenses to the meager income for the agency. Gloria had shown up on his doorstep at exactly the right time. The agency could use a cash infusion from a beautiful broad with deep . . . pockets.

As he prepared to wrap up for the day, he received a call from none other than his new client. Gloria Blendheim's throaty voice announced, "The police have released my home. You're welcome to come check it out any time you want."

He knew exactly what he wanted to check out. He regarded his watch. "How does eight tonight work for you?"

"That would be lovely," came the sultry reply.

His heart skipped a beat as he replaced the receiver. Damn. He would have to be careful with this woman. Anyway, now he could snoop around the Blendheim place with the owner's permission. Unlike last night, Van preferred being invited and not compromising a crime scene. Furthermore, he looked good in clothes.

* * * * *

At five minutes after eight Van rang the doorbell of the Blendheim mansion. As he waited, he turned, and his gaze lifted to the volutes of the Ionic columns lining the front porch. A huge place. No one needed this much space. Off to the side he noticed a tennis court. He wondered if anyone even used it. Then he had an image of Gloria's long legs beneath a skimpy white tennis skirt barely covering her gorgeous ass.

He slapped his cheek to stay focused.

Finally, the door opened and Gloria stood there in a red silk kimono open to stupendous cleavage.

"No butler tonight?" Van gulped, trying unsuccessfully to look at her face.

She gave him a perky smile. "The staff has the night off. Come on in."

*Uh-oh.* He'd have to be extra careful. He followed her into the living room, passing an Oriental vase large enough to contain a dead body. He peered inside, just to make sure. Nothing there.

"May I offer you a drink?" She arched a perfectly lined eyebrow.

"No thanks. I'm fine. Before I check your husband's files, I have several questions for you. Why didn't you tell me that you and Huntington had a thing going before you hooked up with the old man?"

Gloria's gaze dropped. "Oh, dear. I guess you spoke with Hunty."

"And you expected I wouldn't?"

She gave him her little girl's teary look. "You're thorough. I knew you'd talk to him."

"Then why didn't you level with me at the outset?"

She shrugged. "I guess it didn't strike me as that important."

Van rolled his eyes. "Look, Gloria. If I'm going to do any good for you, you need to be upfront with me on everything."

She thrust her chest out. "Okay, I promise."

Van could get used to that way of being upfront. "Any chance Huntington came over two nights ago and killed Cornelius?"

She put a finger to her cheek. "It's possible. He acted pretty steamed at his father. He drives a red Mini Cooper. Maybe someone saw it in the neighborhood. I told Detective Mulhaney he should check that out."

"Yeah, if he'd get past considering you the only suspect. Another question for you. Do you ever wear Shalimar perfume?"

She scrunched up her nose. "Never."

"Okay. Now I'm anxious to take a look at your husband's files. See if I can spot any clue as to who might have held a grudge against him."

"Follow me."

She wiggled down the hallway, and Van's eyes pulled toward her like iron filings to a magnet as her kimono swished from side to side. He thought of a Hawaiian hula as she swayed in front of him. His gaze went lower and he almost whistled. Great calves. Some woman. How the hell was he supposed to concentrate on the case?

"Right in here." She pointed inside a doorway only half a mile down the corridor.

"Did the police take his computer?" Van asked.

"No. They hooked something up to it, I imagine, to suck off all the files." She licked her lips and stared at Van.

"Uh . . . yeah, they copied everything from his hard drive." Van could feel a hard drive in his pants. "I'll take a look as well. Do you know his password?"

"Yes. Bite me. One word and all lower case."

Van nodded. "Okay. Let me spend some time on the computer

looking at his files."

"I'll be in the living room when you want me." She turned and pranced out of the room, leaving him reeling from her fragrance.

Once he heard her footsteps receding along the marble hallway floor, he let out a deep breath. Gloria didn't waste any time in the suffering widow role.

A large mahogany desk in the middle of the room held the computer, telephone and a pen set award from the Denver Rotary Club. A credenza behind the desk had a single object—a picture of Gloria. In it she stood on a cliff with waves crashing in the background. The wind had whipped her hair to the side, and she had a serious, far-away look in her eyes. The only other furniture in the room consisted of a book shelf and a four-drawer file cabinet, fortunately unlocked. The walls contained plaques from various service organizations thanking Cornelius for his contributions. Everybody loved a honcho who dealt out bucks like a big spender in Vegas.

Van began checking the file cabinet. The top drawer contained financial records. Cornelius had approximately twenty CDs at different banks and savings and loans, all in amounts between two-hundred-thousand and two-hundred-fifty-thousand dollars. The government would protect him if any of these institutions went bust. Then your typical stock portfolio worth at most ten mill. A checking account with only ninety-thousand dollars available. Chump change. Then a smattering of bonds and annuities. Tough life.

The second drawer held real estate holdings. The accounts in the top drawer were peanuts compared to these. Old Cornelius had amassed close to a hundred million in assessed property value for a number of commercial properties, a house in the Bahamas and the one Van stood in. Gloria had no financial worries for the future, assuming she didn't end up behind bars.

He found one manila folder with references to a deal being consummated with Bentley Graves, the sleazy real estate guy who had an affair with Gloria. Not surprising.

Van moved on to the computer. Checking the calendar, he saw no indication of a meeting with Bentley Graves the night of Cornelius's death. The day of his murder he had been scheduled for a massage in the early afternoon and had a nine-fifteen P.M. meeting with someone named Greer Lawson. Van jotted her name on his notepad.

Next he checked email. No record of the message sent to Bentley Graves. Cornelius must have deleted it. So the police wouldn't be onto that connection except for the message Van had sent Mulhaney. After another hour of fruitlessly searching through computer files, Van took a break and sauntered out to the living room.

Gloria looked up from a *Mademoiselle* magazine. "Anything interesting?"

Van regarded all the thigh visible through the gap in the kimono. "Yeah . . . several things. Does the name Greer Lawson mean anything to you?"

Her eyes flared. "That conniving bitch."

Van gawked at her for a moment. "Cornelius had an appointment with her the evening he died."

"She was always trying to get her claws into him. Fluttered those fake eyelashes and rubbed her boob implants against him. Didn't have any effect on Cornelius, though."

"Why would he have been meeting with her?"

Gloria gave a little snort. "She claims to be a real estate agent, although I doubt she sells much except herself."

"I'll check her out," Van said. "One other question. Did Cornelius do much business with Bentley Graves?"

Gloria sucked on her full lower lip. "Probably. They both had big deals going on, so I'm sure they had some contact."

"Anything recent you're aware of?"

She shook her head. "Other than with me, no."

"Have you spoken with Bentley since the reception?"

She threw her hands out in a crossing motion. "No way. As I told you before, we're done. Other than seeing him at board meetings, it's over."

"Did Bentley mention any appointment the night of the reception?"

"We never discussed plans for that evening. I told him we were through, and he stalked away. Simple as that."

Nothing was ever as simple as that. Van would see what Mulhaney came up with. Nice having the police working for you. Mulhaney would never divulge what he found, but Van could uncover what he wanted to know with another night visit to Mulhaney's office.

"Anything else I should be aware of?" Van asked.

Gloria looked thoughtful. "Yes. When I returned to my house today, I noticed my diamond necklace and earrings missing."

"Did you report that to the police?"

She nodded. "And to the insurance company."

"Can you describe them to me?"

She stood. "Better yet, I have a picture in my insurance file. Be right back." She returned moments later with a photograph of a string of huge diamonds and a pair of earrings.

Van whistled. "Quite a set of rocks."

"They're worth more than a million dollars. Maybe the murderer stole them."

Van returned the photograph and looked around Gloria's living room. He tried to picture someone entering the house, going into Cornelius's den invited or not, finding Gloria's or Cornelius's gun or having his own, firing a shot and taking off. He'd have to poke around at people with motives to do away with old Cornelius.

With nothing more to be accomplished here this evening, he prepared to make his exit.

Gloria reached for a cigarette.

He held a hand up. "Please don't smoke until I leave. Remember I'm allergic."

Ignoring him, she lit up. "I'm curious about this allergy of yours. Do you break out in hives? Turn red? Puke?" She blew smoke right in his face.

Van reeled as the room spun. Heat shot through his chest and down into his groin. His blood pulsed, and before he knew it, he had taken Gloria in his arms, removed her cigarette and planted a kiss on her lips.

"Oh my. That kind of allergy." She thrust her tongue into his mouth.

His mouth quivered as their tongues met. Then he pressed his body against hers and found his hand on her full breast. She reached down and stroked the emerging bulge in his pants.

They came up for air, and she grabbed his hand. "Let's adjourn to more cozy surroundings." She led him upstairs to her bedroom. He barely caught a glimpse of the blue rug and huge four-poster bed before she doused the light, threw the covers aside and pulled him onto the sheet.

They pawed at each other, and clothes began flying like kites on a spring day. In all his lust Van still made sure to keep on his ring as he grasped Gloria's glorious breasts while their tongues intertwined. She tore into him like a lioness consuming a piece of raw meat. They grappled, engaged and sent the bed into vibrations of delight. Then he entered her as she arched her back and drove him into a new realm of ecstasy. With his one final thrust, Gloria let out a blood-curdling scream to be matched by Van's wild shout of joy. Then they collapsed onto the mattress.

She let out a deep sigh, turned on her side and was asleep like a knocked-out boxer.

Van lay there, panting, a kaleidoscope of colors surging through his sex-sated brain. Then it began. His skin started to stretch over his chest as a fullness set in. A twinge in his groin followed, and his testicles and penis began to shrivel. The hair on his head lengthened and tangled in his face. His dainty hand went to his chin, where soft skin now had replaced the five o'clock shadow. The ring became loose on the now slender finger, and it was slipped off so that Gloria couldn't see the completed result. Van had now transformed into Vanna.

# Chapter 5

Now invisible, Vanna slipped out of bed, careful not to disturb the sleeping Gloria Blendheim. She had not come prepared for this eventuality. When Van had the hots for some dame, he usually brought an appropriate change of clothes along in a sports bag for the aftermath. Fortunately, they both kept spare garments in the trunk of the car. Vanna jotted a note for Gloria explaining the hasty departure, picked up Van's clothes and ring, removed the car keys from the pants' pocket, and traipsed out to The V V Agency's blue Subaru to retrieve her packet of clothes, packed in a red bag. She changed and put on a necklace, glad that Gloria's servants had the night off so no one would see a half-naked woman appear in the driveway.

Although Vanna could give Gloria competition in the looks department, she didn't think Van's client would appreciate waking up and finding a naked woman beside her. Although pissed at Van for letting his prick get out of control again, she allowed herself a moment of gratitude to be back.

She slid into the driver's seat of her car, set the GPS navigator for home. She suffered this little directional challenge and had no clue how to get back to her loft at night. At least during the day she could see the mountains. In Denver, mountains equal west. On a cloudy day with no GPS, she might wander through the city for hours. As she drove, her thoughts drifted back to the first time Van had shape-shifted into Vanna.

Van had been thirteen years old and living in the All Souls Orphanage in Denver. He had heard the older boys describe masturbation but had never given it a try. Then one night as he lay awake, he felt an arousal beneath his pajamas. Careful not to make any noise, he grabbed himself and began rubbing. That felt so good. He increased the friction until he lost control and an incredible warmth passed through his whole body. He gasped and found his hand wet with a sticky substance. So, this was what the other boys had been talking about. Cool. He liked it. He'd have to try it again.

Then another strange sensation came over him. His skin shrank in places, expanded and curved elsewhere. With his hand still holding his dick, he felt it suddenly shrivel up. Oh my god. Had he broken the thing off? No one had ever mentioned a side effect of wearing away a penis by rubbing it too hard. Had he over-masturbated on his first time? Was this what the priest meant by his indirect and indecipherable warnings to the boys?

Then something popped out on Van's chest. He raised his hand and found breast buds. He rubbed them and they tingled. He touched his head. Long hair replaced his crew cut.

What was happening to him? He reached back below his pajamas to find he had no penis, no balls. Where had they gone? He groped around, finding some fuzz and an opening and slipped a finger into the slit. Umm. Good feeling. He inserted it farther and located a small protrusion. He rubbed it. Wow. Not bad. He began stroking and waves of pleasure coursed though his body. He kept at it until he shuddered and slumped onto the mattress. Exhausted, he fell asleep.

When he woke the next morning, everything appeared back to normal. He remembered a strange dream. Or had it been a dream? It seemed too real. Had he really transformed into a girl and back to a boy?

Other than peeing, he didn't dare touch himself down below for two days. Then curiosity got the better of him. Late in the afternoon he snuck away to a favorite place in the woods and disappeared into the undergrowth. When he reached his spot, he took off his clothes, leaving on his ring. He grabbed himself and rubbed. The excitement built in his young body until the release came and he spurted into the leaves lining the forest floor.

Wow. That was really something. He gasped. Then the weird sensation began again. He looked down in horror as his penis and balls disappeared. Exactly like what he remembered from the night in bed. His body changed shape, and he transformed into a girl. He stroked his long brown hair, felt his face soften and ran his hands over the small breasts.

He looked around in a panic. What if the other boys saw him? He couldn't go back to the orphanage looking like this. He remembered what else he had done that night in bed. He reached down and found the opening between his legs and rubbed until the incredible feeling of warmth spread through his body. With a final convulsion, he gasped and removed his finger. In moments the opening sealed up. His breasts morphed back to his normal chest. He felt the top of his head and the short hair had returned, and the right set of gear reappeared between his legs.

Weird and weirder. He moseyed down to the nearby stream to wash off from his sexual explorations. And when the ring slipped off, his hand disappeared from view. This was the occasion he first discovered the attribute of invisibility also accompanied his unique gender transformation.

\* \* \* \* \*

Vanna parked the car in her parking lot and was lugging Van's clothes toward the building when she heard a growling sound. Out of the shadows appeared a large, black Doberman, snarling with saliva dripping from its bared teeth.

Anyone else would have hightailed out of there, but Vanna approached. "Hi there, boy." She held out her hand.

The dog growled but took a step back.

Like Crocodile Dundee, she formed her fingers into horns and waggled them at the dog as she kept her eyes focused on its forehead.

It closed its mouth and sat back on its haunches.

She reached out and patted its head.

It whimpered, rolled over and pawed the air.

She rubbed its belly, as it panted contentedly. "Go on. Get out of here." She whacked it on the side, and it clambered to its feet to trot off.

Vanna took the elevator to her apartment, a separate loft adjoining Van's. It cost more to keep two places, but it eliminated a lot of confusion. Besides, it provided a good real estate investment for The V V Agency.

She punched in the numbers on the keypad. For convenience, both loft doors as well as the agency office were secured with combination locks to provide easy access for naked people who didn't have a place to stash keys.

She needed a good night's sleep. The transformation always exhausted her, but she looked forward to being Vanna for an extended period of time. She planned to avoid sex for as long as possible. Let Van disappear into his never-neverland for a long, long vacation. He'd had too much control over her life anyway. Maybe she'd swear off sex altogether, and Van would never reappear. Nah. She couldn't hold out forever. Besides, she knew Van had less control than she did. He'd have cigarette smoke blown in his face, get horny and she'd be back again.

* * * * *

The next morning Vanna's eyes shot open. The same dream again. She didn't know how many times her brain had been invaded by this specter. Not scary, not enjoyable, nothing sexual—it just happened. She tapped her forehead as if trying to dislodge the image of what she had seen. No, it remained there as clear as could be. She had been standing out in a grassy area as a snake approached. She had no fear of the reptile. When it reached her, she bent her head and picked up its tail in her mouth. She could sense cold scales against her lips. She could smell a strange musty aroma. She had savored an earthy taste, unlike any she had ever experienced except during this dream. The snake didn't struggle but acquiesced to being held in her mouth. The sun beat down, birds chirped, and she and the snake remained in stationary unity. Why did she have this identical dream over and over again?

She went to the sink and spit, trying to rid herself of the lingering taste. She squirted a dab of toothpaste in her mouth, ran her tongue over her teeth and roof of her mouth and spit again.

Feeling the need to cleanse her whole body, she ran water in the tub and allowed herself a luxurious and lengthy vanilla truffle bubble bath. She always kept on her necklace when bathing in order to stay visible.

Afterwards, she let the water run out of the tub and dried herself with a soft crisp towel. Selecting black slacks, a white blouse and comfortable pumps, she dressed.

Next, she planned her day, looking up Greer Lawson's address, but decided to first pay a visit to Detective Mulhaney. She called him and found him in the office. "Detective, I'd like to meet with you regarding the Blendheim case."

"Your place or mine?" He chortled.

"Let's select a neutral site. The Starbucks on Lawrence between 16th and 17th."

"You got it, babe. You coming alone or bringing that dipstick partner of yours?"

"You'll have me all to yourself, Detective."

"Promises, promises. Be there in ten." The phone disconnected.

After a quick visual check to locate the mountains, Vanna set the GPS navigator for extra measure. With the assistance of her electronic tracking, she parked, ordered her mocha latte and sat at a corner table. Minutes later Mulhaney sauntered in, grabbed a black coffee and joined her.

"To what do I owe the pleasure of your undivided attention?" Mulhaney took a gulp of coffee.

She gave him her brightest smile. "I thought you might have received some interesting leads on a murder suspect, other than Gloria Blendheim."

He regarded her warily. "Why would you think that?"

"With all of Cornelius Blendheim's financial dealings, I'm sure he had business transactions that might have been problematic." She batted her eyelashes at him.

It had the desired effect. He leaned toward her and whispered. "Well, I did receive an interesting tip yesterday."

She leaned toward him as well. "Do tell."

"A real estate guy had a meeting scheduled with Blendheim the evening he got whacked."

"Sounds promising."

Mulhaney tilted his hand up and down. "Maybe, maybe not. I checked the guy out. He claimed the scheduled meeting never took place."

"Anyone alibi him?"

"He attended the same reception as your client that night. But he left early. Could have gone to see Blendheim. He can't come up with an alibi for the whole evening."

Vanna sat back in her chair, revisiting what Gloria had told Van. Her client had noticed Bentley leave early. Made him as good a suspect as any. "So that lets my client off the hook."

"Not exactly. Let's say we have multiple persons of interest at this time." He paused and leered at her. "Care to join me for dinner tonight?"

"What would your wife think, Detective?"

"Ex. I'm a free man." He waggled an eyebrow at her.

"Thanks, but I have some investigative work to do. Now if you cleared my client, I might have more free time." She leaned toward him and patted his paw.

He let out an exaggerated snort. "Can't do that, but I'd sure like to see more of you."

She knew exactly what he'd like to see more of, but it wasn't going to happen. "Maybe another time, Detective." She stood. "We'll be talking." She had a brief image of having sex with Mulhaney and letting him find himself in bed with Van. It would serve the prick right, but she'd never go through the displeasure of getting to that point.

Next on the agenda—Greer Lawson. She punched in the address and then followed the GPS map to the destination in Highlands Ranch. She pulled up in front of a two-story brick McMansion, replete with four-car garage, sculpted hedges and fountain gushing water from the mouth of a carved white whale.

Near the sidewalk of the house next door, a little girl in a yellow frock sat playing with a collection of stuffed animals. She moved them around like a ringmaster commanding circus acts. Two braids, tied off with pink ribbon, held her golden hair behind her head.

Vanna sadly shook her head at the sight. She had completely missed a childhood as a little girl. She had popped into existence for the first time at thirteen and had only brief stints before being transformed back into Van. In fact, only at the age of twenty-one did she have an opportunity to really get to know herself. After Van had a one-time romp with a waitress and wannabe actress in Vail, Vanna stayed celibate for six months and learned the life of a young woman. She returned to Denver, talked herself into a job as a receptionist at a PI agency, shopped every free moment her meager salary would allow, taught herself to cook and learned how to apply makeup.

Vanna had treasured that first period of independence. She gained confidence, took a karate class to develop sound punching and kicking skills and dated a number of interesting men, including a doctor, a lawyer, a stockbroker and a rodeo rider. The time as Vanna would have lasted longer except she fell for a gorgeous hunk who appeared at the agency one day, seeking assistance in locating a long-lost brother. One of the private investigators found the missing brother, and Vanna discovered the pleasure of making mad passionate love, with the only drawback being that she transformed back into Van.

She narrowly escaped being detected during the transformation and subsequently lost her job at the agency when she didn't show up for work for two weeks. When Van had his next fling, she pleaded to be rehired, but by then she had been replaced by a redhead who had no intention of giving up her spot.

Still, that six-month period of time introducing her to life as a woman had also sparked the idea for the formation of The V V Agency. With her experience watching private investigators operate plus Van's natural inclination and ability to find lost things and people, The V V Agency was launched a year later. They learned to operate with one and only one of them available to help clients at any time.

The little girl picked up her stuffed animals and raced into the house. Vanna let out a deep sigh and headed up the walkway to Greer Lawson's door.

She rang the doorbell.

A woman in her thirties with her hair held back in a band appeared in the doorway. Her aerobic-sculpted body neatly fit her tights.

Vanna sniffed. Shalimar perfume. Interesting. "Ms. Lawson?"

A sneer. "Yes?"

Vanna held out a card. "I'm with The V V Agency, private investigation. I want to speak with you regarding the death of Cornelius Blendheim."

Her lip trembled. "Dear Corny. What a loss. Please do come in."

In the entryway stood a shining knight in armor holding a diamond-shaped red and blue shield and a lance.

"Are you into medieval decor?" Vanna asked.

Greer waved her hand. "Oh, that. A remnant from my dear-departed husband."

"I'm sorry for your loss."

"Yeah, one parasailing trip too many. Howard loved to take risks. May I offer you some coffee or tea?"

"No thanks. I just made my Starbucks visit."

They sat in an all-white living room, including furniture, plush rug, and curtains. Vanna felt like she had plunked down in a Woody Allen movie. She decided to get right to the point. "I understand you knew Cornelius Blendheim quite well."

Greer dabbed at her eye. "Oh, yes. We even planned to get married once he dumped that bimbo."

Vanna leaned forward. "I never had the impression that Cornelius planned to divorce Gloria."

Greer's chin bounced up and down like a bobble doll. "Oh, he did. Ours was true love . . . and wild sex."

Vanna arched an eyebrow. "I thought Cornelius was happily married."

"Ha." Greer let out a burst of air. "Where'd you hear that? He didn't get what he wanted at home. He needed the right woman." She gave a satisfied grin. Then the smile faded. "But now he's gone."

"Speaking of which, where were you the night of his murder?"

Greer's eyes flared. "I had been to his house that evening. We met while his so-called wife traipsed around at some la-di-da reception. He remained as vital as ever." She actually winked at Vanna.

"What time did you leave?"

"We snuggled on the couch in his den, and I left at nine-forty-five. He said he had some work to do."

"Anyone see you after that?"

She lunged out of her seat. "What is this, some kind of inquisition?"

Vanna gave her most sincere smile. "Only trying to establish your alibi."

"Alibi . . . alibi . . . I don't need no stinking alibi. I had no reason to want dear Corny dead."

Vanna's gaze turned steely. "You haven't answered my question."

"Why I . . . I came back here of course," Greer sputtered.

"Did anyone see you?"

"No . . . o . . . o." She visibly slumped. "Is . . . is that a problem?"

"Could be. The police will be checking all of Cornelius's associates . . . business and otherwise."

"I'd never do anything to harm a hair on his head."

Vanna recalled the picture of Cornelius that Van had seen on Detective Mulhaney's desk. The guy appeared as bald as a cue ball.

"Still you had access to Cornelius on the night of his death. The authorities will be mighty interested in that."

Greer strutted over to the front door and held it open. "Out. I've had enough of this. I need to go to my aerobics class."

Vanna dropped her card on an end table. "If you think of anything else you'd like to share, give me a call." She stepped through the door as it slammed behind her.

Interesting set of reactions from that woman. She'd have to come back at night for a little further inspection of Greer's house. Maybe the missing necklace would be kicking around here somewhere. Vanna looked at her watch. She could grab a sandwich before heading up to Boulder. The Special Collections and Rare Book Room at the Norlin Library at the University of Colorado would be open at one. She had a little time to continue her research. Too bad Van didn't have any interest in pursuing what she had started. Men!

After a tuna sub at a nearby Quiznos, she set her GPS for the library, double-checked to orient herself with the mountains to her left and headed north on I-25 and onto I-36. In Boulder she came to a stop at the light on 28th and Colorado Boulevard. Her GPS flickered and then went out. "Shit." She tapped it, but it remained as dead as Cornelius Blendheim. And she was dead in the water. She knew the library was around here somewhere. She could see the Flatirons, the rock formation to the west of campus, and spotted the collection of university buildings. In the trunk she had a campus map. Previously, she had left her car in a public parking structure somewhere on campus. Using her only other navigation capability, she drove toward the mountains. After stopping to ask three students, she finally found the visitors' parking lot.

With a sigh of relief, she pulled into an available spot on the open air part of the structure. She stared at her GPS. She shook it again. Nothing happened. Then she looked under it and noticed a loose wire. With a screwdriver from the glove compartment, she reattached the offending wire. The GPS came alive. Good. Now she could get home afterwards. Otherwise, she would either have to have sex to regain Van's excellent navigational skills or hire a guide.

The next challenge—locating the library. She opened the trunk. It contained two sports bags—one red and one blue—changes of clothes for Vanna and Van. Other items included a crime scene kit, a blanket, cuffs, a roll of duct tape, a first aid kit, a survival kit, a Beretta 92 hidden in the tire well, a packet of maps and lock picks for special entry situations. She couldn't remember the exact direction to take from the parking garage. Van would be able to find the library with his eyes closed, as opposed to her directional disorder. She thumbed through the maps and found one for the CU campus. She had to orient it to line up with her view of the foothills. She started walking in the direction the map indicated and immediately became confused. She ended up under a portico with a sign for the Alferd Packer Grill, the campus cafeteria named after a real-life cannibal. She stepped out to a fountain with a partial view of the mountains and reoriented herself to her map. She attributed her directional disability to never being a girl. If she had spent time in Girl Scouts maybe she'd have learned how to use a compass and map and be able to get her butt to the right place. With several more miscues and assistance from an eager young man wearing shorts, T-shirt and sandals, she finally found the west entrance to the library. Success.

The building, which conformed to the CU architectural standard, had pink sandstone walls and a red tile roof. Steps led up to an entryway with large columns and the words, "Who knows only his own generation remains a child." Vanna nodded her head at the good advice. Two red pots by the columns on either side of the door contained pink and purple petunias. Another motto right over the door stated, "Enter here the timeless fellowship of the human spirit." Vanna didn't experience much of that timeless fellowship in her chosen profession. On the contrary, she often experienced the mean-spirited side of human nature. Too much of it in fact.

After entering the library, she turned left and climbed a set of cement stairs lined with iron balusters, topped by a polished wooden handrail. The stairs curved back once. She exited on the floor above, actually the third floor, and strode to N345. She stepped into a room with a librarian at a computer to the left and large wooden reading tables in the middle of the room. A worn Persian rug covered the floor. Across the room a glass case resting against one wall displayed a blue on white Afghani burka. Above it hung a large brown tapestry.

Vanna filled out the sign-in card and gave it and her driver's license to the librarian along with the title and Library of Congress call number for the book she wanted to review.

Madam librarian with her gray hair tied back in a neat bun disappeared into the adjoining room to retrieve the requested manuscript.

While waiting, Vanna took a deep breath, reveling in the musty smell of old documents. This had been her home-away-from-home. Whenever she had a spare three hours, she'd come here to continue her research.

Among the dusty tomes, she'd found one particularly intriguing volume. Of course she couldn't remove it from this room. She had once considered sneaking in at night and taking it out to a copy shop, but then decided to honor the library's desire to keep the books in as good condition as possible.

In addition to the rare books, this room always had interesting displays of old curios. In a glass case she viewed a collection of colorful Slavic Easter eggs. Another shelf contained Bakelite purses and on a lower shelf a typewriter used by Jean Stafford. Vanna had previously learned that this section of the library also housed a whole collection of Stafford's writing notes. Under a glass case rested an 1842 table of Mortality. Dead people always generated interest. Quite an eclectic display of whatnots.

The librarian returned and set the book on a wooden cradle lined with felt.

Vanna's fingers shivered as she caressed the lining. She wondered if the Pope felt this way when he stepped up to his ornate lectern to address the masses. She took her notepad and digital camera out of her purse and picked up one of the library-provided pencils (no pens allowed) and sat down at a table to continue her note-taking. This volume was titled, *Shape-shifting Through the Ages*. It had been published in 1893 and written by Harold Munion, an academic who researched mythology. Little did Harold know that it wasn't mythology after all. Still his work provided an interesting background on different types of shape-shifting stories. She had read accounts of a number of Native American shape-shifters. But she had no interest in the transformations between humans and animals.

In this book Vanna had first found a reference to the concept of a transvictus—a transformation between man and woman. Munion missed several critical aspects though. He wrote nothing regarding the ability to become invisible. Furthermore, in his Victorian academic style he neglected to mention anything about sex triggering the transformation between man and woman. Finally, he didn't realize the unique characteristics materialized at puberty. She found the page where she had left off and began reading. She avidly consumed a chapter before another reference to a transvictus appeared. Munion stated he had come across a report of a transvictus in New York City in the mid 1840s. A number of people had claimed to see a sailor get off a sailing ship and transform into a woman. Munion dismissed this as merely being a woman who had disguised herself as a man in order to reach America.

On the next page Vanna found a reference to a person named Charles Rubiar. He had been a wealthy financier in San Francisco during the Gold Rush. Reputedly, he changed into a woman named Charlene who committed a series of murders. She lured men from the gold mines into a wooded estate owned by Charles Rubiar. They disappeared, and Charles became wealthier. But dispute remained over whether Charles shape-shifted into Charlene or if he hired her as an assassin. Interesting.

Van and Vanna used their special ability to help people and hunt down criminals, but they could have as easily applied their talent to the other side of the law. Good thing the nuns in the orphanage beat some morals into Van. Still, he could have rebelled and gone the way of Charles Rubiar.

Vanna brushed her hair back, licked a finger and turned the page. An index card rested in the middle of the next page. It read: "Transvictus? Call 303 555-0172."

# Chapter 6

Vanna stared at the index card left in the library book. Could this be someone who had valid transvictus information? Or merely a kook who wanted to play a prank on people? One part of her wanted to immediately take out her cell phone and call the number. Her more cautious side wanted to gather more information first. She grabbed the card by the edges and turned it over. Blank. She reached in her purse and removed a baggy. She waited until the librarian had her back turned, then still grasping the index card by an edge, dropped it into the plastic bag and slipped it into her purse.

If needed, she could dust the card for fingerprints. Although she didn't officially have access to AIFIS, she could sneak into police headquarters and use Mulhaney's office if required. In the meantime she would check out the phone number. She thumbed through the rest of the book and found no other notes. She filled out the required copyright form and photographed half a dozen pages in the book before notifying the librarian that the book could be returned to its shelved location. Something new to consider here.

As she left the library, Vanna looked across a large grass field toward Flagstaff Mountain. To the right appeared Old Main, the first building constructed on the University of Colorado campus in 1876.

She always enjoyed walking around this beautiful campus, usually having to go twice as far as anyone else to find where she wanted to go. Today she couldn't afford to wander off, other than allowing the usual time for getting back to her car.

With her map correctly oriented, she marched off to find the parking lot, which only required two inquiries and three changes of direction. Back in her car she felt like Lewis and Clark having survived the Oregon Trail. She wondered if other people had the same trouble she did navigating around the civilized world.

* * * * *

Returning to her office before rush hour traffic jammed I-36, Vanna kicked off her pumps, stretched her toes, logged on her computer and checked a reverse phone directory to locate the owner of the phone number she had found in the book at the library. It popped right up with a hit. Turned out to be someone named Harlan Shannon with an address on Marine Street in Boulder.

She Googled the name and found him to be a full professor of history at the University of Colorado who had also received numerous awards and served on the Board of the Boulder Historical Society—all indications of being an upstanding citizen and not some weirdo. She noticed that he would be giving a lecture titled, "Mythology in Modern Society," at the Boulder Public Library the next evening at seven. This would be a way to check him out. She made a note on her calendar.

At that moment the door opened, and Gloria Blendheim waltzed in. She was dressed to kill but scowled at Vanna. "Where's Van?"

"He's . . . uh . . . out of the office on a case."

Gloria tapped her foot. "When will he be back?"

Vanna gave her most engaging smile. "That's hard to say. He had to go out of town, and it could be weeks before he returns."

Gloria slumped into one of the two guest chairs. "Oh. In his absence, who will be handling my case?"

"I'm Vanna. I'm fully briefed. I know everything that Van does. In fact I understand you wanted me to represent you at the outset."

Gloria sucked on her lip for a moment. "Yeah, but I'm now comfortable working with Van."

Vanna refrained from rolling her eyes. This broad had it bad for

Van. One little romp in the sack, and she wanted to make goo-goo eyes at him again. "As I'm sure he told you, we work very closely together. You'll get the same service from me as from him." Well, not exactly the same.

Gloria looked down at the purse in her lap, and then her sad eyes raised to meet Vanna's. "I had hoped to speak with him. He didn't call me this morning."

Vanna had to put this to bed, so to speak. "He's working deep undercover, so you won't hear from him until he returns to Denver. He's undertaken a very hush-hush operation and has to go incognito. I'm sure he'll call you the minute he gets back." Right.

A scowl. Then Gloria narrowed her gaze on Vanna. "And exactly what is your relationship with Van?"

Vanna gave her most sincere between-us-gals smile. "We're business partners. Like brother and sister."

"Oh." Gloria pouted. "I wanted to let Van know, but since he's out of town maybe you can attend. The funeral service for Cornelius will be at three tomorrow afternoon at Continental View of the Rockies Church. There will be a reception at my house afterwards. Do you think you can make it?"

Vanna nodded. "I'll be there. It might be a good opportunity for me to check out who shows up. Odds are the murderer will attend." This would give her a great chance to follow up on her list of suspects.

"One other thing I'll need your help with. That nasty detective questioned me again this morning."

Mulhaney might be crude and always wanted to put his hands where they didn't belong, but Vanna had never used the word "nasty" to describe him. Come to think of it, maybe it fit. She tilted her head to the side. "Really? Tell me what happened."

"He showed up at my house before I even had a chance to get dressed, ringing the doorbell incessantly until I answered. Then he said we needed to talk, so I invited him in. We sat in the living room and he leered at me the whole time. I had to keep bunching my robe around my knees."

Okay, that sounded like Mulhaney. "What did he ask you?"

"He grilled me again on where I had been the night of my husband's murder. He kept after me on when I had been at the reception, what time I left and the route I took home. He then stated I could easily have come home, killed Cornelius and then called 9-1-1. I told him that's not what happened."

Vanna nodded. "Yeah, he'll keep pressing you on that to see if you cave. Keep telling him the facts. What else?"

"He asked me if I knew Bentley Graves." She paused and ran her hand over her eyes as if reliving a bad movie.

Vanna wanted to use a cattle prod to speed her up. "And?"

Gloria let out a long sigh. "I said we were on the Denver Cooperative Art Alliance Board together." Long pause.

Vanna opened her hands toward Gloria. "Keep going."

Gloria's plaintive eyes looked up again. "What else should I have told him? I didn't mention my affair with Bentley."

"That's good. He didn't specifically ask you about it."

"I wondered if I should have confessed that Bentley and I had been . . . you know . . . seeing each other."

Vanna tapped the corner of her desk with a long fingernail. "With the cops, only respond to what they ask. You don't want to lie but never venture more than necessary. If he finds out through other sources, don't deny it."

"Wouldn't that make me look like I had withheld information?"

"All you need to do is bat your eyes at him and say that he never asked you before. You'll be fine. What else?"

"He asked me if I'd ever seen Cornelius and Bentley together. I said no. Then he wanted to know if they had any mutual business dealings. I said that I thought so, but Cornelius kept his financial affairs to himself. Then he pointed a finger at me and demanded to know when I would confess to the murder. I said never, since I didn't do it. He gave me a warning not to leave town and departed."

"Typical Mulhaney. He'll keep harassing you. Stick to your guns."

"There's one other thing you should know." Gloria opened her purse and extracted a letter. "This showed up today. I'm really worried and need your advice on what to do." She handed it across the table.

Vanna unfolded the letter and read: "Leave $50,000 in $100 bills in a black trash bag by the curb in front of your house tonight at 11 or the cops will hear about your affair and how it gave you a motive to knock off your old man."

Vanna wrinkled her nose and handed the letter back. "I assume you haven't mentioned any of this to the police yet."

"No way. From how he harassed me, Mulhaney would consider this evidence to lock me up."

Vanna thought through the alternatives of doing nothing, telling Mulhaney, cooperating, or setting a trap. She quickly formulated a plan. "Let me handle this. Do you have the envelope the letter came in?"

"No envelope. I found the folded letter in my mailbox, stuffed in with my regular mail."

Only one way to play this. "I'll put together a dummy sack of money and bring it to you at seven tonight. I want you to follow the directions and place the garbage bag by your curb at eleven. Then lock yourself in your house and don't let anyone in under any circumstances. I'll take it from there."

"Who could be doing this to me?" Tears formed in the corners of Gloria's eyes.

"I don't know yet."

Gloria took a hanky out of her purse, dabbed her eyes and sniffled. "Do you think you'll catch the blackmailer?"

"I'll give it my best shot."

# Chapter 7

Alone again, Vanna contemplated what had transpired. One interesting observation. The first time Gloria had come into the office and spoken with Van, she hadn't shed a real tear over the death of her husband. On this visit she had actually cried over being blackmailed.

Pushing the thought aside, she proceeded to the next item of business—a visit to the bank to withdraw six crisp C notes from the agency account. Back at The V V Agency office, she put off the further research she intended to do on the CU history professor, Harlan Shannon, instead preparing for the night's work. Using the paper cutter, she cut blank paper into the shape of bills she had collected from the bank and assembled three packets with the real bills on each end. Satisfied that it would pass quick scrutiny in the middle of the night, she wrapped rubber bands around the bundles. Finally, she put the fake money and a garbage bag into a briefcase.

She stopped to grab a quick burger at Wendy's and, while gobbling fries, wondered if she and Van would eventually get old and fat. If Van put on weight would that affect her as well? What if he turned into a real lard ass? If his eating habits started impacting her figure, she'd definitely have to give up sex and leave him in limbo.

She stuffed the rest of the fries in her mouth. Nothing she'd worry her head over today.

Making her way successfully to Gloria's house, due somewhat to keeping the mountains in sight but mainly the result of her trusty GPS navigation system, she picked up the briefcase from the passenger seat, sauntered to the door and rang the bell.

Gloria answered and ushered her in.

"No butler?" Vanna arched an eyebrow.

"I let go all of Cornelius's staff. I'll have a cleaning crew come in once a week, and I can cook for myself when I'm not eating out. I don't need all those people spying on me. Answering the door now and then gives me a little exercise."

"Yeah, we gals need to maintain our youthful figures."

Once inside the house, Vanna removed the money packets from the briefcase, stuffed them in the garbage bag and handed it to Gloria. "You're all set."

"Where will you be?"

"I'll be watching. At exactly eleven put it on the curb and get back in your house ASAP. Don't look out your windows. The blackmailer will be watching. He'll probably wait an hour or so before picking it up. He'll want to make sure no one's around."

"Won't he see you?"

Vanna laughed. "No. I'll keep myself practically invisible. I'll be able to watch the money without being spotted. That's what you pay me the big bucks for."

When Vanna left, she drove through the neighborhood and selected an observation point by a small park across the street on the next block. This would give her an unobtrusive place to watch Gloria's house.

* * * * *

That night Vanna prepared for the surveillance. She didn't share Van's interest in using public transportation and besides, she'd need her wheels after the blackmailer picked up the bag. But she couldn't drive around naked either. Her preferred approach—dress only in a dark overcoat. She arrived at the spot she had selected at nine-forty-five. No other cars on the street. She doused her headlights and shrugged off her overcoat, turning invisible. Now she had no worries of someone walking by the car and knocking on the window to inquire why she was sitting in her car for an extended period of time.

People always thought PIs had such a glamorous life. If only they realized the tedium of surveillance, waiting hours for something to happen. After her first few stakeouts when she squirmed in the seat of a car, tapped her foot and generally drove herself nuts, she had devised a much better approach. Now she kept focused on the target, in this case the curb of Gloria's house, but she allowed her mind to review her life. Tonight her thoughts turned to how she had obtained her identity.

After Van had discovered his shape-shifting abilities, he realized he would need to provide a valid paper trail for his alter ego. One night while in his late teens, he had turned invisible and snuck into the administration office of the orphanage. He began sorting through papers and found the name of a girl approximately his age who had died as a young child. Her name was Vanna Anderson. He removed all the papers from this file. The next day he went to a Kinko's and copied all the documents except for the death notification, which he tore up and threw the pieces into a dumpster. That night he returned the originals to the admin office file. He now had the necessary paperwork to apply for a social security number for one Vanna Anderson.

Vanna's attention returned to the street ahead. At exactly eleven Gloria came to the curb, dropped a bag and dashed back along the long driveway leading to her house. Good. She could follow directions.

Now, nothing more to do but wait. Vanna kept her eyes on the garbage bag while thinking back to how Van had received a scholarship to Colorado State University. He had rented his own apartment, and they took turns attending classes depending on their various sexual encounters. They made sure that Van always took the final exams though, so there would be no suspicion of cheating. After graduation came the idea for The V V Agency. Since Colorado required no PI license, investigative work presented the perfect profession for the two of them to share. If they had tried to set up an agency in California, there would have been background checks, and they would have run the risk of someone asking questions regarding the orphanage records. In Colorado, nada. You only had to say you wanted to be a PI and voila, it became so. No muss, no fuss, no icky personal scrutiny.

Vanna checked her watch, resting on the passenger seat. Midnight. She expected something to happen soon. The blackmailer had had time to check out the street. She had seen three cars drive by. Something should happen at any time. Fifteen minutes later she saw the lights of a car in her mirror. The car drove closely past hers, obviously checking for any occupants inside. Then it pulled to a stop near overgrowth on the edge of the park. A man exited the car and came around to the passenger side. He opened the door and lifted out a woman who appeared inebriated or unconscious. He dragged her toward the bushes. Vanna could see the man tear at the woman's clothes.

Vanna pushed her door open and ran toward the bush. The man remained so intent on fondling the woman's now-exposed breasts that he didn't notice the sound Vanna made.

She pulled back her leg like a soccer player and dealt a crushing kick to his groin. He groaned and toppled over, holding his crotch. She followed with a punch to the face, which knocked him out. She bent over the woman.

She was breathing but had been drugged.

Vanna went to her car and removed a blanket, roll of duct tape and a pair of PlastiCuffs from the trunk. She returned, covered the woman with the blanket, cuffed the jerk and duct taped him to the trunk of a tree. She pulled off his pants and underwear and applied duct tape to his genitals. Good. That would hurt like hell to get off.

She thought back to one time she had almost been raped. She hadn't been paying attention, and a guy snuck up on her in a parking lot at night after she had been searching bars on Colfax for a missing person. Her attacker was big but stupid. He stunned her with a punch, but she didn't lose consciousness. She went limp, feigning helplessness, and he dragged her into a nearby alley. He lowered his pants while spittle flew from his excited mouth. She waited for the right moment and came alive, delivering a karate kick to his balls. Then she knocked him cold and used a rusty nail found in a dumpster to scratch the word "rapist" onto his forehead. That had been preferable to him actually raping her and Van beating the guy to a pulp.

With the current situation under control, she reached in her car to pick up her cell phone resting on the passenger seat and punched in 9-1-1. "There's been an attempted rape." She gave her location, and the dispatcher asked her to stay on the line.

At that moment she heard the roar of a motorcycle. It sped by in a flash of silver reflected from a nearby street lamp, screeched to a halt in front of Gloria's house and then took off. "Shit," she shouted. With a quick glance to assure the attempted rapist remained fully secured and the woman was not suffering, she snapped her cell phone closed and jumped in the car.

By the time she started the engine, the motorcycle had disappeared out of sight. She threw on the overcoat, making sure to completely button it, drove toward Gloria's house and saw that the black garbage bag had been picked up.

# Chapter 8

Vanna drove away from Gloria's house, cursing that she had been distracted by the attempted rape. No sense sticking around and no way she'd be able to follow the silver motorcycle that had picked up the bag of fake money. The cops would be here soon to take care of the rapist, but she didn't want to get embroiled in that diversion. Still, she grinned at the recollection of the expression on the guy's face when she had nailed him in the balls. He never knew what hit him. Served the asshole right.

Then she reviewed in her mind the quick glance she'd had of the motorcycle. Silver. Expensive. Hmmm. The image meshed with something else Van had seen recently. Yes. She snapped her fingers. That could be it. One way to find out. She set her GPS and headed south on I-25. With little traffic at this time of night, her little navigational beauty led her right to the front of Bentley Graves's house. She slowly drove past, parked a block away, took off her overcoat, removed a small kit from the trunk and marched back to his house, taking the risk that no one would be around to see a box floating along the sidewalk at waist height. Knowing she couldn't use the doorbell approach at this time of the early morning, she went around to the back of the house. Taking a pick, she began working on the lock and in a minute had the door open. She set her kit down on the stoop and snuck into the house.

In the dining room she found Bentley setting his motorcycle helmet and the garbage bag on the table. Wifey must have been asleep or away for the night. Vanna stepped right up to him, pulled her fist back and walloped him in the jaw.

He spun like a top and dropped to the floor. For good measure she kicked him in the side of the head. He lay there sprawled out and motionless. Good. Two scumbags out for the count tonight.

She picked up the garbage bag, strolled out the back way and retrieved her pick set. As she rounded the corner of the house, she spotted headlights coming down the street. She dropped the bag and picks to the ground and waited for the car to drive by. A security patrol. Wouldn't have been good for the driver to see a garbage bag and box bouncing in air. Once the street was clear again, she jogged to her car, threw the picks and bag in the back seat and put on her overcoat.

As her GPS led her north, she thought over what Bentley Graves had been up to. He wanted to scam a little off-the-books cash at the expense of Gloria Blendheim. But had he also murdered Cornelius? And wouldn't it be risky for a murderer to play around with blackmail rather than laying low?

Vanna obviously had the distinct displeasure of dealing with some rich people who had no qualms when it came to doing anything to grind out a few more bucks. What a sleazebag. Blackmailing his ex-lover. He assumed, rightfully so, that Gloria wouldn't squeal to the police. But he hadn't counted on The V V Agency. Bentley would be wondering for a long time what hit him and where his money had gone. Vanna let out a shout of joy. Tonight she felt like an avenging angel.

As she followed her GPS navigator back to her loft, she tapped the steering wheel and thought through the list of suspects. Gloria, of course. Bentley who had been scheduled to meet with Cornelius the night of the murder. The estranged son, Huntington, angry at his dad. And Greer Lawson who met with Cornelius the night of the murder and claimed that Cornelius planned to dump Gloria to marry her.

Could Greer have become impatient or been spurned and killed him? From what Vanna had learned so far, any of them might have and could have done it. But right now, she'd back her paying customer and press on to see if one of the others could be nailed for the crime.

* * * * *

The next morning Vanna awoke from her recurring dream and called Gloria. "I want to let you know I tracked down the blackmailer. None other than your old buddy, Bentley Graves."

"Why of all the gall. That sack of pus."

Vanna smiled to herself. "That's a good description of him. Anyway, I retrieved the salted money left at the curb so no additional expense to you. I don't think he'll try a stunt like that again."

"Did he see you?"

"No. I sent him a little message without being identified."

Gloria laughed. "Good. Whatever you did to him, he deserves in spades. I hope you left a lasting impression on various parts of his body."

"That, too."

There was a pause on the line. "Could Bentley have killed Cornelius?"

"Possible. He's on the list. You have anything new for me?"

"Nothing. Just find who murdered my Cornelius."

After they rang off, Vanna looked thoughtfully out her window at a bus stopping at the corner. Van's preferred form of nighttime transportation but not hers. Next step would be checking a little more on Greer Lawson. The ringing phone interrupted her thoughts. She picked it up, "Vanna here."

"Hey, babe."

Vanna's heart leaped. Then a feeling of dread set in. She didn't need Lance Holloway right now. "What do you want?"

"Why, you, of course. I haven't seen you since our last wonderful time together. You bailed on me again. You're going to have to stop doing that."

"Yeah, well, I have a business to run."

"Your partner can cover for you. Let's say you and I run off to Acapulco together. How does that sound?"

"Van's out of town so I have to cover the agency."

"For once he's the one traveling? Usually it's you running out of town—and right after our sensuous times together. When are you going to stay around longer so we can see more of each other?"

"I'm sorry, Lance. You're really important to me, but my private investigation business consumes all my time right now."

"Well, you're here at the moment, babe. Maybe a little get-together tonight, then. Just you and me."

Vanna twitched. Her body wanted to be with Lance, but every time she so much as approached within ten feet of him, they ended up in bed together. She didn't want to transform back into Van. She had too much to do, and Van would never follow up as she would. "Sorry, Lance. As much as I'd like to see you, I have some surveillance to do that will keep me occupied night and day for a week."

"Okay, I'm taking you at your word. A week from today, I'm showing up on your doorstep, and I'm not taking no for an answer."

Hot flashes and cold waves coursed through her body. "Yes, Lance. In a week but not before."

She carefully set down the receiver, then slammed her fist onto the desk. Why couldn't she have a simple affair like other women? Oh, no. Every time she had a fling with Lance, she had to pay for it by turning into Van. She wanted Van to stay "out of town" for as long as possible. Sure, she couldn't wait to get her hands on Lance's Greek god-like body and have him reciprocate, but she'd have to stifle that urge for the time being. Damn inconveniences.

Vanna tapped her foot. She had to wipe the thought of Lance from her mind. She needed to get back on the Blendheim case. One other loose end to tie up.

After putting in the address on her GPS, Vanna drove off to Greer Lawson's home and parked up the block to watch. A late morning smattering of dog walkers and joggers passed, and close to eleven, the garage door opened at Greer's place and her black BMW emerged.

Vanna started her engine, took off and maintained a reasonable distance behind Greer's car. She immediately had no idea in which direction she was headed, but glanced at the GPS to get a reading on street names. Periodically, she spotted the mountains to have some idea. For her, trying to find her way around Denver resembled playing pin-the-tail-on-the-donkey blindfolded after having been spun around six times.

Greer headed into downtown Denver and pulled into the Pavilions underground parking structure. Vanna followed and parked half a dozen spots away.

Greer exited her car without so much as a glance around. Good. She didn't suspect that she had been followed.

Vanna locked her purse in the glove compartment, tucked her hair under a Rockies baseball cap, donned dark glasses, dropped the car key in her jeans pocket and followed Greer.

Greer continued on her single-focused jaunt, apparently still not sensing someone behind her. She entered the Appaloosa Grill on the Sixteenth Street Mall.

Vanna stopped at a kiosk, pretending to be a casual tourist, and waited.

In moments Greer joined a man on the outdoor patio.

Vanna raised an eyebrow. The man was Bentley Graves, sporting a bruise on his cheek and a black eye that made him look like a prizefighter who stayed in the ring one round too many. Good. He bore a visible reminder of the little episode the night before. She wondered what explanation he gave when people questioned him. That must have been some door he ran into.

Bentley and Greer leaned together and exchanged a kiss which would never pass for a business peck on the cheek. Greer took his face in her hands, stuck out her lip and gently patted his good cheek. Then she kissed him again.

After a waiter appeared, listened to them and then disappeared, Bentley handed Greer a document. They huddled together as if scrutinizing a map to the Lost Dutchman's gold mine. Well, well. Seemed like in this crowd everyone did business deals together and jumped in bed with each other too.

Vanna wanted to take a look at the document they were so eagerly perusing. As much as she disliked wandering around naked and invisible during the day, she decided to do it for the cause. She strolled into the restaurant, found the ladies room, entered a stall and took off all her clothes and stacked them neatly on the covered toilet seat. Pulling the stall door closed, she headed invisibly out to the patio. She stopped at the table to view the document resting between the lovey-dovey couple. A legal document of some sort. She saw some numbers and an address. Bentley turned it back to the first page.

Vanna leaned closer, grateful for good eyesight, and saw a contract to purchase the Blendheim Towers.

# Chapter 9

After seeing the sales agreement being connived over by Greer and Bentley, invisible Vanna returned to the ladies room to retrieve her clothes. She opened the stall and did a double take. No clothes. "Shit." She looked all through the restroom. They had disappeared. She kicked the wall. Now what?

Only one thing to do. She stormed out of the restroom and headed back to the parking structure. In her haste, and not paying attention, she bumped into a middle-aged woman holding two huge shopping bags. The woman stumbled and fell to the sidewalk. Vanna reached out a hand to help her up but drew it back when she realized that would really freak out the woman. The lady put a hand to her cheek and looked wildly around. Finally, she slowly stood and dusted off her skirt. She picked up her bags and shuffled off, mumbling to herself and shaking her head.

Vanna had her own problem. She couldn't find where she had parked. How could she get lost when less than a street away? She circled the block and finally found the entrance to the parking structure.

Now she couldn't locate exactly where she had parked her car within the underground structure. She wandered through the spirals for fifteen minutes before spotting her Subaru. With a sigh of relief, she reached under the front bumper to find the hide-a-key fastened there. She opened the trunk and removed the red sports bag containing a change of clothes.

At that moment a car came squealing around the bend.

She paused, not wanting the driver to see a red bag floating in the air.

The car raced past.

Vanna took the bag, let herself into the car and performed a quick change. Good thing she had only worn old clothes today. It would give her an excuse to shop for some new jeans and shoes. And she had another spare car key at the office for such an eventuality.

Back at the office she went online and checked on the Blendheim Towers, which turned out to be a condo complex in southeastern Denver. Ten years old and fully occupied. Upscale and worth a bundle.

Next she called Gloria Blendheim. "What do you know about the Blendheim Towers?"

"Not very much. I've seen it. Not a bad place to live if you like condos. One of Cornelius's properties."

Vanna tapped her cheek with the eraser end of a pencil. "Did Cornelius have plans to sell it?"

"I don't know. I didn't pay attention to the details of his business dealings. He took care of making money, and I spent it." Gloria giggled.

Vanna controlled a gagging sensation. "Who could tell me more?"

"Let's see . . . I guess you could speak with Homer Stiles. He's president of Blendheim Corporation."

"Thanks, Gloria."

"Anything new?"

"I'm following a lead. I'll fill you in when I track it down further."

Vanna next called Stiles.

His admin put her on hold for five minutes.

Finally, a deep booming voice announced, "Homer Stiles here."

"Mr. Stiles. My name is Vanna Anderson. I'm a private investigator hired by Gloria Blendheim. I understand you're planning to sell the Blendheim Towers."

A sputtering sound came over on the line. "That isn't public knowledge, Ms. Anderson."

Really? "As the major stockholder of Blendheim Corporation, Gloria has asked me to look into this matter."

He cleared his throat. "I don't know if you have any experience with the real estate business, Ms. Anderson, but we always have deals cooking."

"I understand. What's cooking with this one?"

"Yesterday the Board approved the sale. We have a financially attractive offer on the table."

"And Cornelius's view on selling the Towers?"

"He wasn't a big fan of divesting the property, but the Board made the decision. We're all saddened by his death, but business must go on."

Greased by Cornelius Blendheim being conveniently out of the way. "I assume you'll be at the funeral this afternoon?"

"I wouldn't miss it."

\* \* \* \* \*

After a stop at her loft to retrieve a spare car key and some old clothes, Vanna went outside to reattach the one she had been using under the bumper and repacked her red sports bag before heading back to her loft to change into a black dress. Funeral show time.

And what a show. All of Vanna's favorite suspects appeared sporting their best funeral garb and somber expressions. Bentley Graves in a dark charcoal suit, which matched his puffy eye; Greer Lawson in a black low-cut dress, well above her knees; and Huntington Blendheim in a ragged sports coat and plaid tie with his unkempt hair still needing a good shampooing. Vanna also spotted Donald Hallett, Gloria's lawyer, slumped in a pew to her right. She turned and saw Detective Mulhaney in his rumpled suit standing inside the back door, scanning the crowd. The grieving widow sat stiffly in the front with a black veil covering her face.

The minister, who had obviously never even met Cornelius, gave a glowing recitation of the deceased's qualities—someone who stood by the right hand of God rather than one who milked the public of millions.

After the florid eulogy finally wrapped up, and no one tried to bump off anyone else, they all adjourned to the reception at Gloria's house. She had a catered affair with tables of goodies and champagne. Cornelius would go to his maker in style. Rather than somber, the mood was now festive. No one seemed to notice that Cornelius had died.

Vanna sidled up to Gloria. "Please introduce me to Homer Stiles."

"Come with me."

Gloria led her over to a group of three and put her hand on the arm of a tall man with intense gray eyes. "Homer, may I borrow you for a moment?"

In his sixties with jet black hair, gold-rimmed glasses and a pinched mouth that looked like it permanently tasted lemon, Homer stepped aside.

"Homer, meet Vanna Anderson."

Vanna shook his hand which felt as warm as the iced bottles of champagne. "Pleased to meet you."

His expression didn't change. "Likewise."

Vanna gave him her best fake smile. "Since I have both of you here, I'm still curious about the sale of the Blendheim Towers. Gloria, did you know a sale's pending, and Bentley Graves and Greer Lawson have their fingers in it?"

"What?" Gloria jumped as if someone had dropped an ice cube down her back. She glared at Homer. "What's going on?"

He harrumphed. "As I told Ms. Anderson over the phone, the Board approved the sale. An excellent price has been offered. It will be a very profitable deal for our corporation."

"But why . . . why are Bentley and Greer involved?" Gloria sputtered.

Homer held a hand up as if trying to stop a charging bull. "They're representing the buyers, that's all."

"Stop the sale!" Gloria shouted. "This sucks. I don't want either of them making one penny from us. Shut it down. Do you understand, Homer?"

Homer shook his head. "I'm sorry. We're finalizing the deal. Negotiations have proceeded too far to back away."

"What? What? I'll see about that!" Gloria stormed off.

"Thanks for setting off that rampage." Homer glared at Vanna.

"Glad to be of service." Vanna turned her back on Homer and headed over to speak with Donald Hallett.

"Do you know this guy Homer Stiles, who's president of Blendheim Corporation?" she asked.

Donald wrinkled his nose. "Cornelius put him in as chief operating officer because of his financial acumen. Wouldn't have been my choice. He's not your most personable executive."

"I'll say. How did he and Cornelius get along?"

"As I said, Cornelius hand-picked him to be his number two in command. I never shared Cornelius's enthusiasm for the guy. He's too cold and calculating for me."

"What does he stand to gain by Cornelius's death?"

Donald gave a sardonic laugh. "Quite a bit. He'll probably take over as chairman and CEO of the corporation."

Not a bad motive for murder. "Thanks for the info." Vanna sauntered over to watch Bentley Graves and Greer Lawson put their heads together in a corner by a potted palm tree. Bentley's black eye had now turned a beautiful shade of purple to complement the grapes on the hors d'oeuvres table.

At that moment Gloria appeared and shook her right index finger at them. "What are you two doing plotting and scheming to buy Blendheim Towers?"

Two mouths dropped open. Bentley was the first to regain his composure. "Just a good business deal, Gloria."

"I want it cancelled!" She stomped her foot.

"Too late for that, sweetheart." Bentley gave a sneer.

"Don't sweetheart me." She slapped him soundly on his good cheek. Now he had a matching set of bruises.

Greer Lawson hauled off and slapped Gloria. "Leave him alone, you bitch."

Gloria lurched, then regained her balance. "Who you calling a bitch, you useless whore?" She drew her arm back and threw it forward, landing a haymaker right on Greer's jaw.

Greer dropped to the floor like a sack of cement and lay there motionless.

Gloria pivoted and stomped away.

Bentley leaned over and softly patted Greer's cheek. In a moment she stirred, and he helped her to her feet. "Let's get out of here," he said and led her away.

Better than a three-ring circus. Vanna took a break from the excitement and helped herself to some shrimp and a glass of champagne. Alcohol had no effect whatsoever on her. She had enjoyed drinking two-hundred pound men under the table at bars. The same couldn't be said of Van. As a teenager he had experimented with alcohol, but after one sip he passed out faster than Greer had from Gloria's punch. Served him right. Still, she would trade her alcohol tolerance for Van's ability to navigate.

Vanna heard a commotion and turned to see Gloria and Huntington shaking fists at each other.

"You bitch. You killed him. I know you did."

"Why you no good little punk." Gloria pulled her arm back and landed a punch right on his jaw.

He staggered back and fell into a fern, knocking it over. He lay on the floor with his head imbedded in the leaves.

This girl had a future in the ring. Vanna vowed never to get within striking distance of that lethal fist.

Huntington raised himself to his feet. "I'm going to sue you!"

Gloria pulled her fist back again.

Huntington's eyes grew as large as silver dollars. He took two steps backward and fell into the fern again.

Gloria dusted her hands together, set her jaw and pranced off.

Vanna reached out a hand to Huntington and pulled him up. "That gal packs quite a wallop."

He rubbed his chin. "Yeah. At least she didn't shoot me like she did Dad."

"What makes you so certain she killed him?"

"It's always the money. Follow the money, like she did." He shuffled off to get some champagne.

Vanna felt a paw on her shoulder and spun around to see the sharp incisors of Detective Mulhaney.

"Care to join me for a drink?" He waggled his eyebrows.

"Sure. Let's have a chugging contest. Care to match me glass for glass with champagne?"

He held up his hands in a crossing motion. "No way. I know your drinking rep. But I'd be happy to treat you to a drink or two plus dinner at a restaurant."

"No thanks. I have a lecture I'm attending this evening." She turned wary eyes toward him. "With all the action here, Detective,

I'm surprised you haven't arrested anyone yet."

He chuckled. "It's only a matter of time for your client. Maybe three assault charges to go along with murder."

Vanna pointed a finger at him. "Be careful you don't get within swinging range of her."

"I prefer the more peaceful types. Like compliant female PIs."

"Yeah. Good luck." Vanna headed off for another glass of champagne and some munchies to suffice for dinner.

A little while later, she spotted Homer Stiles leaving the house. She followed him outside and saw him get into a dark green Jaguar. These rich people and their cars. She returned inside to see if there would be any more entertainment.

After another half hour with no new altercations, she called it an afternoon and drove home to change into more casual clothes for her trip to the lecture in Boulder.

\* \* \* \* \*

That evening, led to her destination by her faithful GPS, she parked in the Boulder library parking lot off Arapahoe, strolled into the glass atrium and across the in-building bridge over Boulder Creek to the auditorium. She found a spot in the first row and settled in to wait for the appearance of Harlan Shannon.

At exactly seven a woman in a tie-dyed dress stepped up to the lectern and introduced the speaker. Vanna heard that Harlan was a full professor, had been at the University of Colorado for twenty years and had received numerous awards and accolades for his outstanding research and academic publications.

Then a man in his fifties, with untamed blond hair and a red bow tie, practically danced onto the stage. He had a twinkle in his eyes and a smile that covered his whole face. "Thank you, Madeline. It's a pleasure to be invited here tonight. Mythology in Modern Society. What is fact and what's myth? I've dedicated my last ten years to research this subject. We all know that dragons are mythical beasts. There has been so much popular literature regarding vampires that some people think they're real." He reached under the lectern and pulled out a black cape which he whipped around his shoulders. He bent over, put something in his mouth and stood erect to display fangs with fake red dripping blood.

A titter ran through the audience.

Vanna rolled her eyes. A real comedian here.

Harlan removed the cape and fake teeth. "But seriously, folks, a number of myths may have a factual base. One that I'm particularly interested in regards shape-shifting."

Vanna shot up straight in her seat as if someone had goosed her.

"Now I'm not speaking of humans changing into werewolves or Dr. Jekyll and Mr. Hyde but people transforming into other people. And one of the most delightful forms of shape-shifting involves a transformation between man and woman. In Norse mythology Odin and Loki both had the ability to change into women. Maybe if more men did that we'd be more sensitive and listen better."

Chuckles ran through the audience.

"In Greek mythology Zeus disguised himself as Artemis. In L. Frank Baum's book *The Marvelous Land of Oz* the princess Ozma had been turned into a boy named Tip as an infant. A wealth of literature and mythology addresses this theme of a change between male and female or as some refer to it—gender bender."

Vanna winced at that label.

"I prefer to call this gender transformation," Harlan continued. "So is there any truth to this tradition and mythology? Most think not, but you never can tell." He winked at the audience. "You may not be able to tell if some professional musical performers are male or female."

He spoke for exactly forty-five minutes and then opened it up for questions. Hands rose like flags at a military cemetery, and Harlan dutifully answered each, until Madeline the moderator stepped onto the stage and announced that the program would conclude with one last question. She pointed. "The man in the back of the auditorium."

A large man with a full dark beard stood. "If someone could change between man and woman what would trigger the transformation?"

Harlan sucked on his lip for a moment. "An interesting question. In mythology, the gods change because they decide to. If a human could change, the trigger would have to be something that causes a significant emotional reaction within the person."

Vanna squirmed in her seat. An emotional reaction like from sex?

Madeline leaned toward the microphone. "That concludes our

lecture. Let's have a warm round of applause for Professor Harlan Shannon."

Harlan stepped off the stage and was immediately engulfed by a crowd of eager questioners.

Vanna waited until the mob subsided and then approached. She handed Harlan a card. "Dr. Shannon, I'm Vanna Anderson, a private investigator. I enjoyed your presentation and would like to meet with you to ask several questions that may assist me with a current investigation."

His eyes widened as he looked from Vanna's card to her face. "A PI. Interesting. You track people down, right?"

"That's correct."

"Hmmm. Yes." He looked around the room. "Would you care to catch a cup of coffee right now?"

Vanna smiled. "That would be great. I don't know my way around Boulder very well so what would you suggest?"

"I live walking distance from here so if you don't mind a cup of bachelor brew, we could go there."

She shrugged. "Sounds good to me."

He gathered his notes, dropped them in a briefcase, and the two of them took off. In a three block walk they reached a small freshly-painted white bungalow. Inside, Harlan put on a pot of coffee, and they sat down in a living room lined with book shelves and old books.

"What kind of investigative work do you do, Ms. Anderson?"

"You may call me Vanna, Dr. Shannon."

"No formality required on my part either. Harlan will do as well."

Vanna shot him a smile. "To answer your question. All sorts. We help clients track down stolen property, check on missing people and cheating spouses, even assist murder investigations."

"You said you had a question for me related to one of your investigations?"

Damn. She hoped he had forgotten that come-on line. Improvising on the spot she said, "I've been following a man who reappears as a woman. He's a master of disguises." She laughed. "I don't expect he's a shape-shifter, but he's mighty effective. I wonder if in your studies you've come across people, like transvestites, who develop this skill."

He chuckled. "Yes. Clearly some people change their appearance because of sexual orientation, for employment or the excitement of appearing as the other gender. Now I also have a question for you. Since you track down people, would you be willing to do some work for me?"

Vanna arched an eyebrow. "What do you have in mind?"

His hands twitched, and then he clasped them together. "I've never discussed this with any of my colleagues. They think I'm already fringe enough with my research on shape-shifting." He looked around the room as if he expected a hidden camera or microphone to be recording what he said. He leaned toward Vanna and in a conspiratorial tone said, "I've come across some information about a unique type of shape-shifting that I'm investigating. Your skills might be of utmost use to me in my work."

Vanna could feel the excitement building in her chest. "Go on."

"In my research I've learned of a specific form of shaft-shifter called a transvictus."

Vanna forced herself to wrinkle her forehead and give him a questioning stare. "Transvictus?"

"Yes. It's a person who can shift between male and female like I discussed in my lecture."

"A mythological creature?"

He shook his head. "Oh, no. I think it's quite real. And I have evidence there may be one in the Denver area."

# Chapter 10

Vanna forced herself not to show any undue reaction to Harlan Shannon's statement that he suspected a transvictus might reside in Denver. "What leads you to that conclusion?" she asked as calmly as she could.

He reached for a pipe. "Do you mind if I smoke?"

"Uh . . . yes. Smoke makes me sick to my stomach. I'd hate to make a mess on your living room rug."

He set the pipe aside. "I guess I can wait until later. To answer your question, I came across some references to this specific form of shape-shifting in some old literature at the university. With further research I discovered an interesting trait of a transvictus." He paused and regarded her warily. "In addition to changing between man and woman, a transvictus can turn invisible."

"Come on, Harlan, no one can do that."

He ran his hand over his chin. "Actually, I think there's a strong possibility. Furthermore, I discovered some interesting reports regarding an orphanage in Denver that closed in 1998 after being around for more than seventy years."

Vanna gulped as she felt a drop of perspiration forming at her hairline. How in the world had he found this out? "An orphanage?"

she blurted out.

"An order of nuns ran it. At any time, between fifty and a hundred children ranging in ages from newborn to eighteen years old resided there. I found a diary kept by a boy who lived there—Marcus Neilson."

It took all of Vanna's willpower to control her breathing. Good old Marcus. Fat, obnoxious, arrogant and the perennial snoop. Always getting into other people's business. Had he picked up evidence of Van's special abilities?

"Marcus wrote that he saw a boy go into a room and later only a girl emerged. He also wrote that he once watched this boy take off all his clothes and disappear. Classical transvictus traits."

Vanna clenched her fist out of Harlan's view. "Did he give the name of this disappearing boy?"

"Only a passing mention of someone called Slick."

*Uh-oh.* Van's nickname in the orphanage. Vanna felt a growing dread. Had Van already been exposed? "Have you interviewed this Marcus Nielson?"

"Unfortunately, it's not possible. He died in an automobile crash in 2005."

Vanna let out a barely perceptible sigh of relief. She was sorry for Marcus but didn't need her and Van's identity discovered. "Have you uncovered evidence of anyone else who appears to be a transvictus?"

"Oh, yes. I came across reports of similar situations in Los Angeles, San Francisco and Seattle. All in orphanages."

Vanna sat, stunned. Could there be others like her? Maybe she wasn't a freak after all. Thoughts swirled through her head. She had never suspected there could be others—people she could speak with openly and not be concerned over the implications of her unique attributes. "You say all in orphanages?"

"Exactly. For some reason each possible transvictus I've discovered has grown up in an orphanage. Interesting isn't it?"

Vanna pictured someone sneaking up and leaving a baby on the doorstep of an orphanage. She and Van had often wondered where they came from. Had orphanages become the repository of transvictus babies? "Why orphanages?"

He shrugged. "I don't know." Then his face opened in a bright smile. "That's why I had this brainstorm to hire you. How'd you like to do some tracking of these slim leads I have, starting with the orphanage in Denver?"

Vanna thought for all of ten nanoseconds. This would provide her an opportunity to research her own background as well as try to find any other transvictus in existence. Still, she didn't want to appear too eager. "I suppose I could work it into my schedule. You know, do some background checking when not consumed by a high-profile case."

"That would be great. This wouldn't have to be a top priority for you. You could work it as time permits." He clapped his hands together. "Let me get my files to show you." He scampered off down a short hallway and returned in minutes with a stack of manila folders that he dropped on the carpet in front of Vanna. He sat down next to her on the couch and picked up the top folder. "Here's what I've found so far in Denver. All Souls Orphanage. Ever hear of it?"

Vanna bit her lip. "Sounds familiar."

Harlan tapped the manila folder. "Around for most of the twentieth century. As the residents aged and graduated, there were fewer and fewer babies without a home, so the need for the orphanage dwindled. The Sisters who ran it decided to put their time and money into other charitable endeavors."

Vanna picked up the folder and began leafing through it. She recognized the name of Sister Mary Ancheles who had been Head Mother and two other sisters who taught the high school kids. Memories of sitting in class while the sisters drilled the students on irregular verbs and geometry pulsed through her brain. Strange how their collective memories worked. She and Van could remember everything that happened to either of them, but their emotional reactions to the events varied widely. For example Gloria Blendheim didn't turn her on in the least. Likewise, Van didn't think much of Lance Holloway. Go figure.

Her mind went off on a tangent recalling how Van and Lance had met on two occasions, once when Van's getaway after her fling with Lance had run into a problem. Van had dropped a shoe while changing in Lance's bathroom. He almost reached the apartment door when a bleary-eyed Lance appeared scratching his ripped abs. Van introduced himself and explained that he had brought a taxi for Vanna who had an emergency meeting and had already left to catch a plane at DIA for New York.

"How'd you find her here?" Lance had asked.

"We have a strict policy in the agency to keep each other apprised of our exact location so that when any emergencies come up, like this, we can locate each other." Fortunately, Lance was so sleepy he didn't question a flight at that time of night or why Van hadn't taken the trip out of town rather than Vanna. They had stared at each other for a few moments before Van excused himself and beat a hasty retreat.

On one other occasion Lance had stopped by the agency the day after a romp looking for Vanna. Van and Lance had eyed each other like two bull elks during rutting season. After a guarded conversation in which Van explained that once again Vanna had been called out of town, Lance stormed out of the office.

Vanna smiled at the memory. Lance really did care for her.

Now her thoughts returned to the file Professor Harlan Shannon had accumulated on the All Souls Orphanage. She read photocopies of pages from the diary of the obnoxious orphan, Marcus Nielson. Good thing Marcus hadn't mentioned Van's name. Several other interview statements from people living near the orphanage described incidents, one from a man who had seen a boy disappear into the woods and then a girl reappeared. Vanna shook her head, remembering times when Van had experimented with the transformation. One time he stayed as Vanna for a whole Saturday and wandered around Denver, flirting with boys. They thought they had never been caught transforming, but obviously some clues had been left along the way.

"And the other cities you mentioned?" Vanna asked.

Harlan selected another folder. "Pretty sketchy. I tracked down a few leads from a Yahoo group on shape-shifting. Corresponded via email with half a dozen other interested parties. Still nothing definitive."

"Any of the other orphanages still open?"

Harlan shook his head. "No. They all seemed to have closed between 1960 and 2000."

Vanna picked up one folder and quickly skimmed a printed email from someone named Jennifer Orloff in San Francisco. "Okay if I borrow these files and make copies?"

"They're yours. Keep them while you do your investigation. Now your fees."

"Sixty dollars an hour." She gave him a twenty percent discount off the agency's normal rates since she would be benefiting from this work as well.

He rubbed his hands together. "Excellent. I can authorize a hundred hours immediately, and then we'll review the progress. I have a grant that will cover this." He winked at her.

She gasped. "A grant to do research on shape-shifting?"

"Oh, yes. You'd be amazed at the organizations out there that will provide funding for academic projects. People have their pet interests, and some of them have amassed fortunes to back up their hobbies." He looked at his watch. "I should let you be on your way. It's getting late, and I have an eight o'clock lecture in the morning."

Vanna packed up the folders and shook Harlan's hand. Once outside, she realized she had no clue where to find the library and her car. Reluctantly, she returned and knocked on his door.

"Back already?" He chuckled.

"I'm . . . uh . . . not very familiar with Boulder. Could you point me toward the library?"

"Sure. Let me walk you part way there."

He shut his door and strolled with her along Marine Street and turned the corner. He pointed ahead. "Go right down there and the street dead ends into the library parking lot."

They shook hands again, and Vanna headed off, wondering if he still had any confidence in an investigator who couldn't even find her way three blocks. Following his directions, she found the parking lot and climbed into her Subaru. With the GPS set for home, she took off to wend her way through the streets of Boulder and back onto the freeway.

Her thoughts turned to an investigation into Van's background. An initial strategy came to mind. She would do independent work for the time being. She'd track down as many Sisters as possible who had worked at the All Souls Orphanage and any other sources she could find. Then later, Van could selectively contact some of these people to see if he could learn any further information on where he had come from under the guise of seeking his parents. The agency wouldn't charge Harlan for that part of the research. Her goal would be to find out some useful tidbits for Harlan but not divulge too much at the outset. She would need to play this very carefully.

She'd also make contacts with the names in the files from the other cities. That would be interesting. She could say she had been hired to follow some information she had been given. She'd start by phone and then determine whether it would make sense to do any in-person interviews. This had been an unexpected evening for her. And the most significant question: Could there really be others like her and Van?

# Chapter 11

The next morning, a ringing phone roused Vanna from a sound slumber. Groggily she answered to hear Donald Hallett on the line. "Our client Gloria Blendheim has been taken in by the police for questioning."

"Something new on Cornelius's murder?"

"No. Someone shot Bentley Graves late last night. She's a suspect in that killing as well. I should have her released within an hour. Meet Gloria and me at her house at ten."

\* \* \* \* \*

Vanna sat in the Blendheim living room with Donald Hallett pacing the floor and Gloria slumping on the couch with her head hung down and wearing a contrite expression on her unblemished face.

Donald came to a stop in front of Gloria and thrust a pudgy finger at her. "What in God's name were you thinking by going to Bentley Graves's house last night?"

Gloria sniffled and looked up with her large doe eyes. "I was mad at him for doing a real estate deal to buy the Blendheim Towers. That's all."

"And the loud argument neighbors reported overhearing?" Donald crossed his arms over his red tie.

Gloria let out a deep breath as if she had been holding it for a week. "As I said, he upset me. He started giving me some highfalutin bullshit, and I shouted at him."

"Saying you'd kill him and cut off his prick?"

She shrugged. "Something like that."

Donald smacked his forehead with the palm of his hand. "I'm trying everything possible to keep you out of jail, but you're not helping any."

Gloria's pleading eyes looked up again. "But I didn't kill him. We had our fight, and we stepped back in the house for a few minutes. He was still alive when I left."

"Well, no one saw you leave or heard Bentley until his wife discovered his body. "The circumstantial evidence indicates you were the last person to see Bentley alive."

Gloria sat up and brushed a strand of hair from her forehead. "But obviously someone came after I left, and that person killed Bentley."

"Obviously. Obviously." Donald kicked at the rug as if trying out to be the new placekicker for the Denver Broncos. "Nothing is obvious to the police except they think you murdered Bentley."

"Well, I didn't." Gloria gave a determined nod.

Vanna jumped in. "Let's review the time sequence. Gloria, when did you arrive at Bentley's house?"

"Oh, it must have been around eight-thirty." A smile played across her face. "Yes. I left my house at eight and it takes thirty minutes to get to Bentley's."

"And when you got there?"

Gloria wrinkled her brow in concentration. "He fixed me a drink, and soon after he handed it to me we started arguing."

"That fits," Donald said. "The police claim they have evidence of you being in the house."

"Well, yeah. I had a bourbon and water with Bentley."

"So they have a glass with lipstick on it, covered with your fingerprints," Vanna added. "Why would the neighbors have heard you threatening Bentley?"

"After the drink, things went kind of downhill." Gloria looked at her red fingernails. "He told me to leave. I said I never wanted to see his slimy face again. He opened the door and pointed for me to get out. I was in the doorway, when my temper got the best of me. That's when I shouted that I would kill him and . . . you know . . . do that other thing."

"And after that?" Vanna asked.

Gloria shook her head. "He told me to calm down. We stepped back inside for a moment. I told him to cancel the sales agreement. He said the deal had already proceeded too far. I shouted at him one last time, opened the door and took off."

"And the time you finally left?" Vanna leaned forward.

"Oh, maybe nine."

Donald glared at Gloria. "And then at ten-thirty Bentley's wife returns from a bridge game and finds him lying on the living room carpet with two fatal gun shots to the head."

"Obviously someone came and killed him right after I left." Gloria glared back.

Donald threw his hands in the air. "Obviously. Gloria, I don't know if I'm going to be able to help you this time. There's too much evidence piling up against you."

She stood and stomped her foot. "Well, you take care of this, Donald. I told you I didn't kill him, and you have to convince the police." She turned to Vanna. "And I need your help in finding who really killed Bentley."

Vanna met her gaze. "That's what you pay me the big bucks to do. I'll follow up today with Bentley's wife and the neighbors." And Greer Lawson. Vanna had a hunch she played a part in all of this. "Is Detective Mulhaney handling this case?"

"Oh, yes," Donald answered. "He can't wait to lock up Gloria on a twofer. It took every trick I knew to keep him from arresting her this morning."

"I'll check in with him," Vanna said. And take a look through his files tonight to find out exactly what he knows.

Vanna left, her day cut out for her. She had hoped to spend some time on the research for Harlan Shannon, but Gloria's situation took precedence, so she'd defer looking into All Souls Orphanage. The professor's work didn't have the urgency of keeping Gloria out of stir.

From her car Vanna called Mulhaney. "Hey there. How's my favorite detective this morning?"

"That sounds promising. You finally recognizing my sterling qualities?"

"Oh, yes. In fact I'd like to get together with you."

"Your place or mine?" He chuckled.

Vanna rolled her eyes. He kept using the same lines and never gave up. "Do you have a few minutes now?"

"For you, sweet cakes, I'll make the time."

"Good. Our regular Starbucks in thirty minutes?"

"I'll be waiting with my dancing shoes on."

She clicked off her phone, wondering why she should have to put up with this walking cliché.

With the successful navigational assistance of her GPS, Vanna parked and sauntered into the Starbucks on Lawrence.

She grabbed a mocha latte and joined Mulhaney with his normal black coffee, no bling added.

"We're going to have to be careful." Mulhaney took a sip and waggled an eyebrow at her. "With all our meetings here, people will think we have something going."

"Oh, we do have something going, Detective. We're both working to prove Gloria Blendheim's innocence."

He gave an eye roll. "Right. She's as innocent as the Pope is Jewish."

"Not a bad analogy. Since Jesus was a Jew and the Pope represents Jesus—"

He swatted his hand toward her. "Don't try to be all philosophical on me. Why do you wanna see me?"

Vanna patted his arm. "In the interest of justice. I'm working on Gloria's behalf. I know you wouldn't want to arrest the wrong person, so I thought we should get our heads together on who really murdered Bentley Graves."

He leered at her. "Now you're talking. Maybe we could get something besides our heads together as well."

"In your dreams, Detective. In your dreams. Now regarding Gloria Blendheim. You don't really think that delicate young lady is a murderer, do you?"

"Delicate my butt. And yes. She did in her old man and this guy Graves." He held up two fingers. "Within a week she commits this many murders."

"She only had a drink with Bentley Graves and then left before the murder occurred."

"Right, screaming threats that woke up the whole neighborhood." He shook a finger at her. "Stay out of this one, Vanna. You'll do your client and yourself no good interfering. She's cooked."

"How do you know someone wasn't in the house already or arrived right after Gloria left?"

"No evidence of anyone else except your client being there."

"And his wife? Graves had a reputation of playing around with women. She could have become fed up and shot him. You know the statistics. Domestic violence leads to a significant percentage of murders."

"Not in this case. The wife isn't a suspect. Instead, we have some very incriminating evidence on Ms. Blendheim."

"Such as?"

He took a last gulp of coffee. "No way I'm sharing that with you or that shark who showed up to get her released."

Vanna showed her dimples. "Why not come clean with me now, Detective? You know I'll find out anyway."

He spit into his empty cup. "Yeah, however you and your partner do it, you may find out. But not from me."

Oh, she'd find out from him. He just wouldn't know it. "When will the crime scene be released?"

He stood up and stretched his arms. "This afternoon, but I doubt whether the widow will let you snoop around."

Vanna also rose. "We'll see. Anything else you'd like to share in your usual forthright manner?"

"Nope. As ever, a pleasure."

Vanna watched him leave and disappear around the corner. She stood motionless for a moment, thinking. Then she pulled out her cell phone and called Greer Lawson who answered on the third ring.

"Ms. Lawson, this is Vanna Anderson of The V V Agency. May I meet with you this afternoon?"

A tone as cold as the North Pole came across the line. "You and I have nothing to discuss."

"To the contrary, we do. Bentley Graves was murdered last night. I know of your relationship with him. I think it would be in your best interest to talk to me before the police get involved."

Greer made no response for a moment and then said, "All right. You can meet me at my house in an hour." The line went dead.

Vanna drank another latte and munched on a scone before navigating to Greer's house. She pulled up in front, picked up a newspaper still on the front stoop and rang the doorbell. Greer, wearing a black Elie Tahari Montana Jacket with black slacks, answered the door. She sported a bruise that makeup hadn't completely hidden on her cheek from her encounter with Gloria's fist.

Greer blocked the door and made no move to welcome Vanna into the house. "I only can spare a few minutes."

Vanna smiled. "This won't take very long. Can we sit?"

Greer looked over her shoulder. "I guess we can go into the living room." She led Vanna to the couch and then settled onto an easy chair facing her. "Now what do you really want?"

"Given the untimely death of Bentley Graves and the fact that you had a business relationship with him . . ." Vanna paused to let this sink in, "it might raise some unpleasant questions from the police."

"If you're implying I had anything to do with Bentley's murder, you're off base. Gloria killed him. You saw how pissed she was at the funeral. That woman can't control her temper." She brushed her hand against her damaged cheek.

"Where were you last night between eight and ten?"

Greer met Vanna's gaze. "Right here. Reading a book."

"Anyone with you?"

"No. I was alone."

Vanna looked around the room, trying to imagine Greer sitting here by herself at night. Not a book in sight. It didn't take a literary genius to see it didn't compute. "What does Bentley's death do to the negotiations to purchase the Blendheim Towers?"

Greer's nostrils flared. "Not that it's any of your business, but the deal is proceeding very well, thank you."

"I bet you'll receive full commission since you won't have to split it with Bentley. Probably pretty lucrative for you."

She shrugged. "What of it? He was handling the transaction as a private matter, not through his corporation."

"And I'm sure the police will want the details of the personal relationship between you and Bentley."

She bit her lip. "That was between him and me."

"Maybe the romance went bad, he dumped you, and you took it out on him with gunshots."

Greer pursed her lips. "Get real. That didn't happen."

Vanna decided to try a different tack. "Maybe his wife got wind of you playing footsy with her husband."

"Oh, please. She was so wrapped up in her own affairs that she hardly gave Bentley the time of day."

Vanna shook her head. "All this hanky-panky. I thought you were in mourning for Cornelius Blendheim."

"Yes, dear Cornelius." She averted her gaze for a moment. "Well he was gone, and Bentley was still around."

"Now both are dead. Zero for two. Your relationships seem to have a way of ending poorly."

"If you're implying I had anything to do with either death, you're dead wrong. Pay attention to that bitch, Gloria Blendheim."

"Oh, the police are. But I'm not convinced she committed either murder."

"Well, don't look at me." Greer regarded her watch. "I really need to get going." She stood, grabbed Vanna's arm and pulled her off the couch. "It's been real." She pushed Vanna to the door, opened it, gave her a nudge out, waved and slammed the door.

Vanna didn't even have an opportunity to look around to see if she could spot the diamond necklace missing from the Blendheim house, so she returned to her car and waited. She was interested in why Greer was dressed up and in such a hurry.

In five minutes Greer's garage door opened and her black BMW backed out, before tearing off down the street.

Vanna followed at a safe distance. Greer led her to Blendheim Corporation headquarters, north of Denver in Thornton. Not bothering to go inside, she drove off wondering if Greer had now turned her attention to Homer Stiles.

Next, her GPS led her to Bentley Graves's home. She parked down the block and watched as Denver police officers removed the yellow tape surrounding the house, climbed into their cars and drove away.

Half an hour later, a silver Mercedes pulled into the driveway. It had tinted windows so Vanna couldn't see the occupants. Their identities were revealed moments later when the driver's side door opened and Eva Graves stepped out. Then the passenger door swung open. To Vanna's surprise, Huntington Blendheim clambered out.

# Chapter 12

Well, well. The plot had thickened. Eva Graves stopped at the mailbox to retrieve a handful of mail and then let herself and Huntington Blendheim into the house. Vanna waited fifteen minutes and then exited her car, strolled to the front door and rang the bell. In moments Eva answered.

Vanna held out a card. "Mrs. Graves, I'm very sorry to hear of the death of your husband. I've been retained to assist with the investigation and would appreciate speaking with you for a few minutes."

Eva snuck a peek over her shoulder. "I'm . . . uh . . . kinda indisposed right now. You'll have to come back later."

"There probably isn't a good time. And I wouldn't worry about Huntington. He and I have already met."

Eva literally jumped. "How do you know . . .?"

"Hello, Huntington," Vanna called over Eva's shoulder into the house.

Huntington stuck his head around the corner. His face turned into a surly sneer. "What are you doing here?"

"Some follow-up investigation. I'm surprised to see you here with Mrs. Graves. Are you two long-time acquaintances?"

"We . . . uh . . . met at Cornelius's funeral," Huntington stammered.

"Right," Vanna replied. "Must have been right after Gloria sent you flying into the fern. Any chance you and Mrs. Bentley spent time together last night?"

Eva jumped again. "How . . . how . . ." She opened her mouth to say something more but then clamped her hand over it.

"Don't be so uptight, Eva. It could be the perfect alibi for you. Huntington, how about you? Care to verify that Eva wasn't here at the time of her husband's death?"

He looked quickly from side to side. "Uh, we hooked up later that night. She called me since she needed a place to stay."

Vanna arched an eyebrow. "Interesting."

"After I came home and found . . ." She gave a tearless snuffle. ". . . found Bentley dead I needed a quick drink so I went to see Hunty."

Vanna wondered if it had been something else quick rather than a drink. "Yeah, that must have been very traumatic for you." Vanna watched the continued performance that included a pout and sniffling. What was it with these people?

"Don't mention to the police that I went to see Hunty."

"Look, Eva. The police aren't stupid. They'll find out these things. You better come clean."

"But I don't want anyone to know about Hunty."

"Too late for that. Were you cheating on your husband?"

She ran her tongue over her lips. "Well, he had his fair share of affairs. I thought I'd get back at him."

"Who did he have affairs with?"

"Half the women in town. Pretty much anything that wore a skirt. I know for sure Gloria Blendheim and Greer Lawson."

One big happy family. "And did you confront him?"

She shook her head. "We had a prenup. I had it pretty good with spending money and didn't want to rock the boat. Besides, with him off having a romp somewhere, it gave me free time to do what I wanted."

"Did your prenup have a provision that covered murder?"

Eva's mouth dropped open. "What do you mean?"

Vanna waved her hand. "Merely my stilted sense of humor. Anyway, the police will find out all of this, so it would be best for you to contact Detective Mulhaney and level with him before he comes up with it on his own."

"You're not going to tell him, are you?"

"I won't need to. He's a big boy. He'll figure it out. Mind if I have a look around the house?"

Huntington stood next to Eva with his arms crossed over his chest, glowering at Vanna but saying nothing. If eyes could send darts, she'd have puncture wounds all over her body.

Eva shrugged. "I guess it's okay."

Vanna strolled into the living room to find a section of rug had been cut away. Everything had been surveyed in the den from Van's nighttime visit, so she headed upstairs. In the master bedroom she looked around. The room had thick brown carpet, with cubist paintings on white walls and a huge bed covered with a gold satin cover.

On the dresser Vanna opened a large jewelry box. Inside rested a diamond necklace that matched the picture of the one missing from the Blendheim house. Another interesting discovery. The police hadn't taken it so they must have missed the connection. She'd give Mulhaney an assignment on this one. She continued rummaging through the jewelry box and drawers but couldn't find the diamond earrings. After a once-through of the other rooms, she headed downstairs. "Thanks for letting me in. I'll get out of your way now. I'll expect you to call Mulhaney."

Eva let out a deep sigh. "All right."

After leaving the house, Vanna visited the neighbors. First, she found someone who corroborated the argument on the porch last night. This middle-aged woman in a housedress and frizzy hair who lived directly across the street gave a full rundown: "This wild woman stood on the front porch screaming and shouting at Bentley Graves. Such a nice man to end up the way he did."

"Did you hear exactly what she said?" Vanna asked.

"Oh, yes. That insane blonde shouted, 'I'm going to kill you and cut off your . . .'" She leaned forward and glanced from side to side. "You know, his thingy."

"I don't know his thingy fortunately, but I understand what you're saying. Did he shout back at her after that?"

The woman in need of a hot oil treatment shook her head which caused her hair to pulsate like broken corn stalks in a breeze. "No. He and the wild lady went back inside."

"Where were you?"

"Right out on my front porch. I saw it with my binoculars." She put her hand to a cheek, which reddened. "You must think I'm a snoop."

Vanna smiled. "That's all right. Without people like you, the police might never know what happened."

Frizz Woman straightened her back. "Why yes. You're right."

"And did you see the woman leave?"

"No, when they both went back inside, I got a call from my friend Mabel. She talks forever. By the time I hung up the phone, police cars had filled the street and cops were swarming all over the Graves place."

"What time did you hear the shouting?"

"A little past nine. I have a cuckoo clock, and it had just chimed."

How appropriate. Vanna was dealing with a fistful of cuckoos on this case.

She rang the next doorbell she came to and an old man with gray hair immeasurably better groomed than Frizz Woman answered. Giving him her card, she asked if he had seen or heard anything last night.

"Darn right. Some crazy woman screamed next door."

"What time did that happen?"

"I don't know. I was reading and didn't check my watch."

"Did you notice anything else unusual?"

"A lot of traffic on the street. Usually not many cars go by. I looked out one time and saw a dark green Jaguar."

"What makes you so certain of the type of car?"

He thumped his chest. "I bought and sold used cars for forty years. I know every vehicle that's ever been built."

"What time did you see the Jaguar?"

He shrugged. "Can't say. I'm not much on time."

This guy obviously needed a cuckoo clock like the previous neighbor owned.

After another interview, which shed no light on the events, and two houses with no one home, Vanna drove away, thinking over all she had heard. A lot of activity around the Graves house last night.

Any number of her favorite suspects could have killed Bentley.

\* \* \* \* \*

Back in her office, Vanna wrote up notes on her day's activities and planned her campaign for that night. Before grabbing some dinner, she decided to follow up on some of the sources from Harlan Shannon. She didn't have time to visit the orphanage and would have to figure out the best way to approach that anyway, but Harlan had given her the name of the Yahoo shape-shifter email loop.

She signed on to her computer and went to Yahoo and joined the group. Then she began perusing some recent messages. One came from someone who called himself Foxmeister. The subject line of his message said, "Another Encounter," and read, "Hey, dudes. I think my chick is a shape-shifter. Last night she disappeared, and when I went to look for her, I found this large shaggy dog on my porch. The next morning my chick was back, but no dog. I think she's a weredog. When I asked her what happened last night, she said she was sleepwalking and woke up a block away. What do ya think?"

Someone with the handle of Averagejoe replied. "Could be, man. I live in a trailer park where two women bailed recently. I hear wild dogs howling in the hills nearby. Strange stuff going on."

Another message came from Joan-of-ark who stated, "You both are nuts. Any woman who's a shape-shifter would change into a cat or a mountain lion. You guys have it all wrong."

Then back to Foxmeister. "No cats or mountain lions. My chick is definitely doing a dog thing. I'm going to keep an eye on her. What should I do if I find her changing into a dog?"

A person named Straight-scoop sent a message, "Give her dog biscuits."

Someone named BlueBeard replied to Foxmeister, "Cool. If that happens, you can make a lot of money. Think of all the people who will pay to see her."

Vanna rolled her eyes. How did Harlan find anything useful with all these fruitcakes? She'd had enough, so she logged off and walked down the street to get some Italian.

\* \* \* \* \*

Donning her overcoat that night at nine, Vanna and her ever

helpful GPS system drove to the police department and found a parking spot on the street a block away. After making sure no vagrants were staggering nearby, she took off the coat, got out of the car and invisibly strolled to the police department entrance. She had to wait ten minutes before she could tailgate inside. Good thing it was a warm summer night. Then up to Mulhaney's office. She sat in his chair and began sorting through the mess of papers on his desk. She never wore perfume. No sense leaving a telltale aroma behind. Besides, she didn't need her own personal scent to attract Lance who couldn't have cared less what she smelled like. He was a sense-of-touch type of guy.

It took her several minutes to locate the report on the Graves case. She read the statements from the neighbors who corroborated what she had heard from her own interviews. Gloria had screamed loud enough to wake up the whole neighborhood. Then she found something new. One of the neighbors had heard two shots and placed the event at approximately nine-thirty. Mulhaney had also checked a statement from Eva Bentley that claimed she had been playing bridge. The three women she had been with all confirmed that Eva had not left the game until after ten o'clock.

Vanna next read that a glass had been found with lipstick and Gloria's fingerprints. But the other damaging piece of evidence contained in the report: Bentley Graves had been killed with two shots to the head, so no suicide. A SIG P210 had been found on the floor next to Bentley's body and had Cornelius's and Gloria's fingerprints on it. The serial number matched the gun that had disappeared from the Blendheim's house the night of Cornelius's death.

# Chapter 13

Back in her coat, Vanna used her GPS navigation system to lead her home. She gripped the steering wheel, her mind churning through the evidence regarding the two murders. Cornelius Blendheim possibly shot with Gloria's gun, which still had not surfaced. Another gun taken from the Blendheim house used to kill Bentley Graves. A lot of circumstantial evidence piling up against Gloria. But nothing conclusive.

If Bentley's murderer had worn gloves, that would explain why Gloria's fingerprints were found on the gun from when she had cleaned it for Cornelius. Other suspects besides Gloria included Bentley Graves, for the first murder only, Huntington Blendheim and Greer Lawson. Vanna also had Blendheim Corporation president Homer Stiles on her person-of-interest list. And the complexity of relationships—Gloria had dated Huntington, married Cornelius and had an affair with Bentley. Greer was messing around with Cornelius and Bentley. Huntington had something going with Bentley's widow, Eva. Bentley and Greer had been working a business deal together that Cornelius didn't favor but Homer did. And big bucks played a part with Gloria's inheritance, Huntington being cut out of most of Cornelius's money and the sale of the Blendheim Towers.

She wished she could lock up all of them and throw away the key.

After parking her car in the small lot next to her loft, she passed a bush not well illuminated by the closest street light.

A hand grabbed her wrist.

She turned ready to plant a fist into her assailant.

"Whoa, babe, don't hit me."

A feeling of relief, desire and anger hit her all at the same time. Anger won out. "Lance, what the hell are you doing here?"

In the dim light she could see the sparkle on his perfect teeth. He took her hand and led her toward the building where she could see him more clearly. He wore hiking shorts that showed his muscular thighs and calves. His tanned arms bulged beneath a short-sleeved Hawaiian shirt, open down to the third button, revealing his sculpted chest.

"I couldn't wait until next week, darlin'." He grabbed her around the waist, pulled her close and kissed her soundly.

She resisted for a split second and then sank her lips back into his. She flicked her tongue against his before coming up for air.

"Let's head up to your place," came his throaty whisper.

Panic seized Vanna. She had too much going on. She couldn't afford to turn back into Van for an extended period. But the tingling in her body told her she couldn't ignore Lance. Damn inconvenience of being a transvictus. Then an idea formed. "Okay, Lance, but let's go to your place tonight."

"That's fine by me, babe." He gave her another kiss.

She felt her nipples becoming erect. She gently pushed him away. "Give me half an hour. I'll drive over."

He held her at arm's length. "You're not going to skip out on me afterwards again, are you?"

"I'm in the middle of an important investigation and will have to leave early in the morning, so I better drive over."

He released her hands. "Have it your way. See you in thirty." He pulled her close again, met her lips with a little tongue that made her shudder before he turned and strolled away.

Vanna felt limp and invigorated at the same time. She staggered to her loft and let herself in. She packed an overnight bag with Van's clothes and picked up her phone to call Gloria.

"I'm glad you're still awake," Vanna said when Gloria answered.

"I'm too keyed up after the discussion with you and Donald today." Then Gloria's tone changed. "You're not calling to warn me of something, are you?"

"Yeah, but in a good way. I found out that Van will be back in town tomorrow, and I need to go to Colorado Springs for the day. He'll want to see you."

"Oh, goodie. I want to see him too."

Good girl. "I think he really likes you, Gloria."

"It's mutual." She giggled. "I'll stop by his office in the morning."

"And here's a little secret that few know. When you see Van tomorrow, light up a cigarette and blow some smoke in his face. That always makes him extra romantic."

"Thanks for the tip. He said he was allergic to cigarette smoke but certainly acted all hot and bothered when I smoked in front of him before."

Vanna hung up. Knowing Gloria, she'd track Van down no matter how evasive he tried to be and then, whammo. He'd be trapped, and she'd be back again. This would be perfect. She'd have Lance tonight and not have to be gone long if Gloria got her clutches into Van again.

Vanna put on fresh lipstick, puffed her hair and dabbed on a dash of Channel No. 5. Not that she needed the perfume or even that Lance would notice it, but what the hell. She wanted to do this right and enjoy herself.

\* \* \* \* \*

At Lance's apartment, he met her at the door with a Margarita. Frank Sinatra crooned from the sound system and the aroma of cinnamon permeated the air.

"Is that what I think I smell?" she asked after taking a gulp of the proffered drink.

"Yup. I know you love sweet rolls."

She set the drink down and put her arms around Lance, feeling his strong chest against hers. "Almost as much as I love you."

He gave her a sensuous, deep kiss. "Then why don't you stick around for a few days? I don't have another gig for the next two weeks. We can lounge around and make love for days. I'll wait on you hand and foot, cook your meals, play my guitar for you, draw your bath, even join you in the tub." He winked at her.

"Tempting. Very tempting." She wished.

He brought her a roll right out of the oven.

She touched her tongue to the frosting and then scarfed every last crumb. "Um, good." She licked her fingers.

Lance took her fingers, kissed them and then began working up her hand to her wrist, arm, shoulder, neck and finally lips.

"Um, good." She shuddered.

Lance ran his hand over her back and danced with her around his living room.

She melted into his arms, all the cares of the day drifting away as she felt his strong body press against hers. Then he lifted her and carried her to his bedroom. She loved this place. Lance defied the bachelor stereotype. In addition to being a good cook, he kept things in immaculate order. She had once looked in his closet. Everything hung neatly on hangers—shirts together, pants in one section, sports coats in another. No underwear or socks strewn on chairs or the rug.

He removed a comforter, pulled back the covers to reveal crisp, clean sheets.

And he never rushed their lovemaking, which was a good thing given Vanna's condition. She needed to savor every moment while she lasted.

He undressed her one garment at a time, as if he had won each round of a game of strip poker. He bestowed kisses after he folded an object of clothing and placed it neatly on a wooden chair. When only her necklace remained, Vanna climbed into bed, pulled the sheet up and patted the mattress. "Well, are you going to stand there with your clothes on?"

Lance slowly removed his robe, obviously enjoying his tempting performance as much as Vanna did.

She gasped at the sight of him. What a firm, solid chest he had, followed by the washboard stomach and then the attractive apparatus below. She reached for him, and he lay down beside her, stroking her back as he pulled her against him. He drew widening circles over her spine and then cupped her breasts while touching her lips with the tip of his tongue. She arched her back as he stroked her hair and then ran his hands over every inch of her body. Finally, he began licking her, starting with her throat and working his way down over her breasts, stomach, and finally lower until he caused her to shudder again.

"Um, good," was all Vanna could say.

She could wait no longer. She climbed on top of him and drew him inside her. She rode him for a wonderful giddy-up and then rolled over with him still inside her. Their bodies gyrated in synchronized rhythm until the moment of mutual release when they both let out shouts loud enough to wake the whole building.

Lance rolled onto his side and began snoring.

Vanna felt the transformation taking place, thankful for this one other good quality of Lance's. After sex he went out like a light.

As Van lay there next to this sweaty naked guy, he unclasped Vanna's necklace from around his neck and slowly slipped out of bed.

Lance smacked his lips once but didn't move.

Good. He hated it the time Lance had thrown an arm out and almost caught him in the nuts. Retrieving the overnight bag, Van entered the bathroom and changed. Tempted to leave the toilet seat up, he slipped on his jeans, T-shirt and tennis shoes and skedaddled before Lance inadvertently woke up.

It was good to be back. He'd have to hold his desires in check for a while and let Vanna have a deserved vacation.

* * * * *

The next morning Van awaked to a call from Gloria. "Vanna told me you'd be back. I'm coming right over to see you. I'll be wearing a very sexy dress just for you."

"Uh, Gloria, let's catch up later in the day. I have some important work to do on your case this morning. You want me to keep you out of jail, don't you?"

"Yeah, that's important. But I miss you."

"I miss you too. Until later."

Having dodged that bullet, he grabbed a quick cup of coffee and piece of toast, dressed and took off in case Gloria decided to stop by anyway.

As his Subaru exited the parking lot, his suspicion was confirmed as he saw Gloria's gold Lexus pulling around the corner. He sped off to make sure she didn't trap him. He really needed to be in his office to check some files on the Blendheim case but couldn't afford a sexual encounter with Gloria at the moment.

Instead, another thought occurred to him. Vanna had come up with the transvictus information from Harlan Shannon and had signed up the agency to do some background work on the All Souls Orphanage. Van clearly couldn't come up with too much there in order to protect his own self-interest, but something had been bugging him for years. Where the hell did he come from and who were his parents? Why had he become an orphan? Had his parents died or had he been abandoned?

The few inquiries he had made while at the orphanage had always been met by indulgent smiles from the nuns, a pat on the head and the admonition to pay attention to the present and future and not the past. Well, what the hell? Why not look into the past a smidgen right now?

The All Souls building had been converted from an orphanage into a parochial school. Not that many orphans in Denver any more, but a definite need for private school education with parents willing to pay top dollar for sound instruction.

He wondered if any of the nuns from his day were still around. They had been strict, but he had benefited from their perseverance. In spite of himself he had received an excellent education, which prepared him for college and his PI career.

As he pulled up in front of the three-story building, memories flashed though his mind. In his earliest recollection, he remembered sitting on the floor playing with a ragged teddy bear. Then the early years of school, learning to read and write. He still had excellent penmanship as a result of the constant repetition insisted on by the nuns.

He also flinched at the image of being whacked over the wrist with a ruler when he had sent a spitball across the room in third grade. Nuns weren't supposed to administer corporal punishment any more, but this order had been slow to receive the message. They had been strong proponents of the carrot and stick. Wallops for misdemeanors followed by gold stars for good performance.

He climbed the stone steps, scene of a scraped knee as he once charged out-of-control for a waiting bus to take him and the other kids on a field trip to the Denver Museum of Nature and Science. A Band-Aid had made the raspberry feel better, and he hadn't missed the expedition.

Inside he found the administration office and stepped up to the counter to be greeted by a young nun with a name tag that read, "Sister Marie Louise."

Van proffered his business card. "Good morning, Sister. I'm a private investigator but also a graduate of All Souls Orphanage. I'd like to speak to whoever might know what happened to the records from the orphanage."

Her eyes widened. "We don't have many alumni of the orphanage stop by to inquire. Let me find Sister Jean Renee for you."

She disappeared behind a door, and in five minutes an older nun with a strand of gray hair peeking out from under a corner of her wimple appeared. She walked gracefully up to Van. "May I help you?"

Van gave her a courteous smile and handed her a business card. "My name is Van Averi. I grew up in this building when it was the All Souls Orphanage. I thought you might be able to help me find some records from the orphanage."

She looked at Van, then at his card and back at him again. "We have retained some documents from that time. As I'm sure you know, we now run a school here."

"Yes. By any chance would Sister Mary Ancheles still be in residence?"

She shook her head. "No. She was reassigned to Boston five years ago."

"She taught me a thing or two." Van chuckled.

Sister Jean Renee gave a knowing nod, and a twinkle shone in her eyes. "She had a reputation for that. What type of records are you looking for?"

Van let out a deep breath. "I've recently developed in interest in exploring my background. I thought there might be some indication of the identity of my parents."

She had a faraway look for a moment, and then her gaze focused again on Van. "No one's inquired about orphanage files. We have boxes from that era stored in the basement."

"I remember that basement. The Sisters warned us never to go there because of spiders. That made us all sneak down to see what was hidden there. We couldn't find any spiders. Nothing but old furniture."

Crinkle lines appeared near her eyes. "I had recently arrived here when the orphanage closed. We gave that basement quite a cleaning and had a huge yard sale before converting the building to a school. But the records kept there have never been sorted or classified. A huge room full of disorganized boxes."

"That's why I thought my profession might help. I'm used to looking through unorganized files to find needed information. I don't want you or the other Sisters to take the time, but would it be possible for me to look through the storage area to see what I might uncover?"

"Why don't you give me your full name and birth date? I do have a list of all the orphans who lived here. Let me check, and I'll let you know what's possible."

"I never had a middle name and Van wasn't a nickname for anything like Vanderbilt." Then he handed her his driver's license. "Here. You can see my birth date is March 10, 1979."

She jotted the birth date on a pad of paper and returned his driver's license. "I can't guarantee that you'll be allowed to do this, but I'll give you an answer in an hour."

"I'll grab a bite to eat and be back. Thanks for helping me."

He drove off to have some lunch, wondering if he'd be given permission to search through the orphanage records, and even so, would there be anything of value.

# Chapter 14

As Van finished his last bite of pepperoni, cheese and crust at Pizza Hut, his cell phone played the theme song from Rocky. He flicked it open. "Yeah?"

"Van, where are you?" Gloria asked.

This woman was persistent. "I told you, I have some work to do today. I'm in the middle of tracking a hot lead."

Her sultry voice made his heart skip a beat. "There something else that's hot. Can I see you later today?"

He had mixed feelings. He hadn't forgotten their romp in the hay and wouldn't mind getting to know her even better, but he didn't want to risk the consequences. "Gloria, I can't wait to see you again, but I'm going to be traveling all over Denver today. I'll give you a call tonight when things calm down."

"You do that, or I'll never forgive you. I hope you're finding clues so you can show the police who really killed Cornelius and Bentley."

"That's my goal."

"You wouldn't want little old me to be incarcerated with all those lowlifes. Call me." She made kissing sounds.

Van closed his phone. Pure trouble, but some woman. He wiped away some tomato sauce from the corner of his mouth, threw the napkin into the trash container and drove back to speak with Sister Jean Renee. What a life. Bouncing back and forth between blonde bombshells and nuns.

While waiting in the former orphanage, he looked around the office. The obligatory crucifix, planted in the center of the wall; neat stacks of paperwork on two administrators' desks replete with industrial strength staplers; a white porcelain vase with slightly wilted daisies resting on the counter; and old chairs that could have been left from the time he lived here and that appeared sturdy enough to support an elephant.

Finally, Sister Jean Renee appeared. She had a frown on her face, and Van deduced she didn't have good news for him.

"I spoke with Mother Superior, and she rejected my request to let you look through the records." She turned her eyes toward Van. "I was an orphan, and I've often had the same questions you have, but Mother Superior doesn't want to set a precedent and constantly have to handle requests such as yours. It could interfere with the operation of the school."

Van met her gaze. "I understand. Thank you for taking my side. I'm sorry it didn't work out."

He strode down the steps and returned to his Subaru. At first this had been a mission of curiosity, but now he was determined to check the old orphanage records. No Mother Superior would stop him.

Part of the woods that had adjoined the orphanage had escaped development. Van parked nearby and opened the trunk. He emptied the blue sports bag of its contents and took it with him into the wooded area. Once far enough into the trees to be unseen from the street, he removed his clothes and ring and stuffed everything in the sports bag. Then he stashed the bag in a bush where no one could find it.

Now completely invisible, he strolled back to the school. With all the problems that had beset the Catholic Church, he knew it wouldn't be well received if anyone knew a naked man was wandering the halls of a parochial school. But he would stay invisible as long as no one threw panties onto his head.

He tailgated into the building and headed down the stairs to the basement. This part of the building hadn't changed one iota. Same musty smell, same bleached wood railing, same creaky stairs requiring him to step lightly, and same cracked linoleum floor. He found the storage area, but the door was locked. He gave it a hard tug—it remained firmly secured. Damn. He had picks in the trunk but had no way to carry them without freaking out people who would see metal objects floating along in the air. He sat down to wait, feeling the cold floor beneath his bare butt. He had visions of spiders crawling over his exposed body. He shivered at the thought. Spiders had never been his favorite type of creature.

No one came into the basement for an hour, and he had almost dozed off when he heard footsteps on the stairs. He jumped up. It would cause problems if someone stepped on him or tripped over his invisible legs. He waited as a young nun, probably in her late twenties, approached the storage room. She extracted a key from a pocket in her habit and inserted it in the lock.

Success!

She held the door open far enough that he was able to scoot inside behind her. The room was pitch black. She flicked a switch, and several overhead bulbs popped on, still not providing a heck of a lot of light.

The nun rummaged through a stack of cardboard boxes near the door, humming as she searched.

Van couldn't make out the tune at first. He stepped closer to her and recognized, *I Want to Hold Your Hand.* Maybe nuns had changed in the last twenty years. In his day the nuns would have been vocalizing Gregorian chants.

The nun finally pulled out a folder, put the cover back, restacked the boxes, turned off the light and departed.

Van stood there in the complete darkness and took a deep breath. Mildew, paper dust and, he suspected, rat droppings. He shook, both from the coolness and the excitement of possibly finding hints of his background. He thought how if Vanna were here, she'd immediately be disoriented and wouldn't know what direction to go to find the light. In comparison, he had excellent navigational abilities. Someone could blindfold him and spin him around, and he'd be able to find his way as if he had a GPS built into his brain. He headed over to the wall, put out his hand and touched the switch, not a fraction of an inch from where he expected it to be.

The dim light illuminated the enormity of his challenge. The room was the size of a tennis court. Metal racks ten feet tall lined narrow aisles. As far as he could see, boxes rested on three levels. He located a stepladder for when he needed it and made a walking tour of his new domain. His slapping footsteps reverberated through the huge room. Four aisles with no markers to identify the contents stored there. He checked several cardboard boxes. Some had dates in black marker, but most only said Weyerhaeuser, Safeway or Target.

Well, Sister Jean Renee had warned him. This wouldn't be an easy task to find the right era much less something useful. Of the marked boxes, most showed dates in the first half of the twentieth century. Nothing to indicate the 1970s or 1980s. And on top of that, he could find no order to the placement scheme. Next to a box labeled 1932, he opened another one that had a picture of kids in tie dye shirts and a roster from 1969. Also, all the boxes appeared to be the same age. Everything must have been packed up when the orphanage closed. That must have been a hell of a challenge—stashing seventy-five years of history. Apparently, once the boxes had been loaded, no one had the energy left to store them in any logical order.

Van rolled his shoulders, cracked his knuckles and began systematically opening boxes. He worked down an aisle at ground level, back at the second level and then used the ladder to reach the third level. Completing the first aisle, the closest date he found was 1998 right after he graduated and before the orphanage closed. In the second aisle he came across records from 1987. He squinted at one picture of a group of kids and spotted himself in his jeans, Bronco T-shirt and short hair. Periodically, he located lists of children being admitted to the orphanage—annual log books stored with other items for that year. His hope remained to find something similar for the year 1979.

He paused to stretch his arms, then put his hands on his hips and arched his back. Damn. Almost as bad as picking strawberries. Despite his thirst, he continued his task, wanting to find the right box. Several false alarms with early 1970s and mid 1980s. He was standing on the ladder going through the top level of the second aisle when he heard the door open. He quickly scurried down the ladder and stood off to the side.

"Someone left the light on," a woman's voice announced.

He heard shuffling sounds, and then the light went off before the door closed. Waiting a minute, he paced off the distance to the light switch and turned it back on. Then he resumed his search.

He checked his watch—four-thirty. He pictured a tall glass of lemonade but pushed the image aside to continue his tedious search. Forty-five minutes later, half-way through the middle section of aisle three, he opened a box and found on top a letter dated August 2, 1979. Not wanting to get too optimistic, he carried the box to a spot right underneath one of the overhead bulbs. He sat down and began removing documents from the box.

He found a letter dated October 21, 1979, from a couple asking to adopt a one-year-old girl. He lifted out a list of capital improvements citing the amount of money spent to repair a sidewalk, replace leaky drains, add a storage shed, and fix the roof after a hail storm. Then he inspected several pictures of groups of teenage kids, before extracting a dusty log book. He opened it and scanned entries with children's names and dates. He ran his fingers down the ledger and then continued to the next page.

When he reached March he found an entry for March 18 with the name Van Averi. He almost dropped the book as his heart raced at a dangerous rate.

A very clean script indicated the name of Sister Helene Claudette. A note in her handwriting stated, "I found the baby on our doorstep yesterday evening. I'd guess a week old."

Van stifled a shout. He remembered Sister Helene Claudette. She had been at the orphanage up to the time he graduated. A friendly woman who didn't whack students with her ruler. She had taught him United States history at the beginning of his junior year. He chuckled. That semester he finally had become interested in his studies. He may have even received an A in her class. He tried to guess how old she had been at that time and did a quick calculation. She must be in her seventies now.

Then another fact struck him and his body sagged. If he had been abandoned, he'd never find his parents.

# Chapter 15

Van continued to search through the box from 1979 but found nothing else useful. Not that he expected to locate anything like a birth certificate that had happened to be left with the abandoned baby boy. He tried to imagine why a baby would be left on the steps of an orphanage. A mother who couldn't afford to raise a child or an abandoned baby that had been discovered and left at a suitable place to be cared for. He thanked his lucky stars he hadn't been aborted or thrown into a trash bin.

But another question nagged at him. Where did the name Van Averi come from? It didn't have the ring of a James, Peter, John, Mark, Luke, Paul or Matthew that the nuns would have selected. His search so far had raised more questions than it had answered.

He repacked everything and put the box back at the correct place on the shelf. Dusting his hands, he returned to the front of the room, turned off the light, carefully opened the door and peered out to make sure no one happened to be coming down the stairs, before he left the storage room.

After departing the building, he jogged to the woods and changed into his clothes. Back in his car he retrieved his cell phone and called the orphanage. "May I speak to Sister Jean Renee, please?"

"One moment please, she may still be in the office."

Van tapped impatiently on the dashboard as he waited.

"Sister Jean Renee. How may I help you?"

He let out a sigh of relief that she hadn't left for the day. "Sister, this is Van Averi. We spoke earlier this afternoon."

"Yes, Mr. Averi."

"Again, thanks for going to bat for me to look at the records. I had another thought that you might be able to help me with."

"Yes?"

"I remember the name of another nun from my time in the orphanage—Sister Helene Claudette. Did you ever meet her?"

She laughed. "Of course. I remember her well. Someone gave her the nickname of Sister Sunshine. A wonderful person."

"I'd like to say hello to her. Does she still work for the school by any chance?" Van crossed his fingers.

"Oh, no. She retired. She's living in the Saint Clements Retirement Community in Fort Collins."

"I hope she's doing well."

"I think so. She's still with it mentally but had difficulty with arthritis the last I heard."

Van bounced around the seat of the car with excitement. "Would you have the address of the retirement home?"

"Sure, give me a second."

He continued to squirm as he waited for her to come back on the line.

"Here it is." She gave him the address.

"Thank you. You've been very helpful." Van closed his phone, drove off and stopped at an IHOP. He dashed in to use the restroom and treated himself to a huge stack of pancakes and a gallon of water. Then he took I-25 and drove to Fort Collins.

When he reached the retirement community, he found a modern two-story building with a large flower garden in front. Van inquired at the desk for Sister Helene Claudette.

A middle-aged woman with a pencil stuck in her hair smiled and said, "You'll find her in the lounge. We have a Wii bowling tournament going on against another retirement community. You can go watch. Down the hall."

Van sauntered in the direction indicated and found a large

commons area full of screaming women. One group wore brown bowling shirts and others had green-striped shirts. He had played a little Wii golf but never tried bowling. He watched as a silver-haired woman on the green team took her hand back and then shot it forward. On the large plasma screen a ball raced down an alley, smashed into the pins and sent them all scattering.

A cheer went up. "Another strike for Eunice." Other green-clad old ladies swarmed around Eunice with pats on the back, high fives and hugs. They acted like they were at a real bowling alley. The only thing missing—no bottles of Budweiser in their hands.

Van saw that the brown shirts bore the tag line, "Nun Miss." He tapped one of the brown shirts on the shoulder and asked, "Is Sister Helene Claudette here?"

"Oh, yes. That's her holding onto a walker. But that doesn't slow her down. She usually bowls over two hundred."

Once pointed out, Van recognized her. She had aged but still had a prim smile on her face. When her match came up, she lived up to her reputation and scored 206 and won against an opponent who only bowled 195. After the tournament wrapped up, all the women drank iced tea and munched on sugar cookies.

Van approached Sister Helene Claudette. "Sister, my name is Van Averi. I knew you when I lived at the All Souls Orphanage."

She bit her lip for a moment, and then a huge smile lit up her face. She shook an arthritic index finger at him. "I remember you. Whenever someone lost something, we'd call on you to find it."

Van chuckled. "That's right. You have a good memory. I put that skill to good use. I'm now a private investigator."

She nodded her head. "That sounds just right for you. Probably track down missing people. What brings you here?"

"Could we sit somewhere to speak alone?"

She pointed to an unoccupied couch across the lounge. "Let's go right over there." She pushed her walker and limped over with Van following. She carefully sat down.

Van plunked down beside her. "I've been trying to research my background. I track down information on other people and finally decided I should do the same for myself. I've learned that someone left me on the steps of the orphanage and you found me. Do you happen to remember any of the details? That was in March of 1979."

She tapped her temple. "I may not move too swiftly any more, but I still have all my marbles." Her eyes showed crinkle lines, and her face lit up with an angelic smile. "I certainly remember that evening. You were wrapped in a blanket. Fortunately, a mild night for that time of year. There could have been a blizzard. You weren't even crying when I found you."

He thought over the note she had written in the log book he had found in the orphanage basement. "I imagine babies were frequently left at the orphanage door."

She shook her head. "No. Some people have that impression, but usually we worked with hospitals and social services. Finding you there was very unusual. That's why I remember it so vividly. I went outside to get a breath of air and almost stepped on you." She laughed. "That wouldn't have done you much good. I bent over and picked you up."

"Did you ever have any idea who might have left me?"

She tapped her lip for a moment. "Nothing directly. But I found a card tucked in the blanket with block letters giving you the name of Van Averi and asking us to take care of you. That and the medallion were the only things left with you."

"Medallion?"

"Oh, yes. I've never seen one like it, before or since. It was gold with the image of a lamb swallowing the tail of a snake while the snake's mouth held the hind hoof of the lamb."

# Chapter 16

Van winced at what he had heard from Sister Helene Claudette. "A medallion of a lamb and a snake?" Then images swirled through his brain. Wait a minute. This struck a cord. His recurring dream of holding the hoof of a lamb in his mouth. He reeled.

"Are you all right?" Sister Helene Claudette's expression turned to concern.

"I . . . I'm surprised at hearing this." Then another realization. Vanna's constant dream of a tail of a snake in her mouth. It all clicked into place in a strange sort of way. "Tell me more."

She adjusted her skirt. "No one I showed it to had any clue either. A strange object to leave with a baby."

Van gripped the arm of the couch, trying to make some sense of this latest revelation. "Do you know what happened to it?"

"I saved it for years, but it must have been thrown away when I cleaned out my apartment to move here."

"That's too bad. I would have liked to see it."

Sister Helene Claudette's eyes twinkled. "That's not a problem. I can show you exactly what it looked like." She tapped the side of her head. "As I told you, I still have an excellent memory and am a reasonable artist. If you give me a piece of paper and a pencil, I'll sketch it for you."

Van jogged back to the main desk and asked for paper and pencil. He returned and gave them to the Sister.

She placed the paper on a table, stuck out the tip of her tongue and drew a large circle. Then in quick, fluid strokes, she filled in the circle and handed the result to Van. A clear rendition of a lamb with a long snake dangling from its mouth and the snake wrapped around so that its mouth held the back hoof of the lamb.

Van laughed. The complementary images of his and Vanna's dreams. Incredible. "Any other markings that you remember?"

"No, nothing else."

"And the back side of the medallion?"

She shook her head. "Pure gold color with nothing engraved. I had a jeweler look at it one time. Not real gold. He said it consisted of bronze and wasn't very valuable. Otherwise it might have provided some money for your college fund." She chuckled. "If it had been pure gold, I would have been more careful not to lose or discard it."

"You've been very helpful." Van thought of one source he could show her rendition to. Something to pursue the next day.

Sister Helene Claudette rose slowly. "Now, if you'll excuse me I really must join my team for the big celebration. We're having root beer floats to toast our victory." She patted his hand. "What a pleasant surprise seeing you again."

"Likewise. Thanks for your help." Van stood as well, shook her hand and watched as she pushed her walker toward the crowd of brown shirts.

Back in his car, he put the drawing in the glove compartment and began the drive to Denver. As he passed the exit marking Highway 34 into Loveland, his cell phone rang. Keeping his eyes focused on the highway, he flicked it open and put it to his ear. "Yeah?"

"Oh, Van. I'm so glad you answered. I tried to reach your office and then called this number." Gloria's voice gave a sob. "Where are you?"

"I'm on I-25 north of Denver."

"I have an emergency. Come to my house right away. That awful detective came here. I'm in real trouble."

"Have you called your lawyer?"

"Yes, but Donald Hallett's at the theater tonight, and I can't reach him. I could be taken to jail at any time. Help!" The phone clicked off.

He watched as the headlights from the other side of the highway zipped by. He had been avoiding Gloria all day, but obviously she needed him. He'd have to stop by to aid the damsel in distress.

When he pulled up in front of the Blendheim house, Gloria raced out and threw herself into his arms, sobbing.

"There, there, sweetheart. Your knight in shining armor has arrived. I won't let anything bad happen to you."

She pressed tightly against him and then turned her teary eyes upward toward his face. "Oh, Van. That detective said the worst things to me."

He pulled away, took her hand and started walking toward the front door. "Let's go inside, and you can tell me all the gory details."

He sat on the couch, and Gloria snuggled up against him. She snuffled, let out another sob or two and wiped away a tear.

"What did Detective Mulhaney say?"

She rested her head on his shoulder. "He showed up at my door with a big smile on his face, saying he had some news for me. I never suspected any problem, so I invited him in. He started by acting very friendly."

"The good cop routine."

She nodded her head. "He said that I was no longer the primary suspect in Cornelius's death. You can imagine my relief over that."

Van thought back to the email he had forwarded to Mulhaney. That had shifted the suspicion to Bentley Graves. "That's good news."

"He was setting me up. He said he knew I murdered Bentley Graves and that I would face a lighter sentence if I confessed. That's when I called Donald and couldn't reach him. I returned to the living room, and Mulhaney said my lawyer wouldn't do me any good now anyway. I should confess and save everyone a lot of trouble. I told him I didn't kill Bentley, but he only laughed. He pointed a finger at me and told me all the evidence shows I killed Bentley. He'd give me overnight to think it over and would be back in the morning to take my confession and arrest me."

"The bad cop routine. Don't worry. If he really had all the evidence, he would have taken you in already. He's trying to strong-arm you and get you to make a mistake. Probably knew your lawyer would be unavailable tonight. That's the way he operates." And obviously Eva hadn't called Mulhaney. He'd have to remedy that situation.

"Oh, Van, you'll stay with me won't you? I'm so afraid and lonely. I can't face this by myself."

"I really need to go back to my office. I've been on the road all day and have some work to catch up on."

She smiled. "I have a better idea." She reached for a cigarette and silver lighter resting on the coffee table.

Van held up his hands. "Don't do that. My allergy."

Ignoring him, she lit the cigarette, inhaled and blew smoke in his face, her lips curling in a devilish grin.

The room begin to swirl. Then a warmth spread through Van's chest, followed by an arousal growing in his pants. He needed to leave. A surge of lust told him to stay. Then all rational thoughts disappeared from his mind. He only wanted Gloria. He reached over and threw his arms around her. She met his lips, and he was done for.

She blew one last puff of smoke in his face, extinguished her cigarette in the obsidian ashtray in front of them. Then she stood, took his hand and let him to her bedroom.

Van had enough presence of mind to turn off the lights so that only a dim glow from an electric clock shone in the room.

Then she was all over him like a bear attacking a beehive.

And he was all over her like man in the desert finding a full canteen. His brain told him not to do this. His groin told him to ignore the brain. The groin won out.

They groped and grappled as they dispensed with clothes. Enough of Van's brain cells still engaged that he remembered to check to confirm he had on his ring before removing his last sock. They fell into Gloria's huge canopy bed and proceeded to make the whole house shake.

Van had one brief moment of asking himself what he was doing before the hormones kicked in and he lost track of everything except fondling, licking and thrusting. At the final moment of ecstasy, Gloria bucked and Van pushed. They both shouted.

Van dismounted, and Gloria sank into the mattress beside him. The transformation began.

Then Gloria opened her eyes, and Van noticed a puzzled expression on her face in the dim light. She shrieked and sat up. His synapses finally made the connection. The ring had slipped off Vanna's more slender finger, and Gloria couldn't see anyone.

"Van, Van, where'd you go? What happened?"

The transformation continued, the shrinking between his legs, the expansion outside his chest, the internal twisting and turning.

Vanna grabbed the ring that had fallen onto the mattress, raced into the bathroom and locked herself inside.

"I heard you go into the bathroom," Gloria said. "What are you doing in there? We're not done. We're just getting started, baby."

Oh, we're done all right. Vanna tried to figure out what to do now.

"I know what will get you right out and up." Gloria giggled.

Vanna heard a click and then cigarette smoke began to seep under the door.

"Here's a little assistance. Vanna told me you couldn't resist cigarette smoke. Sexy cigarette smoke, like an aphrodisiac."

*Uh-oh.* Her comeuppance. Smoke circled up from under the door. Vanna held her stomach, raced to the toilet and retched.

"What's happening?" Gloria pounded on the door. "You not feeling well in there? Honey, you okay?"

With smoke filling the bathroom, Vanna puked her guts out until nothing but bile remained. She wiped her mouth with toilet paper, ran water from the sink and rinsed her mouth. She had returned, Van had disappeared, but she had paid the price.

"Speak to me," Gloria whined. "What's happening?"

Vanna made her voice as deep as possible. "A little stomach problem."

"Your voice sounds funny."

"Yeah. Stomach problem causes that."

Gloria tapped on the door. "Will you be out soon?"

"Yeah. In a few minutes."

"I'll wait for you in bed."

Vanna heard Gloria's footsteps pad away. Good grief. Now what? She waited five minutes, turned off the light in the bathroom, gripped the doorknob, turned it slowly and opened the door without making a sound. She snuck into the bedroom and saw Gloria lying in the bed, facing toward the wall with the covers pulled up.

Invisible, Vanna watched in the dim light to verify that Gloria's rhythmic breathing had turned to sleep. She was as bad as Lance at staying awake after sex. Good thing.

Vanna gathered all of Van's clothes and took them downstairs. Although too large for her, they would cover her body. She dressed, cinched the belt as tight as it would go and left the house.

As she drove back to her loft, she decided she would give up sex forever and leave Van as merely part of their collective memory. That resolve lasted until she saw Lance's pickup parked outside her building. The thought of Lance caused her pulse rate to double. No, she had to avoid him at all costs.

Clenching her teeth, she kept driving until she found the first not-too-sleazy motel. She retrieved the red sports bag out of the trunk and did a quick change inside the car in the darkest corner of the parking lot. Sex was way too complicated when you were a transvictus.

# Chapter 17

The morning light awakened Vanna, and she rolled over in the motel bed. The good news—no bedbug bites. She packed up and headed back to her place, thankful that Lance's pickup was nowhere in sight. Her vow to give up sex had one big problem—Lance. She'd have to find some way to keep him at bay. She needed him to have an extended gig out of town for her own good. That idea had possibilities. She'd work on it.

After a shower, cup of coffee and bagel, she headed downstairs to The V V Agency office. She logged on the Internet and did a quick check for any groups looking for guitarists. She found one promising opportunity in Los Angeles. Her first phone call of the day—to Lance's agent, Nelson Drury. "Hey, Nelson, this is Vanna Anderson."

"Hey, girl. Lance find you last night?"

"No, we missed each other. But I have a lead for you. A group in LA needs a hot guitarist. Thought you might know just the guy."

"Damn right. Give me the info."

She related what she had found. "Let me know if it works out."

"Sure. But I'm not splitting my commission with you." He gave a loud gagging and spluttering laugh.

Vanna imagined spittle shooting out of the phone receiver and almost held it away from her ear. "Wouldn't expect it." Nelson could close deals, but he was pretty useless at spotting them in the first place.

Next, Vanna regarded the drawing she had removed from the glove compartment. A lamb devouring a snake with the snake's mouth on the lamb's hoof. Pretty unusual. She wondered if Professor Harlan Shannon had ever heard of such a thing. Only one way to find out. She punched in his number. His admin said he had an early class but would be back in an hour. Vanna requested a return call.

She was helping herself to her second cup of coffee for the morning when the phone rang.

"Is Van in?" Gloria asked.

"No, he had to go out of town again first thing," Vanna said, oozing sincerity. "He said to tell you he'll be thinking about you and asked me to cover things while he's gone."

"Oh, that rascal. Talk about kissing and running. Did Van mention that yucky detective harassed me again yesterday?"

"Yup. Van briefed me on all the details. I agree with him. Mulhaney threatened you to see if you would break. Stick to your guns, girl."

"I heard back from Donald Hallett this morning as well. He's of the same opinion. He's going to call the detective right away and set him straight."

"I'll also follow up with Mulhaney. Between Donald and me, we'll do our best to keep him away from you."

"Thanks. I need you to keep working to find who killed Bentley Graves."

"I have some checking to do on that today. I'll let you know when I learn anything useful."

After hanging up, Vanna thought through her suspect list. Gloria could have killed both Cornelius and Bentley, but as the agency's client, this was the worst-case scenario. Mulhaney thought Bentley had killed Cornelius and Gloria had murdered Bentley. Vanna's intuition led her to a different conclusion. She suspected one of three people had killed Cornelius. These suspects included Huntington Blendheim, angry at his father for cutting him out of the big bucks in his will; Greer Lawson, a romance gone bad; or Homer Stiles, a shortcut to taking over Blendheim Corporation.

But then did this same person shoot Bentley? And what motive existed for that crime? More facts and motivation needed sorting out.

Huntington had a thing going with Bentley's wife Eva, but that affair only started recently. Could Huntington have killed Bentley to have Eva to himself? Greer had both a business and sexual relationship with Bentley. Had something gone sour there? And then a green Jaguar had been seen in the neighborhood the night of Bentley's death. Good old Homer Stiles owned such a vehicle, and he had been negotiating with Bentley. Lots of opportunities with no clear answers. And why did Gloria's missing necklace show up in Eva's jewelry box?

The ringing telephone interrupted her thoughts. She picked it up to hear Professor Harlan Shannon on the line.

"Hey, Vanna. Have you tracked down anything regarding the All Souls Orphanage or those contacts in other cities?"

"That's why I called earlier. My partner and I have been doing some research, going through the archives left after the orphanage shut down and speaking with several Sisters. We came across one unusual piece of information." Vanna paused to take a sip of coffee while she decided how she wanted to play this. "One of the sisters reported finding a medallion."

"A medallion?"

"Yes. It showed a lamb eating a snake, but the head of the snake bends around to grab the lamb's hind hoof."

"The transvictus icon! That's a link, Vanna. Good job."

Vanna tapped her desk with a finger. "What's a transvictus icon?"

"In my research I found a reference to such a symbol. The lamb represents the female consuming the male snake. But the snake has its jaw on the hoof of the lamb ready to consume it. It's the back and forth transformation between male and female. Any lead to a transvictus living at the orphanage?"

Oh, yeah. But nothing she was willing to share with a man who'd made the transvictus study his life work and wanted to prove it to the world. Vanna hedged. "Not anything concrete yet. I have some other leads to track down, and I'll continue to work those. But I have a question for you. How could a transvictus have a baby?"

"Ah, an interesting question. From what I've learned, transvictus babies are always male. A male past puberty can impregnate a normal woman, but a transvictus can't become pregnant while in the female state."

That would explain why she had never had a period, much less become pregnant after one of her unprotected romps with Lance. She figured she usually hadn't been in the female state long enough to have a period. "It would be complicated if a female transvictus became pregnant and then transformed into a male."

"Yeah. I'm sure that would abort the baby anyway if it happened. All that's avoided since a transvictus is a fertile male and sterile female."

Vanna thought through another implication. "Consequently, only the male passes on the transvictus traits."

"Here's my theory. I think the transvictus genes are dominant and will always be passed on if a transvictus impregnates a woman."

Vanna pictured a woman in a shroud sneaking up to the steps of the All Souls Orphanage at night and leaving a swaddled Van at the door. But who had been the father? "So a woman in Denver got pregnant from a transvictus and gave birth to a boy who ended up in this orphanage."

"That's the most likely scenario."

Then it struck her. She could never become pregnant. Sex for her would only be for pleasure. But sex still led to the unwanted side effect of her being transformed into Van. Maybe she'd stick with her resolution to swear off sex altogether. Nelson had to get that gig for Lance in Los Angeles. That would take the pressure off for the time being. She didn't get the hots for random men. She could control herself if she didn't have Lance breathing down her neck—or on her neck.

"Anything else that you've come up with?" Harlan asked.

"No, that's it for the time being. I'll keep you posted."

After hanging up, Vanna assessed what she had heard. She still had no way to track down the woman who had left Van on the orphanage doorstep, much less a transvictus who had been the father. She'd ruminate on that later. Right now she needed to get back to the Blendheim case. It merited a call to Detective Mulhaney.

"How's my favorite detective this fine morning?" she purred.

"How's my favorite PI tease? What do ya want?"

"I'm longing to see your handsome, chiseled face." Chiseled out of substandard concrete. "What's new on the Blendheim case?"

He gave out a burst of air as if clearing a clogged exhaust pipe. "Yeah, right. Like I'd tell you."

"Oh, come on, Mulhaney. We're old buddies now. Gloria says you're no longer causing her grief over Cornelius's murder."

"That's right, up to a point. She's no longer my number one suspect for whacking her old man. But she shot Bentley Graves."

"Come now. That demure young lady couldn't have killed that slimebag realtor."

"She could, and she did."

Vanna decided to press a little harder. "I bet you think Graves killed Cornelius and Gloria took revenge."

A momentary pause. "Possible."

"And you think Gloria would be dumb enough to use her husband's gun to kill Graves and then leave the weapon on the floor for you to find?"

"You know what they say about blondes."

"Watch your sexist comments, Detective. I'm asking if you really believe a killer would do something that stupid."

"Again, possible."

"I'd surmise it would be more likely that someone else killed Graves and set it up to look like Gloria. That person stole the gun from the Blendheim house. You have three much better suspects than Gloria. I'd suggest you look more closely at Huntington Blendheim, Greer Lawson and Homer Stiles. And then there's always the wife, Eva."

He chuckled. "Quite a list. What makes you think any of them could be involved in the murders?"

"Let's take the demise of Cornelius first. They all have fingers that could have pulled a trigger, may have been at Cornelius's house the night of the murder . . . and, oh yes . . . all had excellent motives."

"Agreed. But Bentley probably committed that crime. Then Gloria paid him back. Simple as that."

"Several interesting items you might want to look into, Detective. Did Eva Bentley call you to give you some information?"

"Nope. Haven't heard from her."

"She and Huntington Blendheim spent time together after Bentley died. They could have been working together. You'd better speak with both of them." She could hear him scratching a note. "And while you're at Eva's house, she has the necklace stolen from Gloria Blendheim."

"What?"

"Get a search warrant to go through the house more carefully. You'll find it in her jewelry box."

"You didn't plant it, did you?"

"No, but you might want to ask Eva how it ended up there. So you have a stolen gun and a stolen necklace both in the Graves' house. Interesting coincidence, don't you think?"

"How do you know . . . damn it, Vanna. Where do you come up with this stuff?"

"Hey, I'm an investigator. Merely sharing a little information that may be useful to you. And let me give you another thought. It might be one of these other people had a reason to want Bentley Graves out of the way after what transpired the night of Cornelius's murder. Work on that and give Gloria a break for the time being. She's not going anywhere, so you can always come back to her if the other leads don't pan out." Vanna twirled a pencil in her hand. "Since the spouse is always a good suspect, why haven't you arrested Eva Bentley?"

"She has a solid alibi."

"Just because a neighbor reported hearing the shots at nine-thirty, and Eva's bridge group said she left at ten, doesn't mean that she didn't have a hand in it."

"Goddamn it," Mulhaney huffed. "How do you know that?"

"Hey, I'm a PI. I'm paid to learn stuff. But check again with Eva and Huntington. Something's fishy there." Satisfied that she had done all she could for Gloria for the time being, she signed off with Mulhaney and took off for Blendheim Corporation headquarters. With her ever-present GPS, Vanna found the modern, glass-covered, four-story building with its large parking lot. Plenty of room here compared to the parking problems in downtown Denver.

Opening the trunk, she retrieved one of her all-purpose picks and put it in her pocket. Although never a Girl Scout, she was prepared. She entered the building, signed the visitor's log, showed her identification and asked to speak with Homer Stiles.

"He's out of the office today," the young brunette informed her, flashing a set of choppers that would make any orthodontist proud.

"I'd like to see his admin in his absence."

"You can go up to the fourth floor. Ask for Jenny Reynolds."

Vanna took the elevator along with a man in a gray suit who kept trying to cozy up to an attractive redhead in a short skirt. The woman obviously wasn't buying. Vanna sometimes wished she carried a stun gun. It would be fun to zap some of these guys who thought they were hot shit.

Exiting the elevator, she found Jenny Reynolds and identified herself. "I'm doing some follow-up investigation regarding the murder of Cornelius Blendheim. I'd like to ask you a few questions."

Jenny frowned, and her eyes opened too wide. "I . . . I don't know what I can do to help you."

Vanna smiled. "Don't worry. I only have a few simple questions. You keep Mr. Stiles's calendar, don't you?"

Jenny looked from side to side as if wanting to escape. "Yes."

Vanna noticed the open door to Homer's office behind Jenny's desk. "Please check to see what appointments he had the day of Mr. Blendheim's murder."

Jenny set her jaw. "I can't do that without my boss's permission."

"Oh, he shouldn't mind. It will be easier for you to show me than when the police arrive with a search warrant and begin going through all your files."

Jenny flinched but held her ground. "I'll wait for the police then."

Vanna flashed a smile. "Your decision. May I use your restroom?"

Jenny gave a relieved sigh. "Down the hall on the left."

Vanna strolled to the women's room. Inside she located a janitor's closet. Making sure she had the place to herself, she pulled out the pick from her pocket and worked on the lock until she finagled the door open. She left it ajar and went in a stall to remove her clothes and necklace. She packed them in a neat bundle and took them to the janitor's closet where she stashed them on a shelf behind rolls of toilet paper. Leaving the janitor's closet unlocked, she closed the door. No sense taking any chances like in the restaurant restroom that someone would take her clothes. Then, invisible, she returned, tiptoed past Jenny and sat down in a visitor's chair in Homer Stiles's office to wait.

When lunchtime arrived, Jenny locked the door to Homer's office and took off.

Vanna figured she now had up to half an hour to herself. She turned on Homer's computer and waited for it to boot up. She hoped that the guy didn't want to bother with a password, but the computer asked for one.

Next, she opened his desk drawer and saw a neat row of filed manila folders. She thumbed through them and found one with the penciled label, "Password." Inside she discovered one sheet of paper with a list of passwords, all crossed out except for the last one which read "reD72aLert." She smiled to herself. The beauty of corporate passwords. The IT jocks always required a combination of lower case, upper case and numbers that needed to be changed regularly, but no one could remember the damn things so they were written down and kept in a convenient place.

She keyed in the password, and Homer's computer came alive. She checked his Outlook calendar for the past week and found a scheduled meeting with Cornelius for nine o'clock the evening of his death. Bingo. Then she checked the evening of Bentley's demise. An appointment with him. Double bingo. The guy hadn't bothered to delete the appointments from his calendar.

Next she scanned through email correspondence. She found a message from Bentley Graves that read, "When can we close the deal?"

She went into the sent mail folder and found a response. "We're set to sign. Cornelius won't be a problem much longer." Sent the afternoon before Cornelius died.

# Chapter 18

Vanna forwarded the email messages sent by Bentley Graves and Homer Stiles to Detective Mulhaney and then deleted them from the sent mail. She should get paid by the city of Denver for all the work she did to assist Mulhaney. Oh well, since Mulhaney provided so much help by keeping needed information on his messy desk, why not reciprocate once in a while?

Continuing through email messages on Homer's computer, she found nothing else of interest. Then noting the clock on his desk, she signed off and shut the system down. She left the office, returned to the restroom, retrieved her undisturbed clothes from the janitor's closet and dressed.

As she drove back to her office, she sorted through the suspects. Bentley Graves had an appointment with Cornelius the night of Cornelius's murder and ended up dead four days later. Greer Lawson had an assignation that same night with Cornelius and was in cahoots with Bentley. Huntington Blendheim had no alibi for the night of Cornelius's murder and later showed up in the company of Bentley's wife. Homer Stiles sent a message that Cornelius would no longer be a problem and had a meeting scheduled with him the night of his death.

A whole hell of a lot of activity took place at the Blendheim mansion that night. Then Gloria returned home and found the dead body with her missing gun as a possible murder weapon. Maybe this would turn out like Agatha Christie's *Murder on the Orient Express* where all the suspects committed the murder. With this crowd it wouldn't be a surprise.

And things remained no clearer regarding Bentley Graves's demise. People coming and going, cars seen in the neighborhood, two shots fired. All this made Vanna think of one suspect who required a social call.

Time to check on Cornelius's son again.

Vanna set the address in Golden on her GPS and followed the instructions. If Huntington were home, she'd have a nice discussion with him. If he didn't happen to be there, then it might be an opportune time to do some uninvited snooping. She didn't have to be constrained by the rules Mulhaney had to follow. The advantage of being a PI plus the additional little boost from also being a transvictus.

Once led to her destination, she parked a block away and strolled back to Huntington's house, giving it the once over. No indication of anyone there, and the garage door remained closed. She stepped up on the porch and rang the bell twice. No answer. She looked around. No one out watering flowers or walking dogs. A walkway led along a fence to the back of the house. She ambled in that direction and came to a back door. She tried the handle. As expected, it was locked. She checked the two houses on either side. No windows facing her and no one peeking a head over the fences. Once again taking her all-purpose lock pick out of her pocket, she made quick work of the lock and let herself inside, closing the door behind her.

The pantry and kitchen appeared as messy as the living room area Van had witnessed on the previous visit. The counter contained a stack of empty Stephanie's Chocolates boxes. How could someone live like this? Vanna wrinkled her nose at the sight of spilled gunk on the floor in front of the refrigerator. Avoiding any other toxic seepage, she wended her way into the hallway and found the den. Magazines in haphazard piles covered the floor. A small path led to the desk where a personal computer perched amid stacks of paper.

She sat on a chair with a torn, spattered, gray cushion oozing stuffing. This place felt as healthy as a landfill dump. She fired up the computer and to her surprise it didn't ask for any password. Huntington was as careless with his security as with the rest of his life.

Opening up the calendar, Vanna checked the last week. On the day of Cornelius's death she found an entry for nine-forty-five P.M. "Dad." Damnation. Another one. Had Cornelius held an open house the night someone shot him? She checked the day that Bentley died. Nothing on the calendar at all that day. She next scanned through email sent and received. It didn't look like Huntington ever took the time to delete anything, as personal messages mixed with junk email. Nothing of interest caught her eye. She logged off and shut down the computer.

Carefully stepping over the debris, she made her way to a file cabinet. No lock. She opened the top drawer and found a five-year-old phone book and a coffee mug full of unsharpened pencils with worn-down erasers.

The second drawer held old *Denver Post* newspapers. The third sported a collection of porn magazines, and the bottom drawer showed empty. Shaking her head, Vanna plodded back and headed up the stairs. Two bedrooms were completely empty, and the master bedroom held a mattress on the floor surrounded by piles of clothes. She peered in the closet. More stacks of clothes with nothing hung up. She sniffed. It smelled like an old gym.

One dresser stood in the far corner. Wading through the clothes, she opened the top drawer and found a single box. Inside rested a pair of diamond earrings, matching the picture from Gloria's insurance file.

At that moment Vanna heard a car with a bad muffler making popping noises. She raced to the window, parted the stained curtains and saw a red Mini Cooper in the driveway. Shit. She had to get out of here.

Hurdling down the stairs, she jumped over the rubble in the hallway, skidded through the kitchen and let herself out the back door, as she heard the garage door opening. She dashed around the side of the house, made sure the car had disappeared into the garage and walked as calmly as possible back to her car.

Then a thought occurred to her. Since Huntington had returned, why not have a little chat. Waiting for her lungs to recover, she sauntered back to the house and rang the bell.

Huntington answered the door and gave her the full body scan with his eyes. "Yeah?"

She held out a card. "I'm Vanna Anderson with The V V Agency. I spoke with you briefly after your dad's funeral and at Eva's house, and you previously met with my partner Van Averi. May I come in?"

His gaze stayed on her breasts. "Sure, why not?"

Vanna suspected Van wouldn't have received this same reception.

They made their way through the refuse to the living room, where Vanna removed a pile of magazines from an easy chair and sat down.

Huntington rested his skinny frame on the arm of the couch.

"I know a great cleaning service if you ever need one." Vanna gave him her best smile.

He scowled. "I like it this way."

She shrugged. "To each his own. My reason for stopping by is my partner and I are still trying to piece together what happened when your dad died. I understand you had a meeting with him that night."

Huntington twitched. "What makes you say that?"

"I found evidence that you had scheduled a get-together with him. How'd it go?"

"We never met."

Vanna arched an eyebrow. "Interesting. Van indicates you claimed to be here that evening. I suspect you actually made a trip to your father's house."

"You can't prove that."

"Maybe, maybe not. But I'm sure Detective Mulhaney will enjoy taking a crack at you." She gave him another smile.

He twitched again. This guy didn't have much control over his body, much less his life. "I don't need any stinkin' cop snooping around."

"Sorry. It's going to happen. And I bet you found Gloria's diamond necklace and earrings."

This time the twitching began at his knees and spread all the way to his face. No need for a polygraph for Huntington. "What do you mean?"

"Oh, I thought you might have seen the missing jewelry."

He jumped up. "I have an appointment downtown. You need to leave."

"Why all the hurry? I'm just getting comfortable."

"I have no time for this crap." He grabbed Vanna's arm and tried lifting her out of the chair.

She swatted his arm away. "I'll leave on my own." She pointed her right index finger at him. "You're in deep shit, Huntington. I'd suggest you level with me before the police tear you apart."

"I'm not saying anything more to you. Get out." His voice raised an octave as his whole body shook.

Vanna regarded him. "Okay, Huntington. I'll be seeing you." She let herself out and walked back to her car. There she placed a call to Mulhaney, who answered.

"This is your special assistant."

"Yeah, you're always so helpful to me," Mulhaney growled.

"Actually I am. You don't appreciate all I do for you behind the scene. I have a lead for you. Huntington Blendheim could have been at his father's house the night of Cornelius's murder. Also, he might be worth some grilling over the missing jewelry. Just a thought for you, Detective."

"Here we go again. You sending me off on a wild goose chase to save your client's gorgeous tush?"

"You'll have to reach your own conclusion, Detective. Nice speaking with you." She closed her cell phone.

Vanna tapped a fingernail on the console as she sat thinking over the next step to take. Huntington was a piece of work and definitely hadn't been dealing from the top of the deck. Maybe she'd stick around for a while and see what he would do next. She settled in for a wait, keeping her eyes on Huntington's house. She didn't even have a chance to get bored for in fifteen minutes, the garage opened, and the red Mini Cooper backed out.

Vanna started her engine, waited for Huntington's car to turn the corner and followed. He drove erratically, first speeding up and then slowing to a snail's pace accompanied by periodically swerving out of his lane. At this rate he'd put himself out of commission by ending up dead in a car crash.

He finally veered onto the on-ramp to I-70, missing a signpost by inches, and headed toward Denver.

Vanna stayed two cars behind him.

Maintaining his inconsistent driving, Huntington drove eighty in the left lane, then slued to the right and chugged along at fifty in the right lane.

At first she thought he might be trying to lose a tail but then realized the jerky movements resulted from him being a crappy driver.

He exited the freeway at Wadsworth, merged into traffic too close to another car, earning a blare of the horn, turned onto Colfax and came screeching to a halt in a small strip mall in front of Burt's Pawn and Jewelry. He jumped out of his car with a box in his hand and strode into the store.

Vanna parked and waited. In ten minutes, Huntington emerged, counting a fistful of cash. She figured she knew what he had pawned but to make sure, she watched him drive away and then entered the pawnshop.

The place displayed the eclectic collection of electronic equipment, jewelry, weapons and sports paraphernalia. Too bad she wasn't in the mood for shopping. The proprietor stood behind a glass case, polishing a silver bowl.

Vanna approached him and gave her most endearing smile. "I'm looking for some diamond earrings."

"You're in luck, lady. I have something that might interest you." He pushed the Blendheim earrings toward her.

"Nice rocks, but I'm looking for something simpler." An idea occurred to her. "You ever see a gold medallion with a sheep and snake on it?"

He shook his head. "Don't do business in that kind of jewelry."

Vanna raised an eyebrow. "What do you mean that kind of jewelry?"

"Medallions and medals and that kind of crap."

"Know anyone who does?"

"I don't give referrals to my competitors."

Vanna slipped a ten dollar bill out of her purse and dropped it on the counter.

He smiled, revealing nicotine-stained teeth. "In that case try Bailey's. Maybe six blocks from here. East on Colfax."

"Thanks." She turned and walked out of the shop, shaking her head. Huntington and this pawn shop guy obviously worked a deal together. Huntington was a thief and an idiot but had he committed one or more murders as well?

# Chapter 19

Mulhaney didn't answer his phone, so Vanna left him a message on where to find the missing Blendheim diamond earrings. The detective could take it from there. She enjoyed the thought of him wondering how she had tracked down the information. Also, nothing wrong with keeping him in her debt.

With no further appointments on her schedule, Vanna oriented herself away from the mountains and drove along Colfax until she spotted Bailey's Pawn Shop. Another decrepit structure in an aging strip mall where the bulldozers had not yet arrived to level the shops and turn the place into apartments or condos.

She parked and strolled into the shop, a bell dinging as she opened the door. An overweight woman, chewing gum and running her hand through stringy bleached hair, sat on a stool reading *The National Enquirer*.

"Any new alien abductions?" Vanna asked.

The woman looked up with narrow, rheumy eyes. "Huh?"

"Nothing. I understand you deal in gold medallions."

She yawned and then scratched her ear. "Got a few."

"Ever see one with a sheep and snake on it?"

The woman coughed and shrugged. "Lemme show you what I

got." She eased off the stool with a grunt and plodded over to a shelf. Reaching up, she removed a tray, brought it over and dropped it on the counter. "Take a look."

Vanna picked up one medallion—a track award. The next one looked like an imitation Olympic gold, followed by a Saint Christopher medal and several commemorative coins. She continued to sort through the tray, until one medallion caught her attention. Bringing it closer to her eyes, she made out the distinct image of a sheep holding a snake. Her heart raced as she almost dropped the medallion. "How . . . how much?"

The woman wrinkled her nose. "You can have it for fifty."

"Can you tell me who pawned this?"

The woman slapped the counter. "Hey, I don't discuss my clients."

Vanna rolled her eyes and reached in her purse to extract four twenty-dollar bills. "Here's a little extra for some information."

The woman grabbed the bills and looked at the tag on the medallion. She rummaged through a shelf under the counter, pulled out a log book and plunked it down on the top of the counter. She turned several pages, ran her finger down a list of numbers, names and addresses. "Jackson Wittich."

"Know him?"

"Nah. Someone pawned it before I started working here."

Using a skill that all good PIs develop, Vanna read the upside down date and Lakewood address that had been written next to Wittich's name in the log book and committed them to memory.

The woman slammed the bound book closed, shoved it back under the counter, padded back to her stool and picked up her magazine.

Vanna left the pawn shop with her purchase and a new clue to check out. After entering the address into her GPS navigation system, she followed the directions to find a small, single-story house two miles away. She parked and knocked on the white peeling door. No one answered. She considered letting herself in but had performed enough breaking and entering for one day. She'd stop by another time. Besides, she didn't need to search the place. She wanted to speak to the man who had pawned the medallion.

Back in her office, she looked up Wittich's name, verified the address and even found a phone number listed. She called and let it ring a dozen times with no voicemail picking up.

She studied the gold medallion and placed the drawing from Sister Helene Claudette alongside it. The Sister had an excellent memory. The two matched. Picking up the medallion she turned it over. Blank back. No other identification or marks.

Vanna caught up on some paperwork and as her stomach rumbled for dinner, she cleared off her desk in preparation for a fast food run.

She had reached the door when the phone rang. She almost let it cut over to voicemail but decided to pick it up. She answered to hear Detective Mulhaney on the line. "Hey, Vanna. For once you may have been onto something."

"What do you mean for once?"

He chuckled. "Because of your info, I've arrested Huntington Blendheim. He's stewing in the back of a squad car. I'm taking him to headquarters for a little chat."

"Good work, Detective. And because of all my assistance, you're inviting me to participate in the interrogation, right?"

"Ha, in your dreams. But I thought out of courtesy I'd give you a little heads up. Maybe we could compare notes this evening over drinks."

Vanna had no intention of spending that kind of time with Mulhaney. "I have a lot going on tonight but thanks for the invite. With Huntington under arrest, I assume my client's off the hook?"

"Nope, but it definitely puts Huntington in the hot seat. Be seeing ya." The phone clicked off.

She put her hand to her chin. She'd love to watch Mulhaney lean on Huntington. The kid acted so twitchy that he'd probably spill his guts after an hour. To be a fly-on-the-wall during that interrogation. She kicked off her pumps. Well, why not? She could use a nice outing to police headquarters.

Deciding to forgo dinner for the time being, she rummaged through the desk drawer, found a granola bar, tore off the wrapper, and devoured the still crunchy oats and chocolate. This would have to suffice. Then she removed her clothes and necklace, set them in a neat pile on a chair and replaced them with her overcoat.

After her GPS led her to police headquarters, she parked two blocks away with a line of sight to her destination. She waited until the street and sidewalk were empty of drivers and pedestrians respectively, removed her coat and slipped out of the car.

At the one corner she had to wait for a light to change, a man on a cell phone came right toward her. She couldn't get out of his way in time, and he stumbled into her sending his cell phone flying through the air. She finally disengaged as he fell against a lamp post.

He looked around, spotted his cell on the sidewalk and reached out to clasp it as if he had found a diamond ring.

Vanna stood stark still and watched to see what the man did.

He fondled the phone and did everything except kiss it, apparently more concerned with its well-being than figuring out what he had run into.

With no more close encounters, she reached the police building on Cherokee, tailgated in and took the stairs to Mulhaney's office. He hadn't returned yet, so she snooped around his desk, careful to keep an eye peeled for anyone walking nearby.

She found some notes indicating Mulhaney had retrieved the diamond necklace from Eva Graves. Knowing she'd learn more when Mulhaney grilled Huntington, she scanned a report on one of Mulhaney's other cases. He hadn't solved this one either and didn't have a PI feeding him clues. The report contained two misspellings. Vanna reached for a pen, tempted to correct the errors but pulled her hand back. No sense taking a chance of someone spotting a floating pen in Mulhaney's office.

With nothing more of interest she sat down in a chair and waited. Twenty minutes later, Mulhaney dashed into his office and set a coffee cup down on the one uncluttered corner of the desk. Then he headed down the hallway with Vanna at his heels.

He pushed open the door to a small interview room, and Vanna scooted in and stationed herself in a far corner. Mulhaney dropped into a chair across from Huntington Blendheim, who looked like death warmed over.

"Okay, kid, let's get started." Mulhaney pointed a stubby index finger at Huntington. "Why the hell did you steal the jewelry?"

"I . . . I don't need to tell you anything. I want my lawyer."

Mulhaney leaned toward Huntington. "You can have your lawyer, but let me make something perfectly clear. You've been read your rights, and it's best if you come clean on the theft. Or would you prefer we book you for two murders?"

"I . . . I didn't murder anyone."

"Unless you convince me otherwise, that's the only conclusion I can reach." Mulhaney whacked both palms down on the worn wooden table resting between them.

Huntington jumped an inch out of his chair and then slumped down. "I took the jewels; that's all."

Mulhaney stood up and paced around the room.

Vanna had to flatten herself against the wall as Mulhaney passed within inches of her breasts. She sure didn't want that type of encounter with him.

Mulhaney dropped back into his chair and faced Huntington. "Why don't you take it from the top? The night of your father's death."

Huntington let out a breath so strong that Vanna could feel air strike her face. "It's like this. I went over to Dad's house to talk with him. He and I didn't get along so hot, but I thought I could reason with him . . . you know . . . since I had run a little low on cash." He fiddled with his hands in his lap, his head down. "I found him sitting at his desk in the den. I told him I needed some money. He stared at me like I was some kind of freak and then laughed at me."

"Is that when you shot him?"

Huntington looked directly at Mulhaney. "I didn't shoot him. When I could see he wouldn't give me anything, I said I needed to use the bathroom. I left him alone in the den. Rather than going to the bathroom, I snuck upstairs and went into the master bedroom. I found a jewelry box and pocketed some stuff. Then I heard a gunshot. That scared me, so I waited a few minutes before going downstairs. Then I saw Dad dead on the floor of the den. I ran out the front door as fast as I could."

"What time did you hear the shot?"

"I don't know. I don't wear a watch. Probably sometime after ten."

"Why didn't you call the police?"

Huntington flinched as if he had been slapped. "Are you kidding? You guys would have accused me of the murder."

"Which I am now anyway."

Huntington shook his head, as if trying to rid himself of unpleasant thoughts. "But I didn't kill him. Someone else came in that room while I was upstairs and did it."

"Did you see anyone?"

"No. By the time I came downstairs the murderer had disappeared."

Mulhaney sat back and crossed his arms. "See any cars?"

"No."

"And then?"

Huntington opened his hands toward Mulhaney. "I got in my car and drove home."

"Very convenient. No one saw you, right?"

Huntington winced. "Er . . . uh . . . I don't know."

"And what did you do with these?" Mulhaney opened a box to show the stolen earrings.

"I figured Gloria would never miss them. She had so much jewelry she had wheedled out of Dad, what was one necklace and pair of earrings. I gave the necklace to a friend and then pawned these earrings to get some cash today. How'd you find the earrings so quickly?"

"I have my ways."

Vanna had to cover her mouth to keep from gagging.

Huntington slammed his fist on the table. "I get it now. That bitch PI. She suspected I had taken the jewelry."

"Now, now, watch how you speak of women. Who was the friend you gave the necklace to?"

"I don't want to say."

Mulhaney leaned forward again. "Look. You're in a world of shit. The only chance you have is to be completely straight with me. Well?"

Huntington pouted for a moment and then scratched his nose. "Okay. I gave it to Eva Graves. She and I kind of hit it off."

"Pretty convenient. Your dad gets shot, and then Eva's husband takes two to the brain, leaving Eva a poor grieving widow with you to console her."

"I didn't shoot her husband. Besides, he played around with every woman in town, and Eva needed some attention."

"And you became the gallant knight stepping in to help her. She ask you to whack her old man or did you decide to do it on your own?"

Huntington came out of his sulk, sat up straight sat and pointed a finger at Mulhaney. "Neither of us had anything to do with his shooting. Someone else did it."

"Yeah, yeah. Always someone else. Who do you think killed your dad and Graves?"

"Obviously that other bitch, Gloria Blendheim. She wanted the inheritance from my father and was pissed at Bentley Graves. There's your murderer. She deserves to be locked up."

"Actually, you're the one who will be locked up. Grand theft along with the suspicion of two homicides. The DA will go lighter on you with a complete confession."

Huntington scowled. "I've already confessed my crime, the theft. I'm not a murderer, so you can stuff the rest of it."

"We'll see. Anything else you'd like to enlighten me on?"

Huntington collapsed in the chair. "No. I want to speak to my lawyer now."

"He'll be able to meet with you at the county jail." Mulhaney stood and opened the door. He stepped back into the room to stare at Huntington. "You're in deep crap, kid."

Vanna used this opportunity to skedaddle so she wouldn't end up locked in the room. As she brushed by Mulhaney her elbow hit the door.

Mulhaney spun around at the sound, but by then Vanna had cleared the doorway. She saw the perplexed look on his face, before she tiptoed away.

\* \* \* \* \*

Back at her office, Vanna dressed and called Jackson Wittich's number again. As before, no answer. With nothing more than the skimpy granola bar in her stomach, she decided to grab a bite to eat. Taking a twenty dollar bill out of her purse, she opened the office door and stepped out. Something came down over her head, cutting off all the light.

Someone grabbed her.

She lashed out with her fist but didn't connect. She tried kicking but also missed. Then she felt a prick in her arm. She tried squirming away. Her muscles went limp. She couldn't move her arms or legs. Her brain became jumbled, and all went black.

# Chapter 20

Vanna awoke and found herself bound to a wooden chair. She tried to focus, but double images reached her muddled brain. Shaking her head, she took a deep breath, and the images formed into one of log walls with faint light coming from behind her.

She shrugged her shoulders and tried to move her hands secured behind her back. She attempted to raise her butt, but found herself firmly attached to the chair. Damn. No way to even shout with duct tape covering her mouth. It would hurt like hell to tear it off, although that was the least of her worries. Her legs were firmly attached to the legs of the chair. Trying to raise her whole body to make the chair hop, she managed to move it only a smidgen.

Vanna looked around. The walls consisted of logs with some kind of putty filling in the gaps. No windows in the direction she faced. To the left appeared another log wall with one boarded-over window. To the right, a solid door. Planks of knotty pine made up the floor. Tilting her head back as far as her neck could bend, she saw log beams.

Where the hell was she? Turning as far as possible, she couldn't spot the source of the dim light behind her. She hopped her chair again while jerking her body to the left and succeeded in moving it a fraction of an inch at a time in a circular motion until she could see a window covered with a thick curtain, letting in faint light around the edges. She racked her brain for any memory that would give her a hint of her location or how she ended up here. Nada.

Then she smelled it. A wood fire. Smoke began to seep under the door. *Uh-oh.* Then she could hear the sound of flames crackling. Not good. She tried hopping her chair again. Hardly more than the width of her little toe each time.

More smoke permeated the room. A rush of adrenalin caused her heart rate to shoot off the charts. To her left she saw a corner of the wood covering the window begin to glow. She could feel heat on her face. She wrenched her body to one side and then to the other with all her strength.

The chair wobbled, and she gasped as the floor rushed to smack her cheek. Momentarily dazed, she shook it off. The back of the chair had broken in the fall. Her hands were no longer completely bound. She wiggled her wrists. She found a piece of loose wood between her hands. She tugged at it. The exertion made her cough as more smoke billowed through the room. She pulled and tore with her fingernails at the piece of wood.

A small amount of slack formed in the duct tape. Finally, yanking the piece of wood from between her wrists, she had enough space to partially free her right hand. She gagged as a puff of smoke rolled across her face. Wrenching her arms as hard as possible, she freed her wrist and brought her hands around in front.

She clawed at the duct tape holding her right foot to the chair leg. Gaining purchase, she made a tear and freed her right leg. With the loose piece of wood wedged between the chair leg and her left leg, the tape came loose. She tore the tape off her mouth, gasping at the pain. As she tried to stand, the smoke covering the top half of the room billowed in her face. She dropped back to the floor and crawled toward the door. Her hand reached up and grabbed the handle. Locked.

Vanna dropped flat on the floor to get out of the smoke again. Then she crab-crawled toward the window. Pulling the curtains aside, she could see trees silhouetted in moonlight outside. A flame licked at the outside of the window. She grasped the curtains and tore them away. Then she scuttled back to the broken chair, picked it up, held her breath and threw it at the window. Glass shattered and a flash of heat struck her face. She picked up a remaining broken piece of the chair and used it as a hammer to knock away loose shards of glass embedded in the window frame.

Then she dove through the window, landed on dirt and rolled away from the building. Flames shot from the cabin twenty feet into the air. Vanna looked all around her. She must be in the mountains. Nothing familiar and no indication of where to go to escape the fire.

She rose to her feet and staggered away from the blazing structure. What if the trees began burning? She would be consumed in a forest fire, a shame after escaping from almost being a victim of a kidnapping and then a cabin fire.

She gulped in a deep breath of air as fear changed into rage at what had been done to her. She wanted to shoot someone. Unfortunately, she didn't know who had brought her here.

She had no water to douse the flames and had no clue where she had ended up. The cabin stood in a clearing with trees approximately fifty feet away on all sides. Her only hope was that the fire would burn itself out and no wind would arise to blow the flames into the forest. Should she wait here or take her chances by dashing into the woods? From the light of the fire, she noticed what appeared to be animal paths but no distinct trail to follow. Yet someone had dragged her here and set the cabin on fire. With her directional disability and lack of outdoor skills, she had no idea what to do.

A hot breeze struck her face. *Uh-oh.* The flames danced to the side, as if reaching out to lick the nearest pine tree. No!

A pine cone exploded as the blaze continued in the center of the clearing. Vanna dropped onto the grass and waited, praying that the forest wouldn't catch fire.

\* \* \* \* \*

Within an hour the flames consumed the cabin, leaving smoldering logs and glowing embers. If she hadn't escaped, her skeletal remains would be there as well.

As her mind cleared from whatever drug she had been given, questions sprouted like spring wildflowers. Who had done this to her? Why had she been abducted? Did this relate to her investigation into the Blendheim case? And most importantly, how could she get out of this place, wherever it was?

She'd have to stay until someone stumbled into the clearing. But what if her abductors returned to verify her death? Then she'd be in deep shit again. She had to get out of here.

At that moment, a black bear the size of a bulldozer lumbered out of the woods. It headed right toward her at a steady pace, growling and tossing its head from side to side.

If it had been Van, he would have been scared shitless. For Vanna animals presented no problem. "Hi, big guy." She formed horns with her fingers and waved them in front of the bear.

It growled again but came to a stop.

She strolled up to the bear, patted it on the head and scratched it behind an ear.

It gave a contented grunt and licked her hand.

Nothing to it. She patted it on the head again and gave it a whack on the rump.

The bear turned and ambled out of the clearing.

Now she had to figure out how to get out of here. Van would be able to find his way out with his uncanny sense of direction compared to her utter lack of directional ability. Van. She could come up with no other solution. Damn. She hated to waste a transformation without Lance, but what other option did she have? Removing her clothes and necklace, she saw her legs disappear. Then she located the right part of her body and settled in to entertain herself.

# Chapter 21

When the transformation into Van had been completed, he looked up at the sky. He found the Big Dipper, followed the pointer stars to the North Star and registered the direction of the moving wisps of clouds, floating in the partial moonlight. He sensed he stood along the eastside of the Continental Divide. He couldn't fit into any of Vanna's clothes, so he left them there, prepared to travel in his invisible state. He next inspected each of the animal paths emerging from the different parts of the woods. He found one path with recent grass damage and set his course to the east. This trail periodically disappeared, and he dropped to his hands and knees to carefully check where it reappeared. Then the path disappeared altogether in another meadow. Van took a new reading, finding the cross of Cygnus and the M-shape of Cassiopeia before continuing on an eastward course.

Mosquitoes buzzed around him in the warm night air, and he wondered if they would bite an invisible person. He soon had an answer when places on his arms and legs began to itch. Damn insects that used a sense of smell rather than sight to find their victims. He wondered if invisible transvictus blood did anything unusual to mosquitoes.

It took him several more hours, but finally he emerged from the woods along the Peak to Peak highway north of the town of Nederland. With another hour of hiking along the highway, he reached the town as light began to appear on the eastern horizon. He slapped his invisible arms in the early morning brisk air, but he knew he could handle it. He wouldn't want to be up here naked in winter, though.

By the time the sun poked above the trees to the east he found the Nederland park-n-ride bus stop. Two men in long-sleeved shirts waited, and he followed them onto the bus, loading to go down Boulder Canyon. He scurried all the way to the last row and dropped down right in the middle. Half a dozen people sat, spread out through the bus, and after only one more stop, no one came near him. Non-crowded buses always provided safe and easy transportation for him. He leaned back and enjoyed the sight of pine trees, steep rocks lining the canyon and the water cascading down Boulder Creek. Although thirsty, he concentrated instead on the scenery.

After exiting the bus at the Boulder Transit Center with no incidents, he waited fifteen minutes for an early morning bus into Denver. He had no trouble getting on the bus as he followed a group of commuters, but once on the bus a challenge awaited him—few available seats. Two men in business casual attire and a teenage girl and boy occupied his favorite back row. The boy had thrown a backpack onto the seat beside him. Van sat down on the edge of the seat in front of the backpack.

All went well until the boy reached over toward the backpack. Van had to scramble out of the seat so he wouldn't be struck by the boy's arm. At that moment, the driver jammed on the brakes, and Van staggered forward. The bus accelerated again, and his arms pin-wheeled as he tried to regain balance so as not to fall into any of the back row occupants. His hand hit a steel post, giving off a twang. People looked around to see what had caused the noise. Fortunately, they soon lost interest and returned to their various reading materials. Once the boy had pulled out a graphic novel from the backpack and settled in to read it, Van returned to his previous spot. After two more stops in Boulder to pick up a few more passengers, the bus took the onramp to I-36, and Van leaned against the backpack knowing he would be safe for the remaining portion of the trip.

His final challenge occurred when the bus reached Union Station in Denver. He had to negotiate the aisle with people leaving the bus. He stood up as the boy grabbed his backpack but didn't time his movement right and the boy's hand whacked his arm. The kid shook his hand like it had been stung. He poked his other hand in the air for a moment as if searching for an invisible object, and Van had to duck to the side.

Then the two men in the back row charged out of their seats and Van had to flatten himself against a seat to keep from being hit. Once they moved forward, he dropped into the side of the back row they had vacated. He waited for nearly everyone to leave the bus, then dashed out at the last minute before the driver closed the door.

From there he had an easy stroll. By seven-forty-five he was punching in the combination to his office door. Nothing to it, thanks to good navigational skills, invisibility and public transportation. On the other hand, Vanna would have been hopelessly lost and on the verge of dying from dehydration.

Not bothering to go to his apartment to put on clothes, he remained invisible and listened to a voicemail message from Gloria, saying she missed him and to call when he returned. He decided to forego that one. He next scanned through email, eliminating the junk mail promotions to reduce or enlarge various parts of his body. Man, where did all these things come from? Then he opened one email with no subject line. It read, "Van. Stay out of what's not your business or you'll end up like your partner. Dead." No name. A Hotmail account xw2g4k7. It looked like an airline confirmation number. He forwarded it to Mulhaney with a note, "Someone kidnapped Vanna and then sent me this message. She's fine, but we've stumbled into one of your suspects who isn't pleased with our involvement. Have your computer geek check this out, but it's probably a throwaway email account. Give me a call when you get this."

Van headed to his loft, chugged a bottle of water and crashed onto his bed to get a few hours of shuteye. Vanna's exploits had drained all his energy.

* * * * *

Van awoke to the sound of his cell phone playing Reveille on his nightstand. He groped for it, almost dropped it, finally thrust it against his ear and groggily muttered, "Yeah?"

"You PIs have such a cushy life sleeping in. Time to join the working world, Averi. It's almost lunch time."

Van regarded the alarm clock. Ten-fifty. "Good morning to you too, Mulhaney."

"I received your email. I hope your cute partner is recovering better than you."

"She's okay, but as I mentioned, she almost got put out of commission. Someone drugged, kidnapped and tied her up in a burning cabin in the woods. By sheer will she escaped."

"Quite a gal. I'd like to speak with her to get a statement."

"Sorry. She went out of town to recuperate. I'll tell her to call you when she gets back. In the meantime, I'm fully briefed. I can answer any questions you have."

Mulhaney harrumphed. "You two. Okay, give me the details."

Van recounted Vanna's exploits of the night before.

"And you say she found her way out of the woods. That doesn't sound like the wrong-way Vanna I know."

"Must have been dumb luck, but after she escaped from the cabin, she did make her way back to Denver. But one of your suspects in the Blendheim case obviously tried to shorten her life."

Mulhaney chuckled. "Why would it be one of my suspects? Surely you must be interfering in some other cases as well."

"Not right now. This is our only big one other than investigating Denver police sexual harassment of female PIs."

There was a momentary pause on the line.

Van laughed. "Just kidding. No, we have nothing else going on right now. By any chance did you release Huntington Blendheim yesterday?"

"Nah, he spent the night in custody with the grand theft charge. Bail should be set this morning, so his lawyer will be springing him shortly."

"Okay, that eliminates him. Others that could have been involved include Greer Lawson and Homer Stiles."

"Or your client Gloria Blendheim. Maybe she's jealous that Vanna is too close to you, Van. If Vanna spent more time with me, Gloria wouldn't be so upset."

Van looked up at a ceiling tile, hoping to be delivered from asshole detectives. Wouldn't it be ironic if Gloria were involved? By eliminating Vanna she'd end up with no Van. "Let's stick with Lawson and Stiles. I'll check them out today. Any other new leads for the two murders?"

"Right. As if I'd share that with you."

Van coughed. "We go over this same ground every time. I'll find out, so you might as well save both of us time and trouble by leveling with me upfront."

"I'll tell you this one tidbit, Van, me boy. After speaking with Huntington, I'm back to thinking Gloria whacked old Cornelius rather than Bentley Graves doing the deed."

"What makes you think that?"

"One of Huntington's statements."

Van tapped the phone receiver. "Don't keep me in suspense."

Mulhaney chuckled. "That's your teaser for the day. Beyond that, my lips are sealed. Stay away from burning cabins." The line went dead.

Damn Mulhaney. Now Van would have to make another trip to police headquarters this evening. The detective had no consideration, making all this extra work for him and Vanna.

After a shave and shower, Van dressed in clean slacks and a crisp white long-sleeved shirt before driving to Greer Lawson's house.

She answered her door and gave him the once over. "Yes?"

Van held out a card. "I'm Van Averi with The V V Agency. You've met my partner Vanna before."

Greer scowled. "What do you want?"

"I thought we could compare notes on the recent events. A suspect has been arrested. I thought you might like an update." He didn't delineate what the suspect had been arrested for.

She arched an eyebrow. "Yeah? Come in. I can spare a few minutes before my next appointment."

She led him to the living room without offering any refreshment. That was fine with him.

Greer sat on the couch while Van settled onto a chair facing her.

He waited.

"Who's been arrested?" she asked.

"Huntington Blendheim."

She pushed a strand of escaped hair back away her forehead. "Cornelius's punk kid? I'd expected Gloria to be nailed."

"No, she's still free."

"Too bad."

"The police took Huntington into custody yesterday. Speaking of yesterday, what were you doing in the late afternoon and evening?"

"I spent most of the day here in my home office. Working on the paperwork to purchase the Blendheim Towers. It's almost finalized."

"Do you have much familiarity with cabins in the mountains west of Boulder?"

She squinted at him and crinkled her nose. She was either a good actor or hadn't been involved. "Huh? I only do commercial, not residential real estate."

"I thought you might have been up in the mountains recently."

"Why would you think that? I've been too busy with this deal to go anywhere." She looked at her watch. "Now, if you'll excuse me, I have a meeting." She stood and led him to the door.

Out in his car he waited. He'd see where Greer went before continuing to his next unscheduled appointment.

Greer backed her black BMW out of the garage and took off like a bat out of Hades. Van had to stomp on the gas to keep up with her, but once he regained sight of her car, she didn't appear to notice him since she made no moves to shake him. She took I-25 north and exited the freeway in Thornton.

Van smiled. He could achieve two purposes on this trip.

Sure enough, Greer pulled into the parking lot for Blendheim Corporation and zipped into a close-in visitor's spot.

Van found a place in the back of the parking lot and watched Greer saunter into the building. Time to do some surveillance. He followed into the lobby and spotted the men's restroom. Inside he took a stall, undressed, left his clothes and ring on the top of the tank and then climbed out under the stall door, leaving it locked from the inside. Then he headed up the stairs to Homer Stiles's office.

As suspected, Greer waited in a chair by Homer's admin's desk.

Van strolled around behind the admin, admiring her platinum

blond hair and curves. He bent close to her and saw her surreptitiously reading a *Playgirl* magazine, hidden from view under her computer keyboard.

In five minutes Homer's office door opened, and he came out with a short, gray-haired Japanese man in a tailored dark blue suit. They shook hands and bowed to each other. After the visitor left, Homer smiled at Greer and waved her into the office.

Van followed close behind her and found a spot to stand in the corner by a golf putter leaning against a credenza. He thought how much fun it would be to wave the putter in the air and scare the piss out of Homer and Greer, but decided he had a job to do.

Homer closed the door and approached Greer. They flew into each other's arms, and more than business pecks to the cheeks were exchanged.

Van wondered if they would do it right on Homer's desk, but they finally disengaged. Van gave an inaudible sigh of relief.

Greer smoothed out her skirt, and Homer adjusted his tie. Then they both took seats at a small round table, which held a stack of manila folders.

Homer smacked his lips. "On to business, although pleasure would be preferable."

"Tonight, darling. I'll be expecting you." She puckered her lips.

"I wouldn't miss it."

Van shook his invisible head. These people were worse than randy, hormone-infused teenagers. Who wasn't copulating with whom?

Homer selected a manila folder and opened it. "My lawyer made three small changes." He pulled out a document and pushed it toward Greer. She in turn removed a document from her briefcase and gave it to Homer. "I've made a few small edits as well. Take a look at these while I look at yours." She winked at him.

Van felt like puking.

They both perused the respective documents as if John Hancock wannabes preparing to sign the Declaration of Independence.

Homer looked up first and nodded his head. "All acceptable to me."

Greer turned a page, read for a minute and then raised her large blue eyes and batted her eyelashes at him. "I'm fine with your changes as well. It's so much easier without Cornelius and Bentley. Both such useless prigs."

Homer chuckled. "Yeah. And Cornelius with his opposition to this deal. I had to make sure to get him out of the way."

Greer gave an eye roll. "And Bentley. He would have kept this dragging on for months. Always one problem after another. He could never close the deal." She giggled.

"I'll have my lawyer draw up the final papers today." He tapped his copy. "I'll bring them with me tonight."

"Excellent. I'll have the Dom Pérignon iced and ready." She licked her lips. "And I'll be ready as well."

They both stood and sealed the deal with a long kiss that appeared to involve much exchange of tongues and saliva. Greer patted Homer's engorged crotch and then headed to the door. "Until tonight, darling."

Van used the opportunity to slip out the door behind her. He jogged down the stairs and returned to the restroom to put his clothes back on. Then he took the elevator back up to the fourth floor. He handed his card to Homer's admin. "I'm a private investigator and need to see Mr. Stiles for five minutes."

She imparted her plastic smile. "I'm so sorry, Mr. Stiles is unavailable."

Van pointed to the closed office door. "I know he's in there, and as I said, this will be brief. You let me see him now, and I won't bother him with the information that you're reading *Playgirl* rather than typing his memos."

She reddened. "Ah . . . give me a moment. Let me see if he has been freed up." She picked up her phone, spoke softly and then put the phone back down. She forced a smile, displaying her perfect teeth. "He can see you for five minutes."

"Great. That's all it will take."

She stood, scooted over and held the door open for him and then closed it none too gently once he had stepped inside.

Van moved over to where Homer sat behind his oval, polished desk. "Mr. Stiles, I'm Van Averi, a private investigator. You've met my partner, Vanna Anderson."

Homer's lower lip puffed out. "Oh, yes. The delightful Ms. Anderson. I remember. Very outspoken."

"That's her. I won't take much of your time. I'm following up in regards to two murders—Cornelius Blendheim and Bentley Graves."

"Yes. Very unfortunate events."

Van leveled his gaze at Homer. "Since you worked with Cornelius and had business dealings with Bentley, I thought you should know what recently transpired." He paused.

Homer continued to show a neutral expression so Van continued. "There have been some new developments with the case as of yesterday. Threats have been made to people associated with the two murder victims. I wonder if you had any similar threats made to you yesterday."

He looked perplexed. "Threats?"

"Any unexpected visitors here?"

He shook his head. "Not that I know of. I spent most of the day out of the office, and no one reported anything unusual."

"And where were you during the late afternoon and evening?"

Homer wagged a finger at him. "Very secret negotiations. Not something I can discuss. Now, I must be on my way to a lunch meeting." He stood and held out his hand. "It was a pleasure meeting you, Mr. Averi."

Van took his hand. "Vanna sends her regards." He sensed no flinching or change in the grasp. He didn't know for sure if he was looking at a murderer and kidnapper or just a greedy bastard.

# Chapter 22

As Van drove away from Blendheim Corporation headquarters, he considered Homer Stiles. Gone the day before. He could have spent that time drugging and carting Vanna up into the mountains and setting the cabin fire. Yet, no visible signs of a reaction during the handshake. Stiles, the consummate corporate vulture, cold and calculating. Maybe he didn't even have blood running in his veins. That was the take on him from Donald Hallett. Maybe Stiles had super control over his emotions.

Homer could easily have decided that Vanna's snooping might cause him trouble and made the decision to get her out of the way. He had a good deal going here with Cornelius dead and wouldn't want the gravy train interrupted by someone looking too closely into his business dealings and relationships.

Then the little side action with Greer. They might have conspired to get Vanna out of the picture.

A number of things to think over.

Van stopped at Teng Fu, his favorite Chinese takeout, for some mushu pork, and then made a pass by Jackson Wittich's house. He parked up the block, walked back, inspected the decrepit structure again and knocked on the door. He waited and pounded again. He had turned to leave when he heard muffled footsteps and then a chain being pulled back from the door. Good. Someone was finally at home.

A hunched old man with sparse gray hair peeked through the two inches he had opened the door. He reminded Van of a shriveled geezer he had seen sitting on a street corner in Denver holding a cup out for change.

"Are you Jackson Wittich?"

The man blinked. "Yes."

Van took out the medallion from his pocket and held the lamb and snake face toward the old man. "I'd like to discuss this with you."

The man's half-closed eyes expanded to the size of the gold disc. "Where'd you get that?" The door opened a foot revealing that Jackson wore a torn undershirt and dirty blue pajama bottoms. He stood no more than five foot six inches tall, had skinny withered arms and gnarled fingers that looked like they had been twisted in a vise.

"May I come in and speak with you for a few minutes? My name is Van Averi, and I'm a private investigator." He handed his card to the man through the opening.

Jackson gasped and dropped the card on the floor. Then gritting his teeth, he reached over, picked it up and looked wildly around. "Give me a minute." The door slammed.

Van stood there, tapping his toe. He heard some sounds inside and then it became quiet. Did Jackson intend to bolt out the back door? Van was preparing to check around the side and the back of the house, when the door opened, fully this time.

"Come, in Mr. Averi." Jackson stepped aside and ushered him in. He had brushed his hair and now wore a yellow polo shirt, slacks and tennis shoes.

In the entryway stood a black table holding a blue and white vase with straw flowers protruding in a haphazard display. This three foot space led to a living room with a leather couch, a folding chair and a coffee table, where a teapot sent steam circling toward the ceiling. Heavy black curtains covered the windows and one pole lamp illuminated the room. A gray carpet lined the floor. The room appeared immaculate—no clutter, no magazines, nothing else.

Jackson pointed to the couch and took a seat on the folding chair.

"Please, forgive my meager furnishings."

As Van sat on the couch, the cushion let out a whoosh of air. He suspected not many visitors had crossed this threshold lately.

The old man cleared his throat. "May I offer you tea?"

Van waved his hand. "No thank you."

"I'll have a cup myself." Jackson poured himself some, took a sip, set the cup down on the coffee table between them and intertwined his fingers, which shook. "Where did you find the medallion, Mr. Averi?"

"I purchased it at a pawnshop."

The old man nodded his head, causing his thinning gray hair to flutter as if in a breeze. "Oh, dear. I guess I forgot to redeem it. Not that I have any money to do so."

Van held it up between his thumb and index finger. "A very intriguing pattern, Mr. Wittich. Can you tell me more about it?"

His eyes narrowed. "Why so curious, Mr. Averi?"

"My partner and I have been retained to do some investigative work for a client. That led us to the medallion, and we owe our client further explanation. That's why I seek your assistance, Mr. Wittich."

"Can you discuss your client?"

"Only that he's an academician and has interest in this from a research standpoint."

The old man's eyes came alive, and a subtle sparkle appeared. "And this is important to you, Mr. Averi?"

Van shrugged. "I'm being paid to learn more."

His eyes met Van's unflinchingly, and finally he sucked on his lower lip before saying, "Why, yes, I see. Let me tell you what I know. This medallion is unusual, don't you think?"

"Yes. I've never seen another like it." Van didn't want to go into the transvictus background of the medallion.

Jackson scratched his cheek. "I've actually seen two of them. This one has a most interesting history. How much time do you have, Mr. Averi?"

Van waved his hand. "As much as it takes to hear your account."

"Fine. Fine. This medallion came into my possession through the boyfriend of my daughter around 1979."

Van leaned forward.

"They were both eighteen at the time. He was a strange young man, very self-contained. They loved each other and wanted to get married, but I must admit, I had my suspicions about him and refused to give my permission. Whenever I asked him to discuss his background, he changed the subject. Very secretive."

Jackson paused, took another sip of tea and replaced the cup on the table. "But they kept meeting secretly, and the inevitable happened. My daughter became pregnant. Rather than seeing that the best course was for them to marry, I became more obstinate and refused to give my blessing for the marriage. My daughter cried and screamed, but I wouldn't give in. She remained very obedient and refused to elope without my permission." He swallowed hard. "I don't know why I took such a hard line. Given what happened, I should have relented. Sure I can't offer you something to drink, Mr. Averi?"

Van waved him off again. "I'm fine. Please continue."

"Yes. As the birth approached, my daughter became more despondent. I forbade her to have anything to do with her boyfriend. One night he appeared on our doorstep. I ordered him away. He said he would be leaving but first had a gift for each of us. He gave my daughter and me each a gold medallion. You hold the one given to me."

Van turned it over in his hand.

"He asked that the other be given to his son. I asked him how he knew it would be a son. He said, and I quote, 'It's always a son.' Very strange statement, don't you think?"

Van shrugged. "Male intuition?"

"Something of the sort. Does this story intrigue you, Mr. Averi?"

Van felt the old man was trying to elicit a reaction from him. He took a deep breath and willed himself to hold his emotions in check. "I'm a private investigator. I hear many unusual stories. I'm not here to judge anything, only collect information. I'd like to hear the rest of your account, Mr. Wittich."

Jackson rose and paced around the room. Then he returned and stood right in front of Van. "Anyway, I never saw him again, as he vanished that very night. My daughter gave birth to a son, and a week afterwards she, the baby and the other medallion also disappeared. I never saw any of them again."

"And the name of this boyfriend?" Van asked.

A strange smiled crossed Jackson's face. "That's what I think you'll find most interesting. He wanted his son named after him. He looked very much like you. His name was Van Averi."

# Chapter 23

Van collapsed farther into the couch at Wittich's revelation. "You're . . . you're my grandfather."

The old man regarded him carefully and then took a seat on the folding chair. "That's possible. Tell me a little about yourself."

Conflicting waves of exaltation and dread coursed through Van. How much should he say? He clearly couldn't burden his newly-found grandfather by describing the legacy of a transvictus. But he wanted to learn as much as he could. He finally decided to be direct, up to a point. "I grew up in the All Souls Orphanage here in Denver. I learned I had been left on the doorstep with a note saying my name was Van Averi."

Jackson nodded. "Could be other Van Averis around."

Van pulled himself out of his slumped position and leaned toward his grandfather. "Yeah, but one of the sisters found me with a gold medallion like the one here." Van held it up so that the gold sparkled in the light from the living room lamp.

Now Jackson gaped. "You are my grandson. But what happened to my daughter, Francie?"

Van felt a hollowness in his chest. "I have no idea where my mother went. But now I know who she was. Do you have a picture of her?"

Jackson squirted out of the chair and disappeared down a short hall. The floorboards creaked, and he returned holding a photograph which he dropped in Van's lap. "Her high school graduation picture."

Van regarded a smiling pretty face, a few freckles, pug nose, dark brown wavy hair. He flinched. It could have been Vanna's identical twin.

Jackson bit his lip and peered closely at Van. "You resemble your dad. Same dark hair and eyes."

"Do you have a picture of him?"

"Nope. I had one of the two of them, but I burned it." Jackson gave a sardonic laugh. "Now that I have a living relative, I'm going to have to change my will. You'll inherit the mortgage on this mansion." He waved his hand toward the far wall. "With my Social Security I barely meet the food bills and monthly payments."

"I have some money saved," Van said. "I'll help you fix up the place. It looks great inside, only needs some repair and painting outside."

"You don't have to do that. But you can do one thing for your old grandpop. Keep that picture. I want you to use your detective skills to find your mother."

Still dazed, Van nodded again. He had a name and description, but how would he track down a missing woman from 1979? Maybe she had run off with his dad after all. But why did she choose to leave her baby at an orphanage? His grandfather didn't know anything regarding the transvictus heritage, and Van would keep it that way. No sense shocking the old man further. "I'll make that a high priority, sir."

"Don't goddamn sir me. But you can call me grandpa."

Van gulped. "Okay . . . Grandpa."

"Now come here and give me a hug."

They stood and embraced. Van held the old man closely, trying to ignore a vague aroma of overcooked onions. He tried to visualize a family with a mother, father, little boy and grandparents. What might have been.

They released each other.

"What happened to my grandmother?" Van asked.

Jackson's chin drooped. "The whole fiasco with Francie did her in.

A month after Francie and the baby disappeared, Glenda had a stroke. She lasted a week and then died."

"I'm sorry I didn't have a chance to meet her."

"She was quite a woman, but she lost her spirit and will to live. A damn shame. I have no one to blame but myself."

"Have you been living by yourself since then?"

"Yup. Just me and my memories."

"Did you have any other children besides Francie?"

Jackson shook his head. "No. She was the only one."

"At least now you have a grandson."

A smile came to his lips. "And I'm grateful for that. Now I need to take a nap. I'm kind of tuckered out. The old ticker can't take all this excitement."

Van looked again at the photograph and then back at Jackson. "I'm taking you out to dinner tonight. I'll be back at six. I want to hear more about my mother."

Jackson yawned. "I have some tales to tell you. Now skedaddle." He walked to the door with Van and let him out.

As he sat in his car, Van again regarded the photo. Francie Wittich, his mother. Vanna's mother as well. He wondered if Vanna had inherited the directional dysfunction from Francie. He couldn't take his eyes off the picture. Finally, he placed it on the passenger seat.

He knew he should work on the Blendheim case, but his head wasn't in it. Instead, he grabbed his cell phone and called Harlan Shannon, who answered.

"Professor Shannon, this is Van Averi. I'm Vanna Anderson's partner and have been doing some research for you."

"Call me Harlan. Anything new?"

"Several interesting developments. Any chance I could meet with you this afternoon to review progress?"

"I have office hours right now but nothing else scheduled this afternoon. When do you think you can be here?"

Van looked at his watch and calculated traffic. "I'm in Denver and could be in Boulder within an hour. Tell me where to come."

"Office 211 in the Hellems Arts and Science Building. If you're not familiar with the campus, the building is northwest of the University

Memorial Center."

Van laughed. "I'll find it."

He drove off, his mind swirling with the latest developments. He would fill Harlan in on some aspects of his investigation but not all. He'd also solicit any new information Harlan might have come across. Then he'd have to determine his next step.

He parked in the same parking structure Vanna had used and walked past the bookstore to Hellems. On the second floor he found Harlan's office and knocked on the door.

"Come in."

Harlan looked the same as when Vanna had seen him, with his bow tie, sports coat with elbow patches and hair slightly askew.

They shook hands, and Van settled into a chair.

Harlan stuck a pipe in his mouth. "It's the image, you know. I have to play the role of the history professor. I'm not allowed to actually light up in the building and can't stand the taste of tobacco anyway."

"That's good," Van replied. "I'm not much on smoke myself. First, I want to show you something." He reached in his pocket, took out the gold medallion and set it on the desk. "Vanna described to you a drawing we came across, but here's the real deal."

Harlan leaned over and reverently picked up the medallion. He inspected it closely like a jeweler appraising a valuable gem and turned it over in his hand. "The lamb and snake. No other markings."

"That's it."

Harlan handed the medallion back to Van. "Excellent investigative work. Where did you find this?"

"Actually in a pawnshop in Denver."

Harlan sucked on his pipe. "Interesting. Any other leads at this time?"

Van decided to play this one carefully. "I'm pursuing several names. Nothing concrete yet. And your work? Anything else you've come across?"

Harlan took the pipe out of his mouth and tapped it on the corner of his desk. "There's someone you should show the medallion to. Let me look up his name." He began leafing through papers in his top drawer and then triumphantly held up a slip of paper. "Here it is.

Daniel Fogart. He deals in jewelry, antiques and relics. You can find him at the Mile High Flea Market. Ever been there?"

Van shook his head as he wrote the name on his notepad.

Harlan pointed his pipe at Van. "The flea market is open every Friday, Saturday and Sunday. Stop by when you have a chance to show Daniel the medallion. He may have some thoughts on it."

"Either Vanna or I will do that. I'm not sure how much more we'll find in Denver. I thought it might be time to try some of your contacts in other cities."

"Fine. In addition to the files I gave to Vanna, I have one new person for you to reach in Santa Fe. A woman I spoke with." He rummaged through his desk again and retrieved another scrap of paper, which he gave to Van to copy. "You may think I'm disorganized, but I know where I stashed every note I made."

Van wrote the name and phone number on his pad. "I wouldn't doubt it." Van checked his watch, now anxious to head back to Denver to have dinner with his grandfather. "Vanna or I will get back to you when we have a further update."

Van ran into congestion on I-36. He looked at his watch and slammed his palm on the steering wheel, hating to be late to see his grandfather. After fifteen minutes of inching ahead, he passed an accident blocking the right lane. The frustration at being delayed changed into relief as the traffic picked up to thirty miles an hour. Then Van felt the anticipation build. He had a living relative, and they would be together in moments.

He pulled up in front of Jackson's house at six-fifteen and knocked on the door. No answer. He knocked again. Then he tried the doorknob. Unlocked.

He stepped inside. "Jackson? Grandfather?"

No answer.

Van looked in the living room. The tea pot still remained on the coffee table where it had been that afternoon. He sniffed the air. Hot and musty, accounted for by lack of air conditioning.

He peeked in the kitchen. A bowl and plate in the dish drainer along with a fork, knife and spoon. The counters wiped clean.

Where was his grandfather?

Van tensed and called out again. Still no answer.

He then moved into the hall, finding scenic photographs mounted on the walls. He passed a small bedroom with the bed made, a dresser with nothing on top and a bookcase containing old books.

In the main bedroom he found the old man lying on the bed. The vacant eyes of his gray face stared lifelessly upward.

# Chapter 24

After calling 9-1-1, Van sat in Jackson Wittich's living room, his face in his hands. To gain and lose a grandfather in one day. He vowed to find his mother, Francie Wittich, for himself and because his grandfather had asked him to do it. He didn't know where he would start, but he would juggle this with the Blendheim case. Right now he needed to make final arrangements for his grandfather.

The EMTs arrived and verified that Jackson had no pulse. As if there was any question. A police officer appeared, and Van explained how he had come to take his grandfather out to dinner and found him in the bedroom. He showed his identification and explained that he worked closely with Detective Mulhaney. Later an assistant medical examiner knocked on the door and came in to check the body.

"Any initial indication of cause of death?" Van asked.

The woman in her thirties brushed a strand of brown hair from her forehead. "I see no signs of foul play. Probably a heart attack, but we'll know after the autopsy." He gave her his card and asked to be informed of the results.

Van waited until the body was placed on a gurney to be taken to the morgue.

He sat in his car replaying the events of the day. When his stomach growled, he finally drove off and stopped to grab a roast beef sandwich at Arby's. After finishing his Jamocha shake, he sadly shook his head. He had so looked forward to a sit-down dinner with his grandfather.

* * * * *

Back in his office Van had just logged onto his computer when the phone rang.

"Hey, Averi, what's this I hear that you found a dead body this evening?" Mulhaney chuckled. "Maybe you're into murder yourself now. I could get you off the streets so your partner could plead for your release."

"Nah," he said trying to force nonchalance into his voice. "I happened by to take a friend out to dinner. The assistant medical examiner thinks the death probably resulted from a heart attack."

"Whatever. After the autopsy I may bring you in for further questioning."

"I'll stay tuned, Mulhaney. You have an enjoyable night."

"Oh, I will. I'll be at home having pleasant dreams about . . . your partner."

Van slammed the phone down. What a jerk. No wonder Vanna couldn't stand the guy.

To look for some hint of his father, he began Googling on the name Van Averi. He found the expected references to The V V Agency and their web site. Even found an article in *The Denver Post* regarding a case he had helped the police crack a year ago. References to him appeared to be all he could find. He continued through twenty pages, reading a summary of a speech he had given to a criminology class at the University of Denver three years earlier. He rubbed the back of his neck and stretched. Nothing that would indicate another Van Averi ever existed. He was preparing to give up when one reference caught his eye, "Mystery man saves three-year-old from flash flood." He had never done this. He opened up the article, dated 2003, from the *Los Angeles Times* and read, "Amid the raging waters of the flooding Los Angeles River, one happy note. A three-year-old girl who slipped down an embankment was saved by a man estimated to be in his forties who jumped in the water and pulled the girl to safety. Both almost drowned. The man pushed the girl to the bank, stumbled out of the water and passed out. According to a passerby who checked his wallet, the hero's name is Van Averi. When he revived, he grabbed his wallet and ran off before he could be thanked by the girl's appreciative parents."

Van printed the page and tapped his thumbs on the frame of his keyboard while deep in thought. This could have been his father. He continued to look through the list of references to Van Averi, discovering nothing else of consequence.

Then he Googled "Francie Wittich." The only relevant thing he found referenced a list of cheerleaders over the history of Denver West High School, with Francie in the class of 1978. Nothing else.

Then a thought occurred to him. He tried a search on "Francie Averi." Only one hit. It referenced a real estate sale in Los Angeles. Francie Averi had sold a house in Van Nuys a year earlier. Intriguing. He jotted down the address. When next in Los Angeles, he'd have to pay a visit to that location.

He next checked telephone directories but could find no listing for either Van Averi or Francie Averi in Southern California. Still, he now had several ties to the Los Angeles area that would warrant future exploration.

With no further information, Van prepared for his nighttime activity on the Blendheim case. First, a visit to Mulhaney's office. With his usual MO he made his invisible way into the detective's office and sat down to survey the detritus on the desk. Pushing aside a stale piece of donut lying on a greasy wrapper, a manual on new state laws, and a crime scene photograph of a bloody handprint on a wall, Van finally found Mulhaney's latest report on the Blendheim murder. It described in detail the interview with Huntington, much as Vanna had heard from the young prick in the interview room when he confessed to being in the house the night of the murder and stealing the necklace and earrings. But even with those admissions, he had not confessed to either of the murders.

The report also included information from a second interrogation session when Vanna had not been present. Huntington had stated that he overheard voices downstairs, one male voice, his father's, and a female voice he couldn't clearly identify right before the gunshot.

The detective had written a note that the female voice could have been Gloria Blendheim's. The reason for Mulhaney's hint in their earlier conversation that Gloria had become a prime suspect once again in her husband's death.

Van considered the information in front of him. Mulhaney was jumping to conclusions to try to fry his client. Instead of Gloria, the female voice could have belonged to Greer Lawson. She had an appointment to meet with Cornelius that night and could have shot him. This of course depended on Huntington not having lied, but Mulhaney must have scared the crap out of the kid, so chances were he had been telling the truth.

Van's thoughts of how all these people should be permanently locked up in the state pen in Cañon City were interrupted when he looked up to see Mulhaney charging down the hallway toward the office.

Van dropped the report back on the desk and stepped out of the office.

Mulhaney skidded to a stop in front of his desk. "Who the hell has been messing with my stuff?" He picked up the report Van had been reading. "This wasn't on top."

Van hoped Mulhaney didn't become suspicious enough to check for fingerprints on the report. He would have liked to have worn gloves when he reviewed the report, but he didn't think finding a naked man in gloves in a police department office would go over very well. Besides, his fingerprints weren't on file anywhere. He'd have to be careful that Mulhaney didn't try to make the connection. Time to leave.

At that moment a huge, industrial-strength polishing machine being ridden by a man in a janitorial uniform turned the corner in the hall, aiming right toward where Van stood. *Uh-oh.* Running into an invisible obstacle wouldn't be received well, to say nothing of what that machine might do to him. He couldn't go toward the elevator and stairs because the polishing machine blocked his path.

Van turned and headed the other way, but at that moment a phalanx of officers came along the hall toward him. He looked around. The only alternative—a janitor's closet with the door open. He quickly ducked inside and waited as footsteps from the group of officers approached. As they passed, someone pushed the door and it slammed shut.

Van waited until the sound of footsteps receded and disappeared. The whirring machine approached and seemed to pause right outside the closet. Then the sound of the machine stopped. Van heard another set of receding footsteps. He waited two minutes, grabbed the door handle and pushed. The door creaked open three inches and hit an obstacle. Van put his eye to the opening and saw the polishing machine blocking further movement. He put his weight into the door, but it wouldn't budge with the behemoth machine blocking his exit. Damn. The cleaning guy must have taken a break. He hoped the machine hadn't been left there for the night.

The closet was hot, the space tight, and Van had to pee. He took a deep breath, telling himself to suck it up—no different than any other surveillance gig. Sitting down on the closet floor to wait, he could hear Mulhaney cussing again, a door slamming and footsteps going toward the other end of the hall. Then all became silent.

Van thought over the suspects in the two murders. Mulhaney had Gloria in his crosshairs again, but Van still favored some combination of Huntington, Greer and Homer. He would have to keep poking.

He settled against the wall of the closet, yawned and closed his eyelids.

Some strange dream of old gray-haired men throwing gold medallions at him morphed into consciousness at the sound of a loud motor. Remembering his predicament, Van peered out the crack in the door and saw the polishing machine moving. After a moment he pushed the door open two feet, stepped out and closed it behind him.

He dashed to the men's room just in time, relieved to not be leaving a puddle to be checked for DNA. Then he dashed down the stairs, glanced at a wall clock in the lobby to see it was almost ten and left the building.

With his memorized RTD schedule, he caught a bus going north and with one transfer, arrived a block from Blendheim Corporation headquarters.

He tested the main door and found it unlocked. Peering through the glass, he spotted a guard sitting at the reception desk. When the man turned his back for a moment, Van moved quickly and quietly through the door. Not wearing shoes came in handy at a time like this unless he stepped on something sharp. Van had calluses from his numerous barefoot adventures, but he still watched where he placed his invisible feet.

Again waiting until the guard focused his attention elsewhere, Van opened the stairwell door and took the steps to the fourth floor. Verifying that no humongous polishing machines impeded his progress, he headed to Homer Stiles's office, finding it locked. He rummaged through Homer's admin's desk, which wasn't locked. Between a box of paper clips and a stapler, he found a key to the inner office.

After opening the door, he sat down at Homer's desk, booted up the computer, verified the password from the folder he remembered from Vanna's visit and logged in. He checked the calendar and found that the afternoon Vanna had been abducted, Homer had an all day offsite meeting scheduled with Greer Lawson. One or both of them could have taken Vanna up to the mountain cabin.

# Chapter 25

With one more part of the puzzle clicking into place, Van left Homer's office hoping someone hadn't tossed away the remaining jigsaw pieces. He was convinced every one of the people involved had committed multiple crimes. He just hadn't figured out which of them committed the two murders.

*  *  *  *  *

The next morning Van went down to the office and found a message on voicemail from Gloria asking if he had returned to town yet. As much as he relished the idea of getting his hands on, and another body part in Gloria, he wanted to remain as Van for a while longer. He conducted some computer research for two other clients, first verifying the credentials of a real estate agent and then completing a background check on a corporate lawyer. Once assured that a little more cash would flow into the agency, he logged off.

Next activity—visit the Mile High Flea Market. Then a thought occurred to him. He had been planning to try out a new disguise. What better place than at a flea market? He applied gray tint to his hair, glued on a gray moustache and goatee, put on a straw hat and regarded himself in the mirror of his adjoining bathroom. He looked like a middle-aged junk collector. Perfect. He locked the door and drove north to the garage sale on steroids.

He exited I-76 at 88<sup>th</sup>, headed east and turned left into the parking area. After paying his three dollars at the toll booth, he found a parking spot and strolled through one of the access points into the grounds of the Mile High Marketplace better known as the Flea Market. The place had a grid of streets—letters running north and south and numbers running east and west. It resembled a huge paved parking lot with permanent buildings near the entrance. The initial wood buildings gave the impression of a western town taken over by painters with an extra budget for wild colors.

The streets between buildings were packed with a summer mob of people wanting deals, seeking key finds or simply checking out legs and asses.

Van passed storefronts offering shoes, jackets, belts, camouflage gear, pants, tools, toys, dark glasses, beauty products, you name it. As he sauntered toward the back of the marketplace, he passed food concessions offering turkey legs, kettle corn, lemonade, funnel cakes and ice cream. His stomach growled, but he ignored it. A large restroom building had mist blowing out by the entryway to cool the shoppers on this hot summer day.

He looked up at the bright blue sky, punctuated by the occasional wisp of white blowing eastward. One of the most popular booths sold umbrellas. Numerous people had succumbed to buying them to provide shade from the fierce sun beating down. He passed a booth with skis and another where he could buy pepper spray and stun guns.

As Van reached the temporary section of the grounds populated with tents and folding tables, sellers displayed more eclectic collections of treasures or junk. He went by a tent with lawn mowers and ATVs, another with appliances including refrigerators and stoves, a third with luggage and backpacks and a fourth with pottery, boom boxes and purses.

A background buzz of conversations included many in Spanish. Young couples pushed strollers, older parents herded gaggles of kids, and seniors limped along using canes. He watched three boys tossing a football.

He stopped at a booth with oil paintings and admired one

seascape. Although it would go with the décor in his loft, he decided he didn't want to lug it around today. Besides, he had enough on the walls for his taste. He shook his head at the thought of the modern art that Vanna displayed in her place. All kinds of twisted sculptures, blobs of paint and geometrical shapes on canvas. Their preferences certainly differed, except when bringing slimebags to justice.

After watching little kids chase each other, he located booth J-118 where the antiquities dealer recommended by Harlan Shannon was supposed to hang out. The stand covered by an open-sided blue tent had antique statues, ornate vases and a collection of coins. He approached a man wearing a deerskin vest. "I'm looking for Daniel Fogart."

The guy scratched a scraggly beard. "Ain't we all."

"Do you know when he'll be back?"

"He took off to grab some chow. You can probably catch him in fifteen minutes or so. Ya wanna buy something?"

"Not right now. I'll be back to see Daniel."

Van wandered around, first buying and consuming a corn on the cob and then taking the opportunity to stop to view a large collection of CDs on display under a green tent. He leafed through the classical selection, considering a Boston Symphony Orchestra collection of *La Mer*, *Prelude a l'apres-midi du'n faune* and *Printemps Symphonic Suite*. Removing the disc from the container he noticed a scratch and decided not to buy it. He then looked at several Beatles selections. Vanna had all of these. They always gave each other Christmas presents, dutifully wrapping one, and only one present and leaving it in the other's loft. One of them would then open the present on Christmas. The other would open it as soon afterwards as he or she reappeared.

He preferred buying Vanna's present at least six months ahead, so he wouldn't be at risk with a last minute transformation. Vanna, on the other hand, always figured that Van couldn't keep his pants zipped that long in December, so she'd have a chance to buy something for him at the last minute.

Finding nothing appropriate to give to his agency partner, Van visited a farmers' market section. He picked up a cantaloupe, thumped it and returned it to the counter. Fresh vegetables and fruit abounded. He stopped to listen to a band twanging guitars and ambled past a slide and small roller coaster entertaining the younger set. Finally, he checked his watch and headed back to see if Daniel had returned.

More people now stood around the tables looking at the objects on display. He asked for Daniel, and the deerskin vest guy pointed to a man in his sixties, wearing a flowing purple robe. His silver hair was combed back over a high forehead above deep-set dark eyes. His crooked nose had a wart on the left side. No smile.

"Harlan Shannon at CU suggested I look you up," Van said as he shook a firm, cold hand.

Daniel nodded his head, still exhibiting no smile. "Ah, yes. The good professor. What interest do you have in antiques and relics?"

"Actually, I have a specific item I want to show you." Van reached in his pocket, brought out the gold medallion and handed it to Daniel. "Harlan thought you might be familiar with this."

Daniel's eyes narrowed. "Where did you get this?"

"I bought it at a pawnshop. Do you know its origin?"

"I've read a description of such a medallion." He brought it close to his eyes, turned it over and ran a weathered finger over the surface. "It's reputed to be a shape-shifting charm of some sort."

"Charm?"

"Yes. I doubt that it has any power." He scratched the wart on his nose. "But it may have been owned by a shape-shifter."

Van arched an eyebrow. "Is there really such a thing?"

"Most definitely." Daniel turned it over again in his hand. "I'll offer you a hundred dollars."

"I'm sorry. It's not for sale. I came here hoping to learn more. Can you can tell me anything else about its history?"

"You now know all I do on the subject." Daniel's eyes dropped.

Van sensed something else going on here. "Why do you think this would have been found in Denver?"

Daniel shrugged. "I'm sure its previous owner must have been strapped for cash. I'll give you two hundred dollars for it."

Van shook his head.

"Three hundred."

"As I said, I'm not selling it."

"Too bad. Now if you'll excuse me, I need to help a customer." Daniel handed the medallion back and turned his back on Van, causing his robe to swish around him.

Van walked away, trying to fathom what was going on with this man. He obviously knew more than he had admitted. Still, Daniel hadn't even asked for Van's name. Evidently, he took at face value the statement of buying it at a pawnshop. This remained as perplexing as the Blendheim case. Would he ever be able to learn more about his transvictus background?

Deep in thought Van strolled past a white tent. He looked down and noticed a quarter lying on the pavement.

As he reached down to pick it up, someone grabbed his arm.

The next thing he knew he was being shoved into the tent. Then he felt a crushing blow to the back of his head and all went black.

# Chapter 26

Van awoke with a searing pain at the base of his skull. He rubbed his head and tried to sit up. Dizziness overtook him, and he dropped on his back to the asphalt surface inside a deserted tent. The top flapped in a gentle breeze. Van remained there motionless, watching the waves of white canvas droop and bellow. He took several gulps of air, turned on his stomach and raised himself to his knees. More deep breathing and he staggered to his feet. The tent swayed, and he braced himself against a pole. He filled his lungs again, and the tent learned to hold still. He touched the back of his head and grimaced as more waves of pain shot from the large, tender knob. He inhaled again.

Remembering a tumble into the tent, he tried to recall any image of who might have done this to him. Only the hand on his arm. Cold. He hadn't caught a glimpse of his attacker.

He reached in his pocket. No medallion. He patted all his pockets. He still had his wallet and keys but no medallion. He smacked his forehead, feeling like an idiot to be stripped of the medallion this way. Reaching in the pocket where the medallion had been, he found only one other thing. On a scrap of paper, block letters stated, "TO BE RETURNED TO ITS RIGHTFUL OWNER."

Van parted the tent flap and staggered outside, blinking at the blinding sunlight. He shaded his eyes and looked around. People of all sizes and shapes scurried in every direction.

A fresh wave of nausea gripped him, and he leaned on a nearby table to steady himself. Once under control again, he teetered back toward Daniel's booth.

The guy in the deerskin vest stood there alone.

"I need to speak with Daniel again," Van coughed out the words.

"He's gone."

"Do you know when he'll be back?"

Deerskin man shrugged. "Can't say. He told me I'd be in charge while he went to Los Angeles."

Van considered going to DIA to try to catch Daniel Fogart before he went through security but realized the futility of finding him at one of the country's busiest airports. Besides, maybe he was driving to LA.

He vowed to catch up with Daniel. Next time the relic guy wouldn't get the drop on him.

Then Van returned to his loft, removed his disguise and slept.

\* \* \* \* \*

The ringing phone roused Van from slumber. He reached for it and croaked, "Yeah?"

"This is Angie Reynolds. I'm calling in regards to the autopsy of Jackson Wittich."

Van blinked. His bedside clock indicated ten A.M. He had slept for sixteen hours. He focused his attention on the caller. "Yes. Has it been completed?"

"I wanted to let you know that he died of heart failure. No foul play. He went peacefully in his sleep."

Van closed his eyes for a moment. "When you have to go, I guess that's the best way. Thanks for getting back to me."

"Do you know who should be contacted to make funeral arrangements?" Angie asked.

"I'll be the one taking care of it. How soon will the body be released?"

"You can have it picked up tomorrow."

After hanging up, he wondered what it would have been like if he had found his grandfather sooner or if his grandfather had lived longer. He grabbed the phone book, looked under funeral homes, made a selection and called to arrange for the disposition of his grandfather's body.

He dropped back in bed, with images of his grandfather alive and then finding the old man dead. Then he fell fast asleep again.

The ringing phone brought him back to earth again.

"This is Donald Hallett. I'm on my way to Gloria Blendheim's house. I need you and Vanna to join me right away."

"What's the rush?"

"Mulhaney will be there shortly. I think he intends to arrest Gloria. I need your assistance in stopping him."

"Vanna is . . . uh . . . out of town, but I'll be there ASAP. You want me to shoot Mulhaney or knock him over the head?"

An exasperated grunt came over the phone. "Of course not. But you may have some pertinent information we can use to hold him off."

"Okay. Give me a few minutes and I'll join you."

Van's head still ached. He downed two aspirin, threw some water on his face, squirted some toothpaste in his cotton mouth, spit it out and determined he was as good as he was going to get. Rush hour traffic delayed his drive and when he arrived, Mulhaney, Donald and Gloria all sat stiffly in the living room, like toy soldiers bent at the waists and knees.

"What a cheery group," Van said. "You all auditioning for circus clowns or something?"

"Your client is going down," Mulhaney growled.

She had done that many times but not in the way Mulhaney intended. "What do you think she's done this time?" Van asked.

"Not what I think. What she did." Mulhaney pointed a beefy digit at Gloria. "She murdered her husband."

"Just because Huntington said he heard a woman speaking to Cornelius right before the shooting, doesn't mean it was Gloria," Van said.

"How did you find out about the woman's voice?" Mulhaney sputtered.

"As you well know, Detective, I have my ways. Personally, I consider Greer Lawson a better suspect than Gloria. She met with

Cornelius the night of his death. Try Greer on for size."

Mulhaney glared at Van. "I think you have a mole in the police department. Someone has been messing with papers in my office."

"Probably a mouse or a rat."

"Yeah, and I'm going to find out who the rat is."

"Speaking of rats, did you know that Greer and Homer Stiles have become cozy?" Van smiled.

"What's that have to do with the price of gold in China?" Mulhaney sneered.

Van rolled his eyes. "Think it through, Mulhaney. Greer kills Cornelius Blendheim over a romance gone bad. Then she hooks up with Bentley Graves. He meets a similar fate. Now she's snuggling up with Homer Stiles to consummate a business relationship to sell the Blendheim Towers, not to mention involvement in the other type of relationship." To say nothing of kidnapping and trying to kill Vanna.

"I don't want that bitch getting any money for the Blendheim Towers deal," Gloria shouted.

"Hush," Donald admonished.

"And one other thing, Mulhaney," Van continued. "How do you know Huntington isn't lying? He stole Gloria's jewelry and was in the house when Cornelius died. He could have murdered his dad out of anger because he wouldn't receive much from the will. That's a pretty good motive."

Mulhaney narrowed his gaze at Van. "How do you know so much? Oh, that's right, your mole."

"I think you'd be way off base arresting Gloria with all these other scumbags and their unethical, dishonest and lust-induced dealings. You'd be best served by incarcerating the lot of them and leaving Gloria in peace."

"Well, young Huntington will serve time for theft." Mulhaney gave a determined nod.

"Good." Van grinned. "Now lock up Stiles and Greer Lawson and you'll make a clean sweep. By the way, any of those three could also have killed Bentley, who, you might be interested to know, came to Cornelius's house the night of the first murder. Bentley received what he deserved. Now how about ridding society of the rest of these menaces?"

Mulhaney wrinkled his nose. "Quite a speech, Averi. Maybe you're the shyster, and Hallett here is merely your bagman?"

Van realized that his headache had subsided. The aspirin had definitely kicked in. He hadn't given a speech like this since he solved the Gallagher case two years ago. A little over-the-counter drugs, adrenalin and an opportunity to perform had brought him back to life.

"I agree with Mr. Averi," Donald said. "Too many loose ends remain and not enough proof of any involvement by my client. With what you have, the DA would balk at bringing charges. I could tear apart any claims made because much more than a reasonable doubt exists in this case. Gloria will continue to cooperate with you, Detective Mulhaney. She isn't going anywhere. You should proceed with finding the real murderer or murderers."

Mulhaney stood and shook his fist at Gloria. "I'm going to get you."

She gave him a sweet smile and blew him a kiss.

Mulhaney turned on his heels and stalked out, slamming the door.

Gloria jumped up, raced over, threw her arms around Van and planted a kiss on his lips. "My hero."

Van felt an arousal in his pants but gently pushed Gloria away. "Mulhaney will keep after you, Gloria. He's tenacious and won't quit. We need to strategize on how to find the real murderer. Donald, any thoughts?"

Gloria patted Van's cheek before returning to her chair.

"You've made a case for any of four people being involved in one or more of the murders." Donald put his hand to his chin. "Huntington isn't a credible witness for hearing a woman's voice with all of his involvement. Van, has your investigation given you a prime suspect?"

"At one time or another each has been on the top of my list. Let's take Cornelius's murder. Huntington remains a prime suspect because of the jewelry theft and being in the house at the time of the murder. Greer had an appointment with Cornelius that night and partook in numerous shady dealings. Finally Homer Stiles made a comment that he planned to get Cornelius out of the way."

Gloria's eyes widened. "Homer planned to kill Cornelius?"

"That's what it looked like, sweetheart. Then we have Bentley Graves before he met his maker. He blackmailed Gloria and could have killed Cornelius as well. I have some ideas, but I'm withholding judgment right now."

"And your thoughts on Bentley's murder?" Donald asked.

Van looked up toward the ceiling for a moment and back at Donald. "I figure one of them stole Cornelius's gun and went to confront Bentley. Someone definitely murdered Bentley. No suicide with two bullets to the brain. Greer had a motive to eliminate a business partner and get a larger share of the Blendheim Tower deal. A car meeting the description of Homer Stiles's was seen in the neighborhood that night, and Homer may have wanted to get Bentley out of the way to have Greer all to himself. Huntington has the hots for Bentley's wife and could have decided to eliminate his competition. And Bentley's wife Eva, can't be ruled out. All good suspects. Again, I have my favorite but will keep looking for more information."

"Does Vanna have any other thoughts?" Gloria batted her eyelashes at Van. "You know, female intuition and all."

"She and I are in synch on this. We've thought this over together. She shares all the views I've expressed to you."

Gloria pouted. "I know. Like brother and sister."

"Exactly."

Donald looked at his watch and stood up. "I have an early meeting tomorrow. I better be on my way. Keep me posted, Van." He headed toward the door.

"Will do." After Donald closed the door, Van slowly raised his tired body and stretched his arms. "I should take off too. It's been a tough day."

Gloria stepped over and grabbed his arm. "Hold on a minute. I have something I want to show you." She raced up the stairs while Van waited in the living room.

Five minutes later Gloria reappeared in a see-through nightgown holding a cigarette in her hand. She took a drag and blew the smoke in Van's face. "Still want to leave?"

Van's pulse doubled as his eyes and one lower appendage grew large. "Uh-oh."

She set the cigarette down in an ashtray and threw her arms around his neck and plastered her body against him. "Uh-oh is right. Something down there is poking me."

Their lips met and Van knew he was a goner. He had the presence of mind before losing use of all his brain cells to do one thing. "Go to your bedroom," he told Gloria. "I'll be right there."

"Don't take long." She sashayed up the stairs, burning lust-filled images onto Van's eyeballs.

He pulled himself out of his trance long enough to dash outside to remove the red bag from the trunk of his Subaru. He stashed it in Gloria's bathroom and then entered her bedroom. She lay on the bed holding her arms out to him. He clicked off the light and dove into bed, ready to let the gymnastics begin.

She made quick work of his clothes and then the flimsy nightgown flew over her head and fluttered to the rug.

He couldn't believe the woman thrusting her voluptuous body against him. His hands explored every inch of her wondrous curves as her tongue wreaked havoc with the remaining functioning synapses in his sex-crazed brain.

She pulled him to her, and he revved up serious friction. At the moment of his release, Gloria let out a wild scream and clawed his back.

Van collapsed on top of her momentarily but rolled off as the transformation began.

Now the part Vanna hated most—being in bed with this slut and trying to figure out how to make a graceful exit after Van had gone wild. Men had absolutely no control over that engorged member between their legs. Well, she had to admit she didn't mind when it belonged to Lance.

She slipped out of bed, removed Van's ring before it slipped off her finger, felt around on the floor to locate and pick up Van's clothes and dashed to the bathroom. In minutes she had changed into the jeans and T-shirt from the red bag, replaced Van's ring with a gold necklace and stuffed Van's clothes and ring back in the bag. What a world she lived in. Would this process ever get easy?

Checking that everything appeared in order, she turned off the bathroom light and stepped out. A bright light flashed on.

Gloria stood there with her arms crossed over her boobs. "What the hell are you doing here?"

Vanna looked from side to side, trying to figure out the best response. "I . . . uh . . . came to get Van. There's been an emergency development in one of our cases."

"Where's he now?" Gloria glared at Vanna, showing no signs of being concerned at standing there buck-naked.

Vanna had to admit that the woman was well-stacked. "I came in a taxi and he just left in it for the airport." Vanna forced a smile. "I had to use your bathroom. I'll be on my way now. Bye." She bolted for the stairs, took them two at a time, jogged to the door and didn't stop moving until she had jumped in the car. Wasting no time, she started it and pulled away. In the rearview mirror she saw Gloria, still naked, standing in the doorway. Busted. In more ways than one.

She slammed her palm on the steering wheel. Goddamn Van and his runaway prick. Then she smiled. Hurray for Van and his runaway prick. She was back!

# Chapter 27

The next day Vanna decided to let things settle a little on the Blendheim case. She had no desire to see Gloria or any of the three slimebag suspects. Instead she took out the files she'd been given by Harlan Shannon. With everything else going on, neither she nor Van had checked out the possible transvictus sightings in three other cities. No time like the present for a little background investigation.

The first manila folder contained email correspondence with a man named Peter Nalley in Seattle. Peter had come across a report of a shape-shifter who once lived in an orphanage in Burien City, south of Seattle. No names were listed.

Vanna logged on her computer and started searching for references to Peter Nalley but could locate no address or phone number in Seattle. The guy must have had an unlisted number. Instead she sent him an email explaining she was a private investigator and had been given Peter's name by Harlan Shannon of the University of Colorado. She provided her contact information and asked if Peter would reply with his phone number so they could speak.

The next folder had the name of Jennifer Orloff. She stated she had seen a boy change into a girl when she worked at the Harbor

Street Orphanage in South San Francisco. Vanna raised an eyebrow at this. Harlan had tried four times with follow-up emails but Jennifer had not replied.

Vanna ran a search on the name and came up with two phone numbers in San Francisco. When she tried the first, a canned recording indicated the phone had been disconnected. After punching in the second number, a creaky woman's voice answered, "Hallo-o."

"Is this Jennifer Orloff?"

"Could be. Who wantz ta know?"

"My name is Vanna Anderson. Professor Harlan Shannon at the University of Colorado gave me your name. Are you the Jennifer Orloff who worked at the Harbor Street Orphanage?"

"Why, yez. I work dere. Den shut down."

"Professor Shannon indicated he received an email from you that you once saw a boy change into a girl."

"Waz dat? Have to speak louder. Hard to hear."

Vanna repeated herself.

A chuckle came over the line. "Oh yez. I remember dat. My daughter show me how ta use computer. I find place 'bout stories of people change into animals and utter people. I send message and nice man send me message back. But after dat too much trouble to use computer more."

"When did you work at the orphanage?" Vanna spoke slowly and loudly.

"'bout twenty years ago I start der. For five years I clean floors. Nice people work with. Do good job."

Vanna clutched the receiver in her hand as if trying to squeeze pertinent information out of this woman. "I'm sure you did. And when did you see the boy change into a girl?"

"Jez before shut down. Boy 'bout fifteen hide in closet. I happen to be watching from 'round corner. In ten minutes, girl come out. Almost drop my false teeth."

"Did you report this to anyone?"

"No. Nobody believe ol' woman so say nut'ing."

"Did you see any other changes take place?"

"Oh, yez. I see broom turn into cat and dog change into tree. Plenty strange tings go on in dat place."

*Uh-oh.* Vanna sensed she had an unreliable witness. "But did you ever see a change between a boy and girl any other time?"

"Nope. Jez dat one time. Dat enough."

"Thank you for speaking with me. You've been very helpful."

After returning her phone to the cradle, she Googled Harbor Street Orphanage. She found a list of references including one that indicated it had shut down in the late 1990s. That part of Jennifer's story checked out.

She picked up the third manila folder. This had a chain of email correspondence between Harlan and a man named Gandolf Sheer who identified himself as a handyman and amateur historian, who researched old buildings in the greater Los Angeles area. While looking into a building that had been an orphanage in Long Beach until 1965, he came across a memoir of a woman who had worked there. In it she referenced seeing a teenage boy change into a girl. No other details. The email had a phone number so Vanna picked up her phone and called.

A woman answered.

"Gandolf Sheer, please."

The woman gasped. "Haven't you heard?"

"Heard what?"

"He had a heart attack and died a month ago."

"I'm sorry for your loss," Vanna said. "Please forgive me for my intrusion."

She hung up and tapped her finger on the corner of her desk. Another dead end. So far the transvictus sightings hadn't added up to a fart in a tornado.

She had one last lead to check. Harlan had also given Van a name and phone number for a Rachel Lewbell in Santa Fe. After calling the number, a man answered and said he would go get Rachel.

Vanna waited five minutes, wondering if the man had forgotten or wandered off in Never Neverland.

Then a tired woman's voice came on the line. "Yes?"

"My name is Vanna Anderson. Harlan Shannon in Boulder, Colorado, gave me your name."

The woman's voice perked up. "Oh, yes. I remember. The professor who's interested in shape-shifters."

"That's the one. I'm doing some work for him, and he indicated you might have spotted a shape-shifter."

"I did indeed. I cover night shifts at the Three Trees Motel. A man and woman checked in around ten. Then around midnight a different woman left the room. A little while after that, the woman who had checked in took off. When I went to look in the room in the morning before going off duty, the man had disappeared. It's obvious the man changed into a woman."

Vanna thought over what she had heard. "How do you know the man didn't leave when you weren't watching and the other woman came in at another time as well?"

"I have that covered. We have a surveillance camera. I forwarded through the tape for the whole night. It takes pictures every two seconds. I could clearly see the man and woman entering the room and the two women leaving, then me going into the room in the morning. The second woman never entered the room and the man never left it. Pretty strange, huh?"

Vanna felt a surge of excitement. "Do you still have the surveillance tape?"

"Nah, we record over it every other day. Too expensive to save."

Vanna let out an exasperated burst of air. "How long ago did this happen?"

"Oh, I'd say six months. I got intrigued and did a little checking on the Internet. That's when I found the professor and spoke with him."

"Did you get the name of the man and woman who checked in?"

"I certainly did. Mr. and Mrs. John Smith."

Vanna rolled her eyes. "I bet they paid in cash rather than with a credit card."

"That's right."

"Did you ask for identification?"

Rachel laughed. "Nope, we're not big on that sort of thing here."

Vanna doodled for a moment on her notepad. "What did they look like?"

"I never got too good a look at the woman. She hung back and had a shawl over her head. Kinda tall and skinny. The man, probably in his fifties, wore a cowboy hat. Maybe six feet, not thin, not fat."

"Any distinguishing marks?"

"No tats or anything like that. Just your regular middle-aged guy."

"Any idea where they were headed?"

"Nope. They showed up carrying backpacks. The video showed each of the women leaving with a backpack. And they left nothing else in the room when I looked."

Vanna asked a few further questions, but it became obvious she wouldn't extract any additional useful information.

\* \* \* \* \*

In the late morning Vanna left the office to conduct surveillance for another client. A woman in her thirties had concerns that her husband, who worked night shifts, disappeared for several hours each day around noon and was spending cash too quickly. Since she had a day job and couldn't check on him, she hired The V V Agency to tail the husband and find out if he was having an affair or gambling.

Vanna parked a block away from the house in Englewood and waited. At twelve-fifteen a man in his thirties matching the picture given Vanna by the wife, strolled out of the house and entered a beat up silver Honda Civic parked by the curb. He roared off and Vanna followed. Within half a dozen blocks the car pulled into a strip mall, and the man headed into an arcade. Vanna waited five minutes and then followed. She found him playing videogames, which he did for the next two hours. When he left, she followed him back to his house.

Vanna returned to the office to complete a short report, which she mailed off to the wife with an invoice.

She raided the small refrigerator in the office to have a strawberry yogurt, apple and iced tea. With hunger and thirst averted, she called Mulhaney next.

"Hey, Detective, what's the latest?"

"That partner of yours come up with any new theories? He was more than his usual asshole self last night."

Vanna laughed. "He's out of town. I'm sitting in my office all by my lonesome thinking of you, Mulhaney."

"Yeah? You want some company?"

Vanna imagined him drooling. "I'm not that lonely, but I want to check on Huntington Blendheim. You release him yet?"

"The kid's out on bail now. He'll be sticking close to home, but I'll see to it that he's locked up after the trial. The DA will throw the book at him, and he's already confessed to the theft, so end of case."

"You still believe him that he overheard a woman with Cornelius right before the shooting?"

"Why not? He confessed to the theft."

Vanna pitched the yogurt container into the wastebasket. "Three to five beats life. He could still be good for the murder as well."

"Nah. I'm still betting on your client."

"And Bentley Graves. Who do you think killed him?"

"Your client's also a person of interest for that one as well. I'll bring her down. Just you wait."

"Thanks for the update, Mulhaney. Be good."

Vanna looked around the office for a moment and decided she might as well visit Huntington. From the file cabinet she removed a recording device disguised as a pen and put it in the pocket of the leather vest worn over her white blouse. She had one additional theory to check out.

# Chapter 28

After stopping at a candy store along the way, Vanna arrived at Huntington's house and rang the doorbell.

Huntington answered looking even more pasty than usual, hair unruly, in need of a shave. "What do you want?"

She handed him a box of Godiva chocolates. "I thought I'd make a friendly visit to welcome you home from your tour of the jail."

He scowled at her but took the box of chocolates, opened it and popped one in his mouth. His sullen expression changed to one of neutrality. "Come on in."

They settled amidst the debris in the living room. Huntington selected another piece of chocolate but didn't offer any to Vanna. No problem for her. With chocolate she could take it or leave it. Now taking or leaving Lance on the other hand . . .

She pushed aside a torn *People Magazine*. "I've been considering your involvement in all these recent crimes."

"Yeah?" He shoved another chocolate into his mouth, so intent on the box that he didn't even raise his eyes.

She clapped her hands together. "Huntington, look at me."

He gave a start, coughed as if choking on the chocolate and jerked his head up.

She pointed her right index finger at him. "It seems you have a knack for being in the wrong place at the wrong time."

He chewed for a moment. "What are you getting at?"

"You're in your dad's house snooping around and stealing jewelry when he gets shot. Not the best of timing."

"No, it wasn't."

"Some might say you killed your father as well as committing the theft but you state you heard a woman's voice coming from your dad's den."

He picked up another chocolate and eyed it. "That's right."

"And you're sticking with that story?"

The fourth piece of chocolate went into his mouth. "Um . . . uh . . . yeah. That's what happened." Vanna saw him struggling, or perhaps it was merely the sticky caramel core glued to his tongue.

"So you waited upstairs and then went downstairs where you discovered your dad's body."

"Yeah."

"And that's when you removed his gun from the drawer."

"How did you know . . ." He clamped his hand over his mouth.

"Look, Huntington. Time to level with me. I figured it out. You took his gun before you left the house."

His eyes narrowed, and he reached under the cushion of the couch. He brought out a handgun, which he pointed at Vanna.

Although her pulse quickened, she feigned nonchalance and gave a dismissive wave of her hand. "Don't act stupid, Huntington. I also figured out what happened after you left the house."

He nervously waved the gun at her. "What?"

"At first you thought no one had seen you, but someone actually spotted you leaving your dad's house that night."

He flinched. "Go on."

"That someone was Bentley Graves. And true to form Bentley, who likes to blackmail people, contacted you to say he had seen you coming out of the house the night of your father's murder. He figured you'd pay up to keep the sighting quiet."

Huntington slumped on the couch.

Vanna knew she'd nailed it. "How much did he demand?"

The gun shook, and he pointed it at Vanna again. "He wanted fifty grand to stay silent. No one yet knew I stole the jewelry. If Bentley told the police I'd been at Dad's, they'd figure out the theft and also consider me a suspect for the murder."

"And you went to Bentley's house four days later."

Huntington nodded his head. "I wore gloves and took Dad's gun with me. I figured I could scare him into calling off the blackmail scheme."

"I bet Bentley laughed at you."

Huntington clenched his teeth. "The bastard said I acted like an idiot, told me to pay up and quit trying to be tough. He called me a wimp."

"And you shot him twice."

"No one calls me a wimp. He got what he deserved. I left the gun there because it didn't have my fingerprints on it. I figured the police would arrest Gloria for both murders. I couldn't believe it when nothing happened."

"Detective Mulhaney thought Bentley killed your father and Gloria murdered Bentley."

"He was wrong on both counts." Huntington tugged compulsively on his goatee. "I don't want to go to prison for the theft. And I won't do time for the murder."

As calmly as she could, Vanna held a hand up like a cop directing traffic at an intersection. Her hand didn't shake. "Don't make things worse, Huntington. Put the gun down and think this through."

"No. I've had enough." He waved the gun in circles.

Vanna tensed.

Then he put the gun to his temple and fired.

# Chapter 29

Vanna's shaking hand dropped her cell phone, but she finally managed to call 9-1-1. Then after several gulps of air, she calmed herself enough to reach Mulhaney. "Get your butt right over to Huntington Blendheim's house in Golden. He just killed himself."

"Jesus H. Christ. I'm on my way."

Vanna scanned the room and replayed in her mind exactly what had transpired. In five minutes two EMTs arrived and realized they could do nothing. Ten minutes later a tall, lanky officer from the Golden Police Department came in the door.

Vanna showed her identification, explained that she had witnessed a suicide and indicated that this tied into a murder investigation being conducted by Denver Police Detective Mulhaney who would be here soon. She could tell the Golden cop had little enthusiasm for the idea of a representative from another department showing up.

Shortly thereafter, Mulhaney appeared and after some interdepartmental haggling and posturing, the two agencies agreed to cooperate. Vanna removed the recording device and handed it to Mulhaney. "You'll find some useful information recorded here. Huntington confessed to killing Bentley Graves."

A plain-clothes detective from Golden arrived and conferred with Mulhaney. Then while a coroner's investigator inspected the body, Mulhaney and the other detective took Vanna's statement. She filled them in on the exact details and told them that it would all be corroborated on the recording. Since the device also doubled as an MP3 player, she activated it so they all could listen. After hearing it, the Golden detective agreed Vanna could leave since a clear case of suicide had occurred.

"I want you in my office at five to discuss this further," Mulhaney said to Vanna. "We now know what happened to Graves, but I want to see how this ties in with the murder of Cornelius Blendheim. I'll need to keep the recording device."

"Fine," Vanna said. "It has a USB connection, so download it to your computer, and then you can get it back to me."

Vanna drove back to her office, pondering all that had happened. As Mulhaney indicated, the Graves murder had been solved, but nothing had been clarified with Cornelius's death. Huntington had stuck with his story of hearing a female voice. Vanna would have to deal with Greer again on that one.

In her office Vanna first called Gloria Blendheim to give her an update on the latest events.

"What the hell were you up to last night?" Gloria growled. "I'm still pissed at you for invading my house and sending Van away."

"Sorry about that, Gloria, but I have some good news for you."

The lioness turned into a kitten. "Oh?"

"Mulhaney says you're off the hook for the murder of Bentley Graves."

"Yeah, I know I didn't off him. Who did?"

Vanna wished she could see Gloria's reaction. Would she act happy or sad? "Huntington."

An audible intake of air. "Why . . . why'd he do it?"

"It seems Bentley went to the money well one too many times. Much like he tried to blackmail you, he pulled the same stunt on Huntington, although more directly since he figured Huntington was a wuss. Bentley miscalculated. Huntington confronted him and shot him."

"Wow. I didn't think Hunty had it in him." She giggled. "I'm impressed."

"A little late for that."

"Yeah, I guess you're right. Is Huntington in jail now?"

"No. He killed himself."

Gloria gasped. "Aw, shit. He wasn't such a bad guy. What a way to go. Maybe Huntington also killed Cornelius?"

Vanna detected a hopeful tone in Gloria's voice. "I'm not convinced on that one. Huntington claimed to hear a female voice at the time of his dad being shot. I'm still interested in Greer Lawson for that one. She had been skulking around your house the night of the murder and could have killed Cornelius."

"Yeah, I wouldn't put it past her. She's a grade A bitch. Her and her conniving to buy Blendheim Towers."

"I'll work on it and let you know."

"Good. Sounds like all of this is nearly wrapped up." Gloria made a kissing sound. "Tell Van I miss him."

Vanna thrust her tongue out and stuck a finger in her mouth. Right.

After hanging up, Vanna checked her email and found a message from Peter Nalley in Seattle with a phone number.

She immediately called the number and a male voice answered.

"This is Vanna Anderson in Denver. I received your email response. Thanks for sending your phone number."

"What can I do for you Ms. Anderson?"

"As I mentioned in my original email to you, Professor Harlan Shannon at the University of Colorado gave me your name. I've been doing some research for him, and he suggested you might have some information on shape-shifters."

His voice dropped ten decibels. "What type of shape-shifting?"

Vanna decided to be direct. "A transformation between male and female."

"Why . . . uh yes . . . I did encounter such an event once."

When he ventured nothing further, Vanna said, "Go on."

"Well, yes. I was on the staff of an orphanage, oh, back in the mid 90s . . ."

Vanna felt like a miner panning for gold with a thimble. She wished she could reach out, grab the guy by his shoulders and shake him. "Please continue."

"You see . . . uh . . . I'm a little hesitant because of the unusual circumstances of this situation."

"I can understand, Mr. Nalley. Anything you tell me will be kept in the strictest confidence."

He wheezed. "All right." Then the floodgate opened. "A very reclusive sixteen-year-old boy lived at the orphanage. In fact we gave him the nickname of Solo Sam. He didn't have any friends, and although he seemed bright enough, he never volunteered answers in his classes and wouldn't speak more than half a dozen words at a time. He did wander around and on numerous occasions had to be taken back to the dormitory when found skulking through the kitchen or classrooms in the middle of the night." He paused. "I'm not boring you with this, am I?"

"Not in the least. Keep going."

Peter cleared his throat. "One time when I drew after-hours monitor duty, I heard a noise in the hallway. I stepped out of my office as Solo Sam slunk around a corner. I followed as he disappeared into the library and shut the door. I went up and tried the door handle, but he had locked it from the inside. I stayed there out of sight, and fifteen minutes later, a girl I didn't recognize came out. I waited until she disappeared and then went into the library expecting to find Solo Sam still in the room after some illicit encounter with this girl. No one was in the library, which had no other doors. I turned to follow the girl. She had already left the building, and I saw her out on the front walkway. In the light from a nearby street lamp, I realized she wore the same baggy shirt and pants that Solo Sam had on earlier. I raced after her. She must have heard me because she ran into the street. At that moment a car raced down the block and struck her. She died instantly. I . . . I've always felt guilty that I scared her right into the path of a speeding car. . ."

Vanna heard a sob over the phone. "Accidents happen, Mr. Nalley. Don't blame yourself. What else?"

He sniffled and made a gulping sound. "She wasn't one of the orphans in our care, and no one ever determined her identity. Also, Solo Sam never appeared again. Because of my role in the death, I never mentioned what I had seen to any of the other administrators. As I've considered it over the years, I'm convinced that Solo Sam transformed into the girl who died."

"And you've never told anyone this story before?"

"I only hinted at it on the shape-shifter Yahoo group and in my correspondence with Professor Shannon."

"Thank you for being so open with me. I'm sorry you had to witness such a tragic accident. Did you ever see any other transformations?"

"I never saw anything myself. I did have one email from someone else on the Yahoo loop . . ."

Vanna rolled her eyes. Back to prying the can open. "Yes?"

"I received a message from a man named Benjamin Randolph. He also worked in an orphanage . . . in Iowa City. He mentioned a situation of a boy transforming into a girl. I never heard from him again."

"Do you still have his contact information?"

"It should be in my email address book. I'll send it to you right away."

After hanging up, Vanna Googled the name Benjamin Randolph but couldn't find any useful references or a phone number in Iowa City. When she next checked email she found a message from Peter Nalley with an email address for Randolph. She fired off a message to Mr. Randolph explaining her interest and indicating she'd like to call him to speak further.

Vanna checked the time and realized she needed to get her butt over to police headquarters to meet with Detective Mulhaney. She arrived at a few minutes before five, and he escorted her up to his office.

"Wow. Look at all that impressive police work." Vanna pointed to the haphazard pile of documents on his desk.

"Don't knock it. I can find anything in there."

She tugged at a piece of lace protruding from the stack of paper and pulled out a pair of pink panties. She smiled at Mulhaney. "What have we here?"

He reddened, swatted her hand away and pushed the panties back into the pile. "Material evidence. Don't touch it."

She tsked and waggled her index finger at him. "Detective, I'm surprised at you. I thought you only had eyes for me."

"Well . . . uh . . . you haven't been too cooperative."

And it would stay that way. "Let's get on with it. What do you need from me?" Other than panties.

"Let's go to a . . . less distracting room. Follow me."

He led the way to a small interrogation room, and they took seats on opposite sides of a marred table.

"First, I want you to know we're recording everything being said."

"That's fine with me, Detective."

"Now, I need you to repeat exactly what happened at Huntington Blendheim's house today."

Vanna recounted the whole episode.

"I'll replay the recording you made to see if it inspires anything else you'd like to tell me." He clicked on the pen in MP3 player mode, and they listened to the events unfold once again.

"Good sound quality," Vanna said after they finished listening to the recording. "You should hire me to do undercover work for you."

"Yeah, not bad. Anything else come to mind?"

Vanna shook her head. "That covers it. Huntington killed Bentley Graves and then himself. He still insisted he hadn't killed Cornelius Blendheim, sticking with his earlier account of overhearing a woman."

"The guy lied so much along the way, that I suspect he made that up. Let me replay some of it for you." Mulhaney found the part he wanted and pushed the play button.

Vanna's voice: "You're in your dad's house snooping around and stealing jewelry when he gets shot. Not the best of timing."

Huntington's voice: "No, it wasn't."

"Some might say you killed your father as well as committing the theft but you state that you heard a woman's voice with your dad."

"That's right."

"And you're sticking with that story?"

"Um . . . uh . . . yeah. That's what happened."

Mulhaney paused the recording. "Right there. Listen to the tone of his voice. He's obviously slurring the words. A sign that he's lying."

Vanna didn't bother to correct Mulhaney's erroneous conclusion, when in reality Huntington had a mouth full of gooey caramel and chocolate. This solved one problem. "So that means my client's off the hook."

"Yeah." Mulhaney snorted. "I make Huntington good for both murders. Case closed."

Mulhaney might have reached that conclusion, but Vanna

remained unconvinced. Why would Huntington lie that he heard a woman's voice when a few minutes later he confessed to killing Bentley Graves? And if he confessed to one murder, why not confess to both? All of this required another conversation with Greer Lawson.

Mulhaney opened the door to the interrogation room, and they walked outside.

"Anything else you need from me?" Vanna asked.

He leered at her.

"Forget it. You have a souvenir from some bimbo on your desk."

"Yeah, but I'd like to collect an even better souvenir."

"And I know one lame ass detective who wouldn't be able to walk upright for a month if he tried."

# Chapter 30

That evening Vanna retrieved another pen recording device and stowed it in the pocket of a light jacket. Time to visit Greer Lawson again. With her trusty GPS navigation system, she entered the destination address and followed the directions.

The sun had set over the Continental Divide, and Vanna watched red and orange wisps of clouds over the mountains. Thunder clouds had threatened earlier, but they had moved off to render havoc in the plains of eastern Colorado. She loved this time of day as light changed to dark—as long as she had navigational assistance.

She parked a block from Greer's house and quickly scanned the neighborhood. No dog walkers or cavorting children. All was quiet. A green Jaguar parked against the curb across the street provided the only color in an otherwise dull street. Maybe she could solve two of her problems tonight.

Greer answered the door and scowled. "Not you again."

Vanna smiled. "Hey, you know what they say about a bad penny. If you have a minute I have some information for you concerning your late business partner, Bentley Graves."

Greer looked over her shoulder.

Vanna peered around her but didn't see Homer Stiles in the living room. "You going to invite me in?"

Greer let out an exasperated groan. "Yeah. But make it quick."

"Just long enough for us to have a heart-to-heart, you know, two women of the world kind of thing."

"Whatever." Greer flounced into the living room and dropped onto the couch.

Vanna selected an armchair and sat facing her. "The police have solved Bentley's murder."

"That Blendheim bitch do it?"

"It was a Blendheim. Actually, Huntington Blendheim."

Greer arched an eyebrow. "Cornelius's son did the deed. No kidding?"

"No kidding. I notice you're over your grieving for dear old Cornelius and Bentley now that your main squeeze is Homer Stiles. You toss them aside like week-old bagels."

Greer stiffened. "How do you know about Homer and me?"

"You get around, honey. First making a play for Cornelius, then once he's dead go for Bentley while you work a sale to Blendheim Corporation. Then you go for the guy who now runs the outfit. Consummate the deal on the Blendheim Towers and provide a little nookie on the side."

"Watch your mouth."

Vanna was enjoying herself. "So why'd you kill Cornelius? Couldn't get what you wanted?"

Greer straightened her back. "I didn't kill Cornelius."

"You were at his house the night of his death."

"So what? I left when he was still alive."

Vanna decided to shift gears. "And then you kidnapped and tried to kill me. You'll get life for all your efforts."

Greer narrowed her gaze at Vanna. "You're right. You are a bad penny and have too big a mouth. Homer should have finished the job in the mountains." Greer reached in her handbag resting on the couch and pulled out a handgun.

Homer stomped into the room also holding a gun. His tie hung unknotted, and his hair looked like it had been combed with a cake mixer. His wild eyes ping-ponged between the two women. "Greer, you stupid bitch. Why did you tell her I was involved?"

"What!" Greer shrieked, her eyes blazing as she turned to point her weapon at Homer. "Who are you calling a bitch, you limp dick wuss?" She fired, hitting Homer in the left shoulder.

The force of the bullet spun him to the side. He recovered and fired a shot catching Greer in the center of the forehead. She dropped to the floor like a sack of cement.

Vanna jumped to her feet.

Homer turned his gun toward Vanna, but she knocked his arm aside, kneed him in the groin and gave a karate jab to his throat. He gurgled and then collapsed.

Vanna kicked his gun away, reached for her cell and called 9-1-1. Then she punched in Mulhaney's number. When he answered, she said, "Get your perverted butt over to Greer Lawson's house. You have one and a half dead people to deal with."

The EMTs could do nothing for Greer, but ministered to Homer before rushing him off on a stretcher. A responding police officer sealed off the house.

When Mulhaney arrived, he pulled Vanna aside. "You have quite a knack for being right in the middle of shit today. Let's hear what happened this time."

Vanna removed the pen from her jacket pocket and handed it to Mulhaney. "Here's another recording of what happened. You can load it into your computer like before."

He shook his head. "Damn. You collect all this information and along the way half the population of Denver dies. You're a dangerous woman."

"You remember that, Mulhaney. The recording confirms that Greer Lawson and Homer Stiles were working together and involved in abducting me."

"The kidnapping Van mentioned?"

"Yeah. Nothing too serious."

"God damn it, Vanna. What have you got into?"

She shrugged. "Nothing more than your usual PI work. Now let me give you my statement." She began her account.

At one point he interrupted. "Why did you accuse Greer Lawson of murdering Cornelius Blendheim?"

"I'm not convinced that Huntington killed the old man."

"Leave it alone, Vanna. She said she didn't do it, and she was right. Huntington shot his father."

"You don't know that for sure."

Mulhaney winked at Vanna. "Since it's all resolved I guess I could share an interesting piece of evidence with you. You want to trade information for a little affection?"

Vanna raised her fist.

Mulhaney put his hands up to defend his face. "All right. Only kidding. Here's the tidbit you'll get a kick out of. After finding you with Huntington's dead body earlier today, I searched his car. You'll never guess what I found under the driver's seat?"

Vanna waggled her eyebrows at Mulhaney. "Pink panties?"

He reddened. "No. God damn it. I found Gloria Blendheim's missing handgun. The ballistics lab ran a quick test this afternoon and guess what else?"

Vanna's mind raced. How could this be? "It matched the bullet that killed Cornelius?"

"Bingo."

Vanna thought over all that had transpired. "I'm still not convinced that Huntington killed Cornelius."

Mulhaney did a little tap dance. "Case closed. All wrapped up."

"Have it your way, Mulhaney."

He smiled. "Okay. Let's have the rest."

Vanna ran her hand through her hair, took a deep breath and continued giving her statement.

In a few minutes Mulhaney held up a hand to stop her again. "Go back to you being kidnapped."

"As I said before, no big deal. Greer and Homer Stiles drugged me, took me up into the mountains, tied me up with duct tape, set a cabin on fire to burn me to death, but I escaped."

"You gonna press charges?"

Vanna gave a gagging cough. "Won't matter with Greer. Let's see what happens with Homer."

# Chapter 31

Vanna slept fitfully and awoke in the morning with what felt like a humongous hangover. She never experienced this aftereffect from alcohol, but she hadn't overdosed on dead bodies before.

Once again she had dreamt of holding a snake in her mouth. Same as the damn transvictus image on the medallion. What quirky things went on in her brain anyway? The dream had been so real she could still taste it. She spit into the sink and washed her mouth out with Listerine to get rid of the snake scales.

Lacking the energy to change and go down to face the responsibilities in her office, she puttered around her loft for an hour. Finally, she called Mulhaney.

"What's the latest?" she asked.

"The grim reaper also took Homer Stiles. Lost too much blood."

Vanna held a hand to her pounding head. "Saves the state the money for incarcerating another scumbag."

"Ah, what a sentimental woman. Everybody involved in this case is now dead except for your client. I wonder if she needs some male companionship."

"Forget it, Mulhaney. You're not her type."

"Yeah, I figure she prefers a PI like your partner, Van."

"Something like that. Anything else for me?"

"Oh, lots but you never act interested."

"And it will stay that way. Have a good life, Mulhaney." She set the receiver down gently so as not to set off her headache like an avalanche of roaring rocks cascading down a sheer cliff.

She went back to bed and woke up again right before noon, feeling half human again. She lay in bed for ten minutes letting her mind wander over what clothes to wear and finally put her feet down on the rug and pulled on jeans and a T-shirt.

Over a cup of strong coffee she reviewed all that had transpired. Cornelius murdered. Mulhaney attributing that act to Huntington who said he heard a woman. That woman could have been Greer Lawson, but Greer claimed no dice. Huntington stole jewelry and got caught red-handed. Bentley Graves saw Huntington going out of the house and blackmailed him. Huntington gave the necklace to Bentley's wife, Eva, to encourage their romance and killed Bentley using Cornelius's gun. Huntington killed himself when confronted. Mulhaney found Gloria's gun in Huntington's car, and the lab identified it as the weapon that killed Cornelius. Greer and Homer Stiles kidnapped Vanna to get her out of the way for their nefarious dealings, and then in a moment of rage killed each other. Five dead. It would take a phalanx of lawyers years to sort out all the wills, deals and implications of it all. Enough to give her another headache.

She gulped down another cup of coffee, refilled a mug to take with her and staggered down to the office. There were no new voicemail messages, so she logged onto the computer to check email. She blinked at the screen, which was filled with a bunch of spam trying to sell her Canadian pharmaceuticals, reduce her mortgage and solicit a payment for the two million dollars awaiting her in Nigeria. She needed to install a spam filter one of these days or Van could do it when he returned, if she ever decided to let him return. One item of interest—a message from Benjamin Randolph. He indicated he would be happy to speak with her today and included a telephone number.

Vanna picked up the phone and punched in the digits. It rang and rang, and she was ready to hang up when a man answered.

"Is this Benjamin Randolph?" Vanna asked.

"It is."

"Excellent. I'm Vanna Anderson, and you responded to my recent email. Peter Nalley referred me to you."

"Oh, yes."

"I'm a private investigator doing research for Professor Harlan Shannon of the University of Colorado. He asked me to track down some leads on reports surrounding shape-shifting. That's what led me to you. I understand you had an interesting experience at an orphanage in Iowa City."

"Well . . . um . . . yes. It's not something I freely discuss. Not many people would believe my story."

Vanna took a sip of coffee. "As an investigator, I'm used to maintaining the strictest confidence in these matters. I'd appreciate your full account. I'm not here to judge, only to collect information."

"In that case let me recount the events. I hired on as an art instructor at the Rose Hill Orphanage in the 1970s. I had an uphill battle because the administration favored standard academics versus the more creative endeavors. In addition, not many of the children acted very interested in painting and drawing, except for one teenage boy. He had a very unique style and focused on variations around a common theme. He drew obsessively and all his pictures entailed lambs and snakes."

Vanna almost spewed out the mouthful of coffee she had just taken. "Lambs and snakes?"

"And always in a very strange position. The lamb had the snake in its mouth and the snake had its fangs around the lamb's hoof. I've never seen anything like it before or since . . ."

Vanna dabbed the corner of her mouth with a tissue. "Go on."

"This boy's drawings became more refined and realistic, but I became increasingly concerned over the obsessive nature of his one theme. I couldn't convince him to draw anything else. On one sunny spring morning I took my drawing students outside to draw flowers and trees. The boy I mentioned refused to draw anything except his usual lamb and snake. When we completed our lesson and the kids had free time, he wandered off into the adjoining woods. I later saw a girl emerge wearing the same bulky overcoat the boy had worn. She disappeared, and I never saw either her or the boy again."

"And the name of the boy?" Vanna asked.

"I'll never forget his intense eyes. His name was Van Averi."

# Chapter 32

Vanna's headache returned at the revelation of a Van Averi having been at an orphanage in Iowa City in the 1970s. Her surrogate's history intertwined with an orphanage and now this new piece of information.

After thanking Benjamin Randolph for his disclosure and hanging up, she reviewed the timeline. This teenage boy in Iowa City in the 1970s. An eighteen-year-old boy in Denver named Van Averi getting Francie Wittich pregnant. The next generation Van Averi being left on the doorstep of the All Souls Orphanage in 1979. It all tied together but still gave her nothing concrete to deal with.

She locked up the office and returned to her loft to eat a tuna sandwich, down a large glass of apple juice and take a nap. When she awoke in the late afternoon, her headache had been reduced to a minor background pressure around the base of her skull. At close to a hundred percent for the first time during the day, she decided to take a walk.

Outside she relaxed as the sun shone on her arms, making them tingle. She took in a deep breath, spotted the mountains to the west and strode off to the north where she thought Coors Field would be. She stopped at a light and when it changed, she made a move to enter the crosswalk when a hand grabbed her wrist.

She whirled around, right hand ready to punch the offending person, when she saw it was Lance.

He stepped back and put his hands in front of his face to defend himself. "Whoa, babe. Put your fist down. What kind of greeting is that?"

She glared at him. "Lance! You scared the crap out of me."

He pulled her to him and planted a kiss that truly woke her up for the day. He tilted her chin and gazed into her eyes. "I missed you."

Her initial anger evaporated. She gulped, realizing her heart was racing. "I missed you too, but I thought you were in LA."

"Yup. A darn good gig. But it's over, and I flew right back to be with you. Now you and I are going to have a fancy dinner and a night of recreation." He kissed her again. "I'm not going to let you out of my sight for a month."

Not likely. She didn't want to transform into Van, but her body ached for Lance. Oh, hell. She relaxed and stuck her tongue into his mouth and thrust her body against his.

"Get a motel!" someone shouted.

That sounded like a good suggestion to Vanna, but first she wanted dinner, realizing how famished she was. "I could use a thick steak."

Lance brushed his lips against hers once again and released her. "A steak it will be. Let's go to Morton's."

"It may be difficult to get in."

He put his arm around her and steered her along the sidewalk. "Hey, it's early and you're with a celebrity. We'll get a table."

She had no idea which direction to go to the restaurant, but Lance had no difficulty leading her to Morton's. They waited in the bar for half an hour, downing two glasses of Glenlivit apiece, which had no effect on Vanna, but she had to be careful that Lance wouldn't get drunk. She wanted him in peak form for the later festivities.

After taking their seats, ordering wine and filet mignon double cuts, Lance raised his glass. "To the purtiest girl in the universe."

"To my handsome guy," she answered.

They clinked glasses.

"Man, it's great to be back in good old Denver." He took a sip and put his glass down. "I had one strange experience in Los Angeles."

Vanna raised an eyebrow. "I hope not with one of your groupies."

"Nothing like that, babe. I save myself for you. And besides the groupies are more interested in the singers than the backup guitarist. No, something completely different happened. I noticed a guy who showed up at one of my performances."

"You aren't switch hitting on me, are you?"

"No way, babe. I'm a confirmed heterosexual." He reached under the table and gave her thigh a squeeze.

Vanna shuddered at his touch. She wanted him so much. She had this strange mental picture of them clearing the table and doing it right there in front of everyone in the restaurant. She gave herself a mental pinch on the cheek to regain focus. Then she reached down, patted his hand and removed it. She would wait until after the steak and in a more private setting. "You mentioned a man you saw in LA."

He took the hand that had been under the table and ran in through his wavy locks. "Yeah, this guy right in the front row during my gig. He looked a lot like your agency partner but in his fifties."

Vanna set her glass down. "He resembled Van?"

"Spittin' image. Could have been brothers except for the age difference. He sat with a weird older dude in a purple robe."

Vanna put the pieces together immediately. "Did the guy in the robe have silver hair and a crooked nose with a wart on it?"

"Yeah. How'd you guess?"

"Female intuition. Anything else you noticed?"

Lance speared a piece of lettuce. "Let me think. Ya know, I get a good chance to watch the first few rows of the audience during the show. This robe guy didn't look anything like the regulars." He chewed for a moment and then his eyes lit up. "Hey, babe. One other thing. The Van lookalike wore a gold medallion around his neck."

# Chapter 33

Vanna realized she or Van would have to go to Los Angeles one of these days for some work on behalf of Harlan Shannon—and for themselves. She pictured all the links from Iowa City to Denver through Santa Fe to Los Angeles. Van's contact with Daniel Fogart, the medallion being stolen and now this latest news.

Lance took her hand and brought it to his lips. She could feel her mind and emotions being tugged in a different direction. Finally, the mind lost. Los Angeles and medallions could wait. And to hell with solving the Blendheim case right now. That could also wait.

Making sure to not drink Lance under the table, she concluded her meal with a piece of key lime pie before they adjourned.

As they left the restaurant, Lance wrapped his arm around her. "I'm taking you to my place right now."

"You can take me anywhere and any place, but first I need to pick up an overnight bag. I'll meet you there."

He held her so tightly, she gasped. "No way, babe. I'm not letting you out of my sight. I'll come with you."

Vanna didn't want to risk taking Lance up to her loft, so she stopped in the parking lot, opened the trunk of her Subaru and removed the blue bag. Armed with the necessary change of clothes, she accompanied Lance on the six block walk to his apartment. She never would have been able to find it on her own. "Good thing we live so close together," she commented as she held his arm.

He nibbled on her ear. "Not exactly a chance occurrence. Why do you think I picked out this place, darlin'?"

With several stops along the way to explore each other's mouths, they arrived at Lance's condo. He unlocked the door. Once inside, he poured each of them another scotch while Vanna stashed the blue bag in the bathroom. She downed her scotch in one gulp, and he tried to match her, choking on it.

She whacked him on the back. "Don't try to keep up with me, Lance. You know you can't."

"Damn, woman. I used to have quite a rep for holding my liquor. You're the only lady I can't drink under the table."

"And don't try. I want you fully conscious tonight." She kissed him again and began unbuttoning his shirt.

"Now you're speaking my language." He began to reciprocate with the buttons of Vanna's blouse.

Two pairs of lustful hands began groping at two willing bodies. Then Lance stopped before he had fully removed Vanna's blouse. "Why don't you go into the bedroom and get ready. I'll fix us two fresh drinks and be in momentarily."

Vanna scampered into the bedroom, removed her clothes, stacked them neatly on a chair and jumped into bed, adjusting her necklace to make sure it was firmly attached. She heard some rattling noises in the living room and something that sounded like the tingling of Christmas bells. She shrugged. Unpredictable Lance. No idea what he might be up to. As long as he didn't wait too long. Her whole body wanted him and wanted him now. She snuggled under the sheet.

Moments later Lance appeared and handed her a drink. She gulped it down as he did a little striptease in front of her, which fully captivated her attention. He finally tossed his boxer shorts into the corner and turned off the light before diving into bed.

They caressed, and he planted gentle kisses all over her body, starting with her thigh and working upward, ignoring the spot she most wanted him to touch. He continued over her stomach, breasts, neck and back down until he found the location that made her shudder. She grabbed his long, wavy hair as his tongue worked its magic. His kisses moved upward again until their lips locked. He dropped gently on top of her, and she guided him inside. His smooth thrusts thrilled her, and she let out a low moan.

They rocked back and forth, until she began to lose control. He slowed, and she took a deep breath. Then the ebb and flow increased as their bodies moved in syncopated rhythm. Vanna held him tight as warmth spread through her whole body. The motion increased in intensity until she lost all control and shouted, "Yes! Yes! Yes!" as they both burst at the same moment.

Colorful lights flashed through her brain like images of Fourth of July sparklers. She pulled him close to her one last time before squirming away as the transformation began.

He smacked his lips, turned on his side away from her and was out for the count.

She never really got used to the strange feeling as her breasts shriveled, her hips shrank and the protrusions began to grow between her legs. She grasped a strand of long hair and felt it slip through her fingers. She placed her hand to her chin, and the soft skin turned to stubble. A scientific mind would want to study this strange transformation. For her it was something to get over with.

Van waited a minute to make sure Lance didn't regain consciousness. He stuck his tongue out. Yuck. The thought of being in bed with the guy made his stomach turn.

Then Van's gaze caught the bedside digital clock which gave off a faint blue glow. It changed from 9:59 to 10:00. Time to get out of here. He started to put his foot down on the rug, but his eyes remained riveted to the digital numbers showing exactly ten o'clock. Something clicked in his brain. That was it! He slapped his forehead. How could he have missed it? Always look for the most basic answer. The pieces fell into place like the tumblers aligning to open the lock of a safe.

# Chapter 34

Van climbed out of Lance's bed, removed the necklace from around his throat, picked up Vanna's clothes and strode out of the bedroom toward the bathroom, grateful to have escaped lying next to the snoring lout. The idea of being naked next to another naked guy didn't appeal to him in the least. He had no problems with people who lived the gay lifestyle, but it wasn't for him.

He took two steps into the hall and ran into something that felt like a strong spider web. Bells began to tinkle. Hell. He swatted his hands and they became entangled in more web. Bells jangled. He grasped the web and felt a thin filament. Fishing line with Christmas bells attached.

"Gottcha," Lance shouted from the bedroom. "You tried to sneak off again."

Van dropped Vanna's clothes on the floor. The lights went on and a naked Lance appeared in the bedroom doorway.

Van stood invisible as still as he could, trying not to stare. Man, that guy was well hung. No wonder Vanna went ape shit over him. A few bells still swayed.

Lance scratched his head. "What the heck? Woman, where are you? Vanna?" He craned his neck, trying to find her. "Where'd ya go?"

Van remained frozen, the bells now hardly swaying.

Lance scratched his stomach, turned off the light and retreated into the bedroom, muttering. "Doggone. I thought I'd catch her this time."

It seemed like Van had to wait forever, but finally he heard snoring. Carefully, he extricated himself from the tangle of fishing line and bells, trying to keep as quiet as possible. Good thing Lance hadn't armed his booby trap with razor wire and knives.

He ducked under the last strand, reached back along the floor to slide out Vanna's clothes, before tiptoeing into the bathroom. He changed and put Vanna's clothes into the bag. Then in full stealth mode he left the apartment and closed the door.

Only after he had walked away, did he relax with a sense of relief over escaping Lance's booby trap. Vanna and her trysts were becoming too dangerous, but it wasn't like he could do anything about it. To say she was part of him was an understatement. At least he had returned, and Vanna could go on vacation. And he now had an idea of something important to check on in the morning.

* * * * *

The next day Van woke up from his recurring dream of biting the hoof of a lamb, reflecting that he at least had become familiar with the symbolism if not the rationale behind the dream.

His first order of business entailed a visit to the Danvers Building. He parked and approached a woman in a dark blue uniform sitting behind a curved reception desk. She had a knockout figure and bright green eyes, which Van had no problem staring into. He gave her his card and explained he'd like to check out the room where the Denver Cooperative Art Alliance had held their most recent reception.

She gave him a provocative smile. "That would be the Gold Room. At the end of the hall on the left."

He thanked her and marched off in the direction indicated, glad that no smoking was allowed in the building. He'd have to watch himself. He had some work to do and couldn't risk transforming back into Vanna.

With his footsteps reverberating on the marble floor, he entered the Gold Room, finding two waiters adding silverware to white-clothed, round banquet tables set to accommodate ten people each. Every table held a vase of flowers.

Van found the clock above the inside doorway and checked it against his watch. Accurate within one minute. He sucked on his lower lip. One hypothesis eliminated. Then it dawned on him. He snapped his fingers. Of course. He had been on the right track. It was even more obvious than he had first thought.

He pulled out his cell phone and called Gloria. She answered.

"I'm back in town."

"Oh, goody. We need to get together."

"That's why I'm calling. So much has happened that we need to debrief. When can I see you?"

"You can see me any time," she purred.

Van rolled his eyes. He'd have to be careful this time and not let her blow smoke up his . . . not blow smoke at him at all. "I can be there in half an hour."

As he drove to her house, he planned how he wanted to handle the conversation. He owed his client a full explanation of all that had transpired in the last few days. That in itself would be a lengthy conversation.

He entered the circular driveway, parked right in front of the house and raced up the walkway. He reached for the bell when the door flew open.

Gloria stood there in a tight fitting gold-sequined pants suit. "Baby, it's so good to see you. I watched you drive up." She threw her arms around him and gave him a passionate kiss.

He returned the kiss but quickly disengaged and took her hand. "You'll never believe what has happened since we last saw each other. I have all kinds of news to share with you. Let's go sit down."

They walked hand-in-hand into the living room like two young lovers and sat next to each other on the couch.

Van looked around the room. He noticed three new impressionist paintings on the wall. "You been redecorating?"

"Oh, yes. Time to change some of the artwork. Did you know that Cornelius had a whole storage room full of famous paintings? I thought I'd display some of them." She patted his knee. "Now for your update."

"Where should I start? Well in this case there have been a number of persons of interest. Mulhaney considered you his prime suspect for quite a while in the death of your husband."

Gloria's lower lip puffed out in a full pout. "That nasty detective harassed me so many times. I hope you've set him straight."

"He no longer considers you a suspect in Cornelius's death."

"Oh good." Gloria grabbed Van's arm and snuggled up against him

"Back to the murder of your husband. In my mind the suspects included Huntington, Bentley Graves, Greer Lawson and Homer Stiles."

She stuck out her tongue. "They all deserved to be locked up."

"No need for that. They're all dead now."

Her eyes widened. "I knew what happened to Bentley and Huntington, but the others?"

"As I said at the outset, a lot has happened. Let's review a few of the pertinent facts. First, Huntington. As you know, he stole your diamond necklace and earrings. The necklace he gave to Eva Graves—"

"That gold digger."

"The police have the necklace so you'll be getting it back soon."

She smiled at him. "That's a relief."

"Huntington was upstairs stealing your jewelry at the time of Cornelius's murder. I'll get back to that later. Anyway, Huntington also pawned your earrings."

"Why the little scumbag."

Van held up a hand. "Not to worry. They have been retrieved as well. Vanna told you that Bentley tried to blackmail Huntington."

"I don't know what I ever saw in Bentley. What a weasel."

"He saw Huntington leave this house at the time of the murder. He threatened Huntington. Huntington took Cornelius's gun and went to Bentley's house and shot him. Vanna figured this out and confronted Huntington. That's when he killed himself."

Gloria grabbed Van's knee. "Wow. She never went into those details with me. She's quite a woman."

"Exactly. She's tough and put a lot of this together."

"I'm sure you helped solve your fair share as well." Her hand moved up Van's thigh.

He squirmed and picked up Gloria's hand so it wouldn't distract him further. "Next, as you also know, Bentley and Greer Lawson were working the deal to buy Blendheim Towers."

"Yeah, that really pissed me off."

"It gets even more complicated. With Bentley dead, Greer took over and became cozy with Homer Stiles. Vanna once again interfered with their plans, and they kidnapped her and tried to kill her. Fortunately, she escaped."

Gloria sighed. "I'm going to double the fee to your agency for all the risks you both have taken on my behalf."

He nodded his head. "For what Vanna has been through you should triple the fees."

"Done. What else?"

"Vanna confronted Greer and Homer. A little disagreement ensued. Greer shot Homer, and Homer killed Greer. Homer died later as the result of his wound. So, a clean sweep. Bentley, Huntington, Greer and Homer all dead."

Gloria jumped up from the couch. "Before you continue, what can I get you to drink?"

"Seltzer water, please."

She stepped over to the bar and fixed a vodka tonic for herself and a seltzer water for Van. She brought the drinks back. "You've never told me. Why don't you drink liquor?"

He took a gulp of the seltzer water. "I have no tolerance. One sip of alcohol, and I pass out within ten minutes."

Gloria took a long swallow of her drink and smacked her lips. "I'm glad I don't have that affliction. Continue."

"So with all of this, Detective Mulhaney has the answer to Bentley's murder, and the jewelry theft has been solved. All that remains is who killed Cornelius."

She snuggled up against him. "You're getting to the punch line."

"Exactly. As I mentioned earlier, Huntington admitted being in this house at the time of the murder. He didn't admit to killing Cornelius, though. He said he heard a woman's voice right before the gunshot."

Her blue eyes widened. "And what does Detective Mulhaney think?"

"He thinks Huntington killed Cornelius. He found your missing gun under the seat in Huntington's Mini Cooper. The police ballistics lab verified that the bullet killing Cornelius came from your gun. Huntington had means and opportunity, being in the house and had the motive of being angry over the changed will. Mulhaney figures that Huntington had lied along the way and the statement of hearing a woman's voice was another subterfuge."

"Do you buy that?" Gloria asked.

Van shook his head. "No. When Vanna confronted Huntington, he stuck with his story. He proceeded to admit killing Bentley, so he had no reason to lie about what happened the night of Cornelius's death. Because of this, Vanna and I suspected Greer Lawson could have killed Cornelius."

Gloria sneered. "Another gold digger."

"Yeah. She played along all the men for her own objectives. Several things pointed to Greer. She visited here the night of Cornelius's murder. A crime scene investigator noted the aroma of Shalimar perfume. You don't use Shalimar."

"Darn right."

"But Greer did. She had means and opportunity and her motive—Cornelius became a bottleneck to closing the deal on Blendheim Towers. For a while I had her as my prime suspect."

Gloria disengaged from Van, turned to look into his eyes and furled an eyebrow. "What do you mean for a while?"

"That's the confounded thing with this whole case. Mulhaney has closed it, but Huntington didn't kill Cornelius. And Greer didn't either."

Gloria jumped up. "Before you get to the punch line, let me freshen our drinks."

"Okay. I also need to use your bathroom."

"Down the hall first door on the right."

Van stood and ambled into the hallway. When he returned Gloria handed him his seltzer water, and they sat down again.

She grabbed his arm and leaned her head on his shoulder. "You were saying."

"One interesting part of Cornelius's murder relates to the timeframe. Mulhaney has the death set at approximately seven minutes after ten. That's based on the clock found on the floor in the den with the battery knocked out. Then you called 9-1-1 at ten-twenty-eight. Mulhaney first considered you his prime suspect because of finding blood on you and your gun being missing but the right caliber to have fired the bullet that killed Cornelius. But you left the reception at ten o'clock and couldn't have been back to the house at seven minutes after ten. I even verified it. It takes more than twenty minutes to drive that distance."

She squeezed his arm again. "Thanks for checking."

"Gladys Roons, who saw you leave the reception at exactly ten, noted the time from the clock in the reception room at the Danvers. I thought that clock might have been wrong. I looked at it this morning, and it's accurate. But then I realized how convenient for a clock to fall and knock out the battery to leave visible evidence of the time of the murder. Mulhaney bought it, but the murder didn't happen at seven minutes after ten. The murderer changed the clock, took out the battery and threw them on the floor." Van took a big gulp of seltzer water and licked his lips. "Tastes funny."

"I used different ice. Now tell me. Who killed Cornelius?"

"You did, Gloria. You came home at approximately ten twenty. You went into the den where Cornelius was working, fired a shot into the back of his head, messed up the room to make it look like an altercation had taken place, removed the battery from the clock, changed the time and threw it on the floor. Huntington was upstairs at the time and heard the shot. You wore gloves so no residue would be on your hands. You disposed of the gloves, hid the gun under the driver's seat of Huntington's red Mini Cooper that you found parked outside. You waited to see Huntington leave the house and returned to call 9-1-1 at ten-twenty-eight. As simple as that."

Gloria leaned her head back and laughed. Then she pecked Van on the cheek. "I knew you would be the only one to figure it out. You missed one other point, though. The clock at the reception was actually ten minutes fast, as you at first suspected. I set it that way earlier that day. Then the next morning I went back and reset it. My insurance in case the clock in the den didn't fool anyone. I actually left the reception at nine-fifty and made sure Gladys saw the wrong time on the clock. I drove home, parked around the block, snuck into the house, killed Cornelius and reset the clock. Then I snuck out again, hid the gun in Hunty's car, dropped the gloves in a neighbor's trash, retrieved my car and drove up in time to find the body and call 9-1-1 at ten-twenty-eight. Pretty neat, huh?"

Van wanted to agree, but the room started swimming. "What . . . what's happening to me?"

She put her arms around his neck and gave him a kiss. "Don't worry. I put vodka in your seltzer water. I want to see how you pass out."

Van tried to stand up. He crashed back on the couch and all went black.

# Chapter 35

Van woke up with a pounding headache. At first he didn't know where he was. Then he noticed the Monet painting on the wall and remembered he had passed out on Gloria Blendheim's couch. Daylight seeped in through the curtains. He opened his cell phone and checked the time and date. He'd been out for almost twenty-four hours. "Gloria," he called. No answer. He staggered up and went into the bathroom to pee.

He walked through the downstairs. Deserted. He slowly climbed the stairs, having to stop once from the hammering pain in his head. He resumed the ascent and checked each room on the second floor. In Gloria's bedroom he found no jewelry. Her bed didn't look like it had been slept in. He returned downstairs and sat on the couch, trying to regain his thoughts.

Finally, he took out his cell phone and called Donald Hallett. "Have you heard from Gloria?"

"As a matter of fact I did. She left me a message yesterday afternoon. She said that since she's no longer a suspect in her husband's death, she would be traveling. She had me transfer some money to a Swiss account and indicated she would be in touch with me soon. She also authorized a substantial payment to your agency."

After he signed off, Van sat on the couch for another ten minutes, reflecting over all that had happened. Gloria had made a clean getaway. Nothing he could do. Mulhaney had his case closed and wouldn't want to hear any more. No one suspected Gloria, so she had escaped scot-free.

Then he stood and went to find his car. Nursing his headache he returned to his loft, downed two aspirin and sank into his bed for more sleep.

* * * * *

That afternoon when he had returned to a half-human state and after lamenting that he couldn't hold his liquor a thousandth as well as Vanna, he called Professor Harlan Shannon.

"Any new information for me, Van?"

"Vanna and I have been tracking additional leads, but all have led to dead ends. We followed up on all the names you gave us. Some turned out to be crackpots and some appeared credible. We found indications of transvictus sightings but nothing definitive."

"Sorry to hear that. Tally up your time and send me a bill."

"We didn't spend that much time on it, Harlan. It was an interesting exercise, and we'll write it off to academic assistance."

"You sure?"

Van couldn't justify charging Harlan for work they'd done. Besides, he didn't want to tell him the truth regarding the transvictus at the orphanage in Denver. "Yeah. If we ever come across any interesting leads we'll pass them your way."

"Let's stay in touch."

After hanging up, Van thought over these two investigations. In one, the client had ended up being a murderer. Yet, he had been paid handsomely for the work done. In the other case, he and Vanna had tracked down information for the client that really benefitted them. Only fair to not charge Harlan.

One thing Van knew—he and Vanna would be going to Los Angeles sometime in the foreseeable future. Some leads definitely needed to be worked there. But they would be doing it independently and not for Harlan. That would be another day. Right now he needed to recover from Gloria.

* * * * *

The next day Van called Detective Mulhaney.

"Your partner around today?" Mulhaney asked.

"Nah. She's out of town. But she sends you her love."

"Give her my best." He chuckled. "What can I do you for, Averi?"

"Just checking in on the Blendheim case. You have any doubt that Huntington killed his dad?"

"Nope. All wrapped up, sealed and delivered."

"What if some new evidence showed up?"

"What new evidence? We have everything we need. Case closed."

Van felt conflicted. He had been paid well but knew the truth. He also had strong feelings for Gloria that went beyond the wild sex. He missed her. He might even be in love with her. How crazy was that? To be in love with a woman who had murdered her own husband. He decided to press on. "You even suspected my client at one time."

"She was a damn good suspect for a while."

"So do you have any second thoughts about Gloria?"

Van could hear Mulhaney licking his lips. "Damn good-looking broad. Gives your partner a run for the money. But Gloria's free."

"You found blood on her shoe, and her gun killed Cornelius."

"The blood ended up on her when she found her old man's body. Huntington stole her gun and used it as the murder weapon. Besides, we checked Gloria's hands for gunshot residue that first night. Nada. And she couldn't have raced back from that reception in time to kill her hubby. I must say I enjoyed questioning her, but that's all over now. She has a clean bill of health. Now I have some work to do, not like you lazy PIs."

The line went dead. So much for trying to get Mulhaney to reopen the case. Van remained torn. He owed it to his client to represent her, but he wasn't a lawyer bound to maintain his client's confidentiality. On the other hand, PIs wouldn't be in business long if they turned in their clients to the cops. All a moot point with Gloria gone and Mulhaney not open to new information. He decided to take a few days off and go camping in the mountains. Wander off in the woods and then find his way back.

* * * * *

Two weeks later Van was still moping around the office. He had deposited fifty thousand dollars from Gloria Blendheim, which would keep the agency solvent for the next six months. He had also taken a case to check on a cheating husband. He followed the husband around for three days and nights. The guy did have an affair going. It turned out to be another man and not a woman as the wife had suspected. Van preferred murder cases to snooping around to find people having sex.

He thought back to the week before when he had buried his grandfather. Half a dozen mourners showed up for a service at the Methodist church Jackson sporadically attended. The minister gave a traditional sermon—the from dust to dust kind of message. Much like at Cornelius's funeral, the minister didn't really know much about the deceased. A few platitudes, a solemn hymn and lots of organ music.

Van thanked those in attendance and learned that none of them had more than a passing acquaintance with the old man. Sad that he had become so isolated in his waning years.

If only he had made contact with his grandfather sooner, things might have been different. The story of his life. What if? What might have been?

The daily mail arrived. He sorted through the Xcel Energy, telephone and office rent bills and came to a large manila envelope addressed to him. It bore no return address but had a collection of colorful bird stamps. Van squinted at the stamps and saw the imprint: Repoblican'i Madagasikara. He didn't know anyone in Madagascar.

He carefully opened the envelope and found a typed letter along with pictures of beautiful beaches, rain forests, lemurs, chameleons and geckos. He shook the envelope, and a check for ten thousand dollars fell out. He began reading the letter.

Dearest Van,

I miss you so. I'm sorry I had to knock you out, but it was time for me to leave Denver, and I didn't want you trying to stop me. As you can see from the accompanying pictures, I'm now in Madagascar. I'm staying at the Tsarabianjina on Nosy Be, a beautiful island off the northwest coast. A wonderful resort with snorkeling and white sand beaches. I flew from Denver to JFK to Johannesburg to Anatananarivo. A grueling day and a half of travel.

Although Donald Hallett says I probably have no worries, I

thought it best to go to a country with no extradition treaty with the United States. And I couldn't have picked a more wonderful destination. The only thing lacking is you're not here.

I'm shopping for a new home and will settle in within the next several months, but for the time being I'm enjoying being on vacation and being waited on hand and foot. After all the stress of the events in Denver, it's nice to relax on the beach without a care in the world.

I should also explain to you that I'm not a heartless murderer. Cornelius had been abusing me. He had a fetish that included beating me on parts of my body you would have seen if the lights had remained on. I vowed to take it no longer, and that's why I did what I did. It may not justify my actions in your mind, but I have no regrets. Besides, I now have a lifestyle with no wants.

The enclosed check will cover the airline flight for you and Vanna to come stay with me. I mention Vanna because I figured out about you and Vanna. It's very convenient that the two of you can fly on one ticket. We both have our little secrets. I will be happy to provide an attractive male companion for Vanna. We can enjoy our time together, and then she can have her turn. I think it would be a wonderful arrangement. We'd never be around each other too long to get tired of one another.

When you're ready, I'll be waiting for you.

And by the way, one other little item. Your son will want to meet his father. I'm pregnant. I'll name our baby boy Van. I'm looking forward to being a mother.

All my love,
Your Gloria

\* \* \* \* \*

Van stared at the letter for another fifteen minutes. Then he threw his head back and roared with laughter until tears ran down his cheeks.

What a woman.

He considered having a shot of alcohol to knock himself out for two days but thought better of it and instead paid his bills. He was getting ready to go grab a bite to eat when the door creaked open. He looked up as Eva Bentley sashayed into his office. Va-va-voom. She had sumptuous legs visible practically to her hips, sparkling hair flowing down to her shoulders, tits out to . . . well out to there, and azure eyes like deep wells he could fall into and never get out.

She looked him up and down and licked her lips. "I need you to help me with a little problem . . ."

# About the Author

Mike Befeler writes humorous novels, and THE V V AGENCY is his latest offering—a paranormal mystery. His previously published books include CRUISING IN YOUR EIGHTIES IS MURDER, a finalist for The Lefty Award for best humorous mystery of 2012; SENIOR MOMENTS ARE MURDER; RETIREMENT HOMES ARE MURDER; and LIVING WITH YOUR KIDS IS MURDER, a finalist for The Lefty Award for best humorous mystery of 2009. Mike is president of the Rocky Mountain Chapter of Mystery Writers of America.

http://www.mikebefeler.com

If you would like Mike to speak to your book club, you can contact him at mikebef@aol.com.

22360556R00133

Made in the USA
Lexington, KY
27 April 2013